THE DEAD DON'T DREAM

A MIND GAMES NOVEL

MEGHAN O'FLYNN

PYGMALION
PUBLISHING

THE DEAD DON'T DREAM

Copyright 2022

Distributed by Pygmalion Publishing, LLC

WANT MORE FROM MEGHAN?
There are many more books to choose from!

Learn more about Meghan's novels on
https://meghanoflynn.com

For Emerald O'Brien
who is the best thing to come out of Canada since poutine. Ask a
Canadian to make you some, trust me.
Poutine, not an Emerald. She's mine.
But not in a creepy, possessive way.
In an awesome friend way.
She's at least a thousand times better than poutine and six
million times better than Canadian geese. Those fuckers can kiss
my ass.

I guess what I'm saying is:
Em, I'd cage fight a goose for you if you ever needed me to. I
cannot wait to see what twisted set of circumstances might lead
to that inevitable feathery beat down, but please visit me in the
hospital after.
And bring poutine.

CHAPTER
ONE

M<small>OONLIGHT</small> <small>FELL</small> in harsh blades of white against the hardwood floors. It bleached the oak, but it made the filth on his hands appear black, inky and shiny and somehow heavy—tacky against his flesh. It was caked around his wrist, too, pressed into the tiny crevices of his jewelry, smashed into the circular gilded edge, smeared over the leather band. The piece was old as the dirt itself, as reliable as the ground beneath his feet, but it felt... compromised. Soiled.

He stilled, held his breath and strained his ears, but he could not hear the steady *tick, tick, tick* that usually echoed through the room like a second heartbeat—the antique clock from the night table was on the floor. Ticking away for a century, and now it was dead.

Dead. The word ate at the soft spot between his shoulder blades for reasons he could not immediately place. Though he was unable to feel his own heart throbbing in his chest, *he* wasn't dead. He was in his bedroom. A dream—just a dream. But the expanse between the area rug and the floor-to-ceiling window was covered in scattered bits of grass and pebbles. He could smell damp earth, the musk of worms. His feet were bare, cold against the rug. His toes were... wet.

Mud.

He closed his eyes, trying to force his brain to understand, but slivers of memory slipped by without offering explanation. And though he was quite sure that he was alone, he could hear the wet hiss of breath against his ear, less like air and more like the rush of some unidentifiable pent-up emotion. He could still feel the sultry damp of her lips against his earlobe, her teeth like knives, the canines of a hungry animal, tearing his throat as if she intended to sever his windpipe. His wrists hurt as if he'd been tied.

Was it really just a dream? Some of it was. The woman, her long blonde hair, her blade-sharp teeth—those couldn't possibly be real. No injuries marred his neck; no bloody ribbons of skin hung beneath his hairline. Though his wrists were sore, he could not make out any abrasions that might indicate he'd been the victim of some attack. But there were parts that felt more vital—details that stuck out in sharp contrast. He could see the moon in his mind's eye, the outdoor world gray beneath its glare. He could hear the heavy weight of silence broken only by the crackling whisper of skittering leaves. He could feel the rocks, sharp beneath the knees of his sweatpants—he could feel those abrasions even now, the enduring sting from road-rashed skin. And the dirt...

The mud was real. That was definitely real.

He opened his eyes. The dirt... it wasn't only on him, nor was it merely on the floor as if he'd tracked it inside. It was *everywhere*. A swipe of grime marred the window, obscuring the night beyond. The bedspread was crusted in fine streaks of thick black and wider smears of filthy gray.

He touched his face, his fingertips gritty and sticky—mud in his facial hair. The top edge of his cheekbone felt sharper than usual, but the dirt there was dry.

The blood was not. And though the world was a black-and-white movie in the silver gleam of the moon, he knew now that it was blood. He could smell it, woven through with the damp musk of petrichor, the metallic tang of congealing life... or recent death.

Bile rose in his throat. He gagged, his heart thundering to life, pumping furiously as if his body had only now realized that he was being pursued by some predator, his meat snared in a frenzied dance of ichor and panic. Then he was running, wobbling and lopsided, off the rug, over the dirty floor to the marble tile of the bathroom—frigid against his feet. Gooseflesh shivered along his spine. He threw himself onto his injured knees in front of the toilet.

Bile and the bitter remnants of vodka tonic poured over his tongue and dripped past his lips. But the dirt... oh, the dirt. That was far worse.

This was supposed to be over.

He retched again, again, then slumped back against the wall. He inhaled deeply, trying to steady the frantic throb in his temples, trying to ease the pulse that was turning his vision into a strobe, but he only succeeded in lodging dirt deep in his sinuses. He gagged and snorted, staring in horror at the earth still crusted beneath his fingernails and the slippery weeping chasm along the pad of his thumb. He had tried so hard to stop, but perhaps he'd only been lying to himself. The proof was here, everything he needed to know.

He'd done something terrible.

Again.

CHAPTER
TWO

THE PROPENSITY TO feel watched is a common one, the sensation intimately connected to the sensitive bones in the inner ear, the tiny hairs along the spine, the tugging synapses deep inside the brain—an amygdala overworking itself. A useless system when there were no enemies to fight. But that didn't stop Maggie Connolly from squinting out the window at the oak tree that stood vigil across the courtyard, then at the wide sidewalks meant for wheelchairs or walkers. The decorative gravel embedded in the concrete glittered like bits of broken glass. Not a single person plodded over the walk; no grandmother sat beneath the dappled sunlight that leaked through the oaks. But something felt wrong. Maggie just couldn't put her finger on what.

Maybe she was overthinking it. If she ever wrote a book, it'd probably be called *Something a Tiny Bit Weird Happened, and I Made it a Thousand Times More Awkward: An Autobiography*. Or maybe she'd just call it *#DorkLife*, and lose every bit of street cred right up front. It was usually easiest to keep expectations in check.

"Are you new here?"

Maggie turned to the man who'd spoken, his back rigid as a drill sergeant, though his musculature was beginning to slacken. He leaned a little, too, had since her teenage years when he'd gotten a bullet lodged in his rib. A maverick, a risk-taker—that was her father, like *Sons of Anarchy* without the gangs or anarchy or misogyny or the constant propensity to "watch yo back, sucka." Okay, he was not like the *Sons* at all, and even if he had been, he would not recall so now. Despite the bullet lodged in his bone, he did not possess the modicum of self-preservation necessary to escape death for a second time.

So if someone had been peering through the wide bay window, Maggie's dad would be blissfully unaware. He was also unaware that his wife had left him years ago, probably unaware of the bullet, too, even when it ached. That type of forgetfulness insulated you from some forms of pain; it made you gratefully ignorant of the traumas already passed, if you were lucky. If you weren't, the traumas were all that remained. She sometimes wondered what camp she'd fall into in her later years, but it was probably best to be surprised—in her father's case, over and over again.

Maggie's nose burned with an astringent lemon scent, like the public restrooms at those freaky southern gas stations where people bought dinner instead of filling their tanks. "No, I'm not new," she said. "I'm just here to spend some time with you. Is that okay?"

Grant Connolly appraised her, the shrewdness in his brown eyes familiar but oddly distant. It sometimes felt like her life was split into two parts—the time before the stroke and the time after. But she knew that was a trick of the mind. This was just life, a persistent roller coaster of ups and downs, and damn if she didn't love the feeling at the top of the first hill. Here, they were halfway to the bottom, and when the worst happened, it would be less like a roller coaster ride and more like smashing her car straight into a brick wall. The pain might ebb and flow, but the highs would be hidden beneath the rubble for quite some time, the agony of loss enmeshed in every inch of her like the glittering beads driven into the walk outside. It took a while to dig yourself out of grief. Even if she hadn't been a psychologist, she would have known by the ache in her chest that still acted up on pivotal days—Kevin's birthday and their anniversary being the most recent additions.

She should have said yes when he'd asked her to marry him six months ago instead of letting him leave. It wasn't her fault that Kevin had relapsed, not her fault that he'd driven his car straight into the river by way of the Fernborn bridge where they used to watch the sun set. But when the worst events of your life were all linked directly to choices you made, you started to take things personally. The one saving grace about her father's condition was that he didn't remember Kevin, her almost husband. He also didn't remember that she'd killed his son.

"Are you the librarian?"

Maggie glanced down at her outfit, brushing her flaming red curls off her shoulder. She did look like a librarian, according to her mother. Long skirts or suit pants, button-down blouses, and the closest she got to those fancy nighttime "cat eyes" were the thick black frames on her reading glasses. She'd donned a suit today, but her polka dot blouse didn't exactly scream "fashionista." Her father shouldn't mind that —his apartment at the retirement village had strong *Golden Girl's* energy—but Maggie was no Betty White. *If only.*

"No, I'm not the librarian. I do love to read though."

Grant's nostrils flared. His eyes narrowed, then relaxed. "I suppose you can stay," her father said finally. "Do you like *World's Most*?"

World's Most—aka *World's Most Baffling*—was a knock-off *Unsolved Mysteries* type show, hosted by Harris Overstreet, a man who would never be as intensely interesting as Robert Stack. Three growly words from Stack, and you half believed you were the one lost. Overstreet was like the impression you got if you pressed newspaper comics into silly putty. "*World's Most* is one of my favorite shows," she said. "The producers wanted to replace the host, but I think they changed their minds."

He harrumphed, combing his fingers through his fine white hair, and it made the patches of brilliant rust curls along his temples stand out all the more—hair the same color as hers, though she'd as yet managed to avoid the beard. She had his amber eyes, too, even if he didn't see that now.

"That's ridiculous, replacing Overstreet," he grumbled, but he wasn't looking her way. She followed his gaze to the wall-mounted television at the front of the room. The TV was off. Only the wallpaper surrounding the blank screen was animated, the same paper he'd had in his old living room. She'd fought for a month to install it before resorting to cash—a high price to pay for the "sneezed flowers all over the wall" aesthetic.

"He's no Stack, but there's no one better suited," her father muttered. "What are they trying to pull?" His gaze stayed locked on the blank television.

"I agree. No reason to mess with a good thing." She scanned the squishy well-loved La-Z-Boy, the only chair he'd sit in, but the remote was not wedged behind the arm where it usually was. Nor did Maggie see it in the tiny living area. It was not on the coffee table topped with a chess-board—five moves in, where his memory had paused the game three weeks ago. She did not see it on the electric piano that held a photo of her and her brother, a potted plant, and a stack of sheet music. She accompanied Dad's piano with her bassoon on days when he remembered both that he could tickle the ivories and that his daughter played an instrument that sounded like a wounded goose. Probably best if he forgot the latter. But the potted plant...

Amidst the spires of Mother-in-law's Tongue, the remote stuck from the dirt like a shiny black flower. She retrieved it and returned to sit beside her father in a newer, but much stiffer, La-Z-Boy.

She aimed the control at the screen as he turned to her, his eyebrows furrowed. "Have you seen Joyce?" he asked.

Her mother. *Ouch.* "No, I haven't." It wasn't a lie; while she usually had breakfast with her mother once a week, Joyce had been indisposed the past two weeks. And she wouldn't come here. Even if she hadn't been under house arrest, Mom had divorced her father a year before his first stroke.

"Are you new here?" her father asked.

She hit the button on the remote, and the screen lightened. *Not a good day*, the nurse had said, and it was definitely a hot-garbage kind of day when the only thing you recalled was your ex. Better if he could remember his daughter. Or maybe his work. Grant had been an outspoken psychologist, volunteering with projects that freed wrongly convicted felons—he still got Christmas cards from some of them.

He narrowed his eyes at her. "Well? Are you?"

"No, I'm not new. I'm just here to spend some time with you, if that's okay."

He sniffed brusquely, then nodded. "I suppose you can stay."

The opening sequence for the show crossed the screen, walls of creepy looking trees, exactly the kind of place a jogger might go missing—exactly the kind of place you'd tell a big-breasted blonde to steer clear of. They always died first. But red-headed librarians usually came out okay.

Usually... but not always. Her eyes cut to that wall of windows again, the hairs on the back of her neck tingling.

"Trees never get to the root of the problem," her dad muttered, and she chuckled, then tapped the button to unmute the television as Harris Overstreet appeared on-screen—he was no Stack, but he did have the smoldering-eye thing down. Overstreet's low voice blared: "With your help, these riddles might finally be solved."

She tried not to wince at the volume. Louder televisions were par for the course with aging, but at this rate, she'd be deaf well before her time.

"Are you new here?"

Maggie turned to see her father staring at her, one eyebrow raised.

She shook her head and smiled; even forced happiness could help you to avoid drowning in sorrow. When he frowned in response, Maggie glanced at the piano—at her and her brother, smiling, smiling, smiling forever. Aiden had been the first in a series of losses, but he wasn't the last. Her father was leaving, too; he was just doing it more slowly than most. Certainly more slowly than Kevin.

Her throat clenched, but she forced out: "I just came to watch *World's Most Baffling* with you." She nodded to the screen. "Is that okay?"

He sniffed. "I suppose. I hear they tried to replace that Overstreet fellow. Morons, all of them." His eyes sharpened;

his brow furrowed. "You have very pretty hair, darling. Almost as pretty as mine." He ran his hand over his curly beard like a cartoon villain. "I'm not sure how anyone resists it, quite frankly. You'll probably need a bat to beat the men off. Or a well-placed pun." He leaned closer to her, eyes glittering as if ready to impart a juicy secret. "People *hate* puns. I always keep a few in my back pocket for the assholes."

She smiled, and this time, it was as natural as the rust in her hair. Yeah, her dad was in there. Somewhere.

CHAPTER
THREE

THE NEXT STOP on her "let's see how much we can cram into a Friday" agenda came all too quickly, and the watchful-eye sensation she'd felt at her father's retirement home did not dissipate as she sped across the city and into the outskirts of Fernborn. She saw no one in her rearview, though—nothing of concern. The sensation was probably just strangers checking out her DeLorean. Yeah, the radio was busted, and the whole frame creaked when she opened the door, but she and her brother had been obsessed with *Back to the Future*. Plus, eighty-eight miles per hour was basically her normal driving speed, and the car made her feel like going back was possible—like mistakes were somehow impermanent, though nothing could be further from the truth.

And no one knew that better than the man she was visiting today.

The air inside the penitentiary reeked of lye-rich soap, sardine-packed bodies, and the salty-sweet musk of desperation. A taupe-clad caterpillar-mustached guard stopped just outside the barred cell and nodded her inside.

14

The cell door slammed shut with a heavy metallic clank that made her legs tense to the point of pain. It wasn't that she was locked inside with a killer; it was that being trapped at all was an affront to the human psyche. Some people needed to be here—pedophiles were difficult to rehabilitate, and there were other exceptions—but she was a firm believer in redemption for a good portion of the population.

If only it were so easy for Mannie Koch.

The man across the stainless table had olive skin covered in bluish-gray prison ink: the Virgin Mary, grinning skulls, and a series of birds on his left temple that were probably blue jays but looked like flattened pigeons—his tattooist wouldn't be up for the Prison Artist of the Year award. Mannie also had an enormous tombstone across the back of one shoulder blade, his wife's name in heavy, uneven lettering.

Mannie Koch appraised her with the deep black eyes of a rattlesnake. He outweighed her by a hundred pounds, with a chest as wide as her shoulders and finely honed muscles that her daily yoga practice would never create. But she knew his rattlesnake eyes and clenched fists weren't meant for her.

"What happened, Mannie?"

He flinched at the sound of his name; she was the only one he allowed to call him that. To everyone else, he was Mark. Mark was not his middle name, or some westernized version of Mannie. "Mark" referred to the slashing *X*s he'd gouged into his victims: his wife and her mother. *X marks the spot.*

Maggie had worked with a lot of violent sociopaths. She could feel their diagnoses in the fine hairs between her shoulder blades, the itchy tingle of being in the room with someone who didn't care whether she lived or died. Mannie wasn't one of those. She felt his depression like a pit in her belly, but she did not feel threat.

She had been wrong before, though. The scar at the base of her skull throbbed, just once, like a flutter of a heartbeat, then settled.

Mannie shrugged one heavy shoulder, but his jaw tightened. He planted his fisted hands on the metal table between them. Keloids writhed like worms over the small bones on the underside of his wrist; she could see the patterned scars from his teeth if she squinted. His eyes darted to the iron bars and back again.

"Mannie?"

"She won't talk to me," he finally whispered.

Maggie didn't need to ask who. There was only one female he cared about. His daughter, Izzy, had walked into her grandmother's house and found him standing over her mother's corpse. He'd waited until she was in New Orleans with a friend to start the process, though maybe if the children had been in town, he'd simply have killed his victims more quickly. As it was, it had taken his wife six days to die.

"She's trying to forget, Mannie."

"She ain't never going to be able to forget. But I did it for her. I just want her to be..." His eyes hardened again—pain this time, not fury.

"Thankful? At peace?" She wasn't guessing; he'd expressed both in the past.

He sniffed. And nodded. "Yeah, maybe both of those things."

"She did testify on your behalf. That says a lot about her state of mind." Maggie might have additional insight if she'd watched the trial, even looked at Izzy's social media accounts, but Maggie preferred to treat using unbiased observations. It was an invasion of privacy to poke around on a patient or their family, no matter how public the information might be. And that was if social media was reliable... which it wasn't.

"Fat lot of good it did," he scoffed. His fists clenched; the tops of his knuckles paled where the skin stretched tight over the bone—so thin. "It just doesn't feel right. The way those kids are actin'."

"The right thing doesn't always *feel* right. And you can't force them to open that door right now, not with all that's happened." She waited while he took a large shuddering breath, then said, "What do you want for them, Mannie?"

He lowered his big head—the top of his skull shone through the sparse hair at the crown. "I want them to be safe," he said to the tabletop. "I want 'em to be okay, more okay than I ever was. Than their mother was."

"And what do you think they need to achieve that?"

"Maybe they need to... figure out how to deal with what happened to 'em. Especially my boy. He acts like I don't exist, but he also acts like *that* don't exist." He raised his face. His thick lower lip quivered, and he fought to stiffen the muscles around his mouth. But his eyes remained glassy. Mannie still cried himself to sleep. Lots of inmates needed help, but she suspected the crying—and disturbing the other inmates—had kept him on the short list for her sessions. That, and when he'd been referred a year ago, he'd still been chewing through his wrists every time they left him alone.

A year ago, he'd still been refusing to tell anyone why he'd killed them. Even now, no one knew but Maggie... and, of course, his children.

She reached a hand across the table and laid her fingertips against his forearm—his skin was hot, sticky. The guard stationed outside the barred door grumbled, "No touching," but he said it with the half-hearted energy of a sullen child kicking a deflated ball, an activity which was a good five steps better than gym-class dodgeball, twenty-five steps better than any gym class for nerds.

Maggie ignored the guard. There were cameras everywhere—no one could accuse her of being inappropriate. Sometimes, a person just wanted to feel human.

"Mannie, give them time. You didn't remember your own abuse until you caught your wife and her mother hurting your kids." She squeezed his arm, and he gently laid the fingers of his other hand over hers. Mannie had done what most sane people would want to do: kill the women who had been sexually abusing his children. But he'd spent six days delighting in their pain, watching them bleed out from their wounds—"cut them where their damn hearts should have been." That pushed it too far for a jury, especially because he'd refused to give them a reason for the crime. He hadn't told anyone what his children had experienced, hadn't tried for a temporary insanity plea, refused to let Maggie petition to get him into a psychiatric hospital. He'd protected those children the only way he knew how: by giving them their privacy, even if it meant he never saw the outside world again. To the guard, to the world, her patient would always be a sadistic murderer; he'd always be Mark.

Perhaps he was onto something. It was safer to maintain a hard shell to keep others away from your soft bits. Some people had bruises on their balls from a misplaced dodgeball kick.

Some people wore a cup.

CHAPTER
FOUR

A PAINTING from an incarcerated patient graced the back wall of Maggie's office, an abstract of blues and oranges, a single sharply lettered word: TRUTH. It felt aggressive, but the artist had said she was the first person who hadn't tried to "blow smoke up his ass," which seemed a dubious and maybe impossible activity. How hard would you have to blow to get smoke through a colon?

"I don't really know where to start," the man sitting across from her said. "Do I just tell you that I have a thing about Elvis, and you tell me how to get my life together?" His eyes were not on her; they were glued rather suspiciously to the tank that sat behind her desk. To be fair, a lot of her patients didn't like Fluffy, a gift from her father in one of his rare moments of lucidity—a low-maintenance friend for when his brain opted out. She could have kept him at home, but her business partner hated spiders, and she never missed an opportunity to screw with Owen.

"If Elvis is a problem for you, then yes, we'll talk about him. Are you getting lost thinking about his blue suede shoes? Or maybe it's a *Can't Help Falling in Love* situation, though I'm pretty sure you'd have a hard time seducing a dead man."

He pulled his gaze to her and blinked. Attractive if you liked high cheekbones and strong jaws and meticulously close-cropped facial hair with lines so straight they looked drawn on. He had broad shoulders, too, but not Army-prison-guard square, the kind honed at the gym instead of in the service. Based on the smug cock of his eyebrow and sandy brown hair cut on the too-long side of professional, he wouldn't let anyone, even a drill sergeant, tell him what to do.

Then again, maybe he just reminded her of Kevin—he had that same crooked smile. She'd have to watch that. Connecting new patients with known associates was a good way to skew your thinking.

She sipped from her glass water bottle—hand-blown, a gift from Alex—then set it aside. The uneven bottom rattled against the mahogany desktop.

"You're saying that I can't seduce Elvis... because of the security at Graceland?" he asked.

She touched the winged corner of her glasses to adjust the frames. "I was thinking because necromancy is implausible. But sure, let's go with security concerns." Even in Dungeons and Dragons, it was tricky to raise the dead. It was tidbits like that which had made her *so popular* in middle school.

Her patient's emerald eyes appraised her as she picked up her pen, humor glinting around the irises, but there was a shrewdness in the set of his mouth. Owen had called Tristan Simms a "tricky patient" when he'd handed her the referral, which usually meant he'd tried therapy in the past, and it hadn't taken. And Simms had refused to see anyone but her. She had a few referral services that sent patients to her and her alone. Sammy, for one—her prosecutor best friend had sent Mannie Koch her way. But Sammy would have emailed her if he had given Simms her number.

"Why don't you start at the beginning," she said, flipping the intake file open to expose the first page of background questions. "What brings you here today, Mr. Simms?"

"You can call me Tristan." His pressed blue suit and cream-colored button-down were as carefully manicured as the razor-sharp lines of his beard. Shiny shoes. A perfectionist. His words would be just as carefully maintained unless she caught him off-guard. Strange for a man like that to forgo a tie, though.

"I'll call you Tristan when you trust me," she said. She'd call him whatever he wanted, of course, but his response would tell her more about his state of mind. Tricky patients sometimes required thinking outside the box.

"Fair enough." He leaned back against the chair, crossing one ankle over the opposite knee, then laced his fingers on top. Though the rest of him was put together, his nails and the tips of his fingers looked rough—chewed on. And *too* clean, like he'd attacked his hangnails and close-bitten nails with a scrub brush full of bleach. She'd seen that before.

"I'm having trouble sleeping," he said, when she remained quiet.

Maggie waited for him to elaborate. When he just stared, she said, "Lack of restful sleep can be triggered by any number of things. From the state of your hands"—*and the sleep issues and the nervous twitch at the corner of your eye and the tight muscles along your mandible*—"I'm guessing anxiety." Perhaps on the obsessive-compulsive spectrum, though maybe sub-clinical. She set the pen aside. "But I don't really like guessing, Mr. Simms. And you don't either. You strike me as someone who tries to maintain control over every aspect of your life—who likes to know what he's getting into." *Who chooses a psychologist and makes her partner rearrange the schedule to get in.* But she didn't believe this was a function of narcissism as his well-put-together exterior might suggest; it was often desperation that made people unyielding.

"Let me explain how this works, Mr. Simms. I'll ask you some questions. We'll make some goals together. If you don't like my style, I can refer you to—"

"I don't want to see someone else." His eyes locked on Fluffy again. "I heard you're good at keeping secrets. That you help... victims."

That was an unusual statement, and it certainly hadn't come out of nowhere. Perhaps he knew a past patient... or her mother. But like Sammy, Mom would have called her directly. "Do you consider yourself a victim, Mr. Simms?"

His left eye twitched harder. "Yeah. The police have it out for me. They're always watching me, poking around my life."

Hmm. This might be more pressing than anxiety or OCD-spectrum issues. Delusions of persecution often involved the police or some other authority figure—the FBI, the government. It was a red flag. His shiny shoes tapped the wood floor like the restless ticking of a metronome, and the lyrics for Elvis's *Suspicious Minds* floated into her brain. She had the sudden notion that perhaps he'd elaborate if she sang it to him; maybe he'd start talking just to shut her up.

"Do they have a reason to watch you, Mr. Simms? Have you done something wrong?"

"They come after me even when I don't do anything wrong. I think they'd rather frame me than do their jobs."

Well, that wasn't a no. It implied that the police also came after him when he *did* do something wrong. Unless she was overthinking it. "What would they like to frame you for, exactly? Sleepwalking isn't a crime."

"Do you deal with a lot of crazy people?" he asked in lieu of answering her question.

"My patients are just normal people in abnormal situations." She cocked her head. "Do you believe you're insane, Mr. Simms?" Did he suspect that he was delusional, that the police were unlikely to be after him? If he was psychotic, she'd need to take more extreme measures to ensure his safety.

"You're the doctor." He pressed the tip of his ragged thumb to his middle finger and squeezed so hard the muscles in his jaw tensed. He released the pressure, unclenched his jaw, then did it again, using the hot ache of chewed cuticles to distract himself. But what exactly was he distracting himself from? "And whether I'm crazy or not, you can't say anything, right? Can't tell the police?"

Ruh-roh. But the statement wasn't a red flag on its own. People with anxiety often believed that scary thoughts meant they had intention to harm; that they'd end up arrested if they told anyone, including a therapist. But— *Surprise!*—it's normal. If she called the police every time she had a patient with a scary thought, all her clients would be in cuffs. She only worried when people told her those thoughts didn't *bother them.* If someone thought killing their neighbor was a great idea, then there was a problem.

She slid her hands off the desktop and rested her palms on the knees of her suit pants—the tips of her fingers were damp. "Thoughts are not illegal. I am required by law to contact authorities if you have a plan and a means to harm yourself or someone else—there has to be imminent danger. If you've already hurt someone, I'm not obligated to report it unless you're still a risk to the community." Admissions of past violence and homicide had happened a few times during sessions, but usually the confessors were already in jail.

"It's nothing like that," he said. "I don't want to hurt myself, and I don't want to hurt anyone else."

Excellent—anxiety thoughts for the win. Logically—and legally—his words were enough to maintain his privacy. The last thing she wanted to do was call the authorities and end up with a dead patient and a bullet in her rib like her father.

She retrieved her pen and made a note on the assessment page, checking boxes about suicidal and homicidal ideation: *none.* But by the time she looked back up, his eyes had gone faraway—blank.

Her hackles rose, instinct more than training. "Mr. Simms, if you're telling me the truth, then you have nothing to worry about in terms of confidentiality." Simms— Tristan Simms. The name was familiar, she realized, but she couldn't place it. His face was familiar, too, now that she really looked, but that might have been the knife-blade cut of his cheekbones, and that smirk—Kevin's smirk. He was much paler than Kevin though. Like if you took Tom Cruise, bleached the Scientology fervor out of him, then roughed him up Brad-Pitt-*Moneyball* style.

He raised an eyebrow, but kept his gaze on a spot beyond her shoulder. His nostrils flared. "*If* I'm telling the truth?"

She'd worded the question that way on purpose, to see how he'd respond. Defensive, but not surprised; between that and the whole "Mr. Simms" thing, trust was a sore spot for him. "It's a reasonable disclaimer. I won't make you promises that I can't keep."

"Ah yeah, because of the..." He gestured to the painting over her shoulder—*TRUTH*. "I thought it was your job to trust what I say and tell me how to fix it."

"It's my job to listen." She shrugged. "You insisted on getting in today, which leads me to think there's a pressing situation you'd like to discuss. But I can't read minds. That ambition is just a dream."

"With a V8 engine," he said. Humor flared in his eyes, then vanished. He *was* an Elvis fan. But he was avoiding her gaze again, staring at Fluffy.

Maybe they needed to start smaller. "What do you do for a living, Mr. Simms?"

His green eyes hardened into chips of emerald. "I already told your secretary that I'm paying cash."

From the suit... attorney? But why hide that? Maybe he was a high-priced escort. Sex work was just work, but it was useful information to have when trying to build a personality profile. And the fact that he'd called her business partner her secretary was *awesome*. She'd buy Owen a mug today that said "Best Secretary Ever," and from now on, every Secretary's Day would be a true celebration.

"That wasn't a billing question," she said, pulling the file closer. "I know very little about your situation, Mr. Simms." She leveled her gaze at him. "Tell me why you think your sleep habits are a secret worth sharing."

The muscles in his jaw hardened to stone, but his shoulders slumped. He sighed. "I don't know what I do when I'm asleep. And I'd really like to avoid... whatever happening again."

Her pen paused above the new patient paperwork—

Well, that's a new one. The silence stretched, his eyes drifting to the long sofa table on the far wall that held her brother's baseball glove and a picture of her and Aiden, taken the week before he'd vanished. He was nine—she'd been thirteen. Sometimes she wondered if he might be alive out there, but the things people did to kids... he was dead. Had to be.

Her guts twisted; she straightened, and the knot eased. She'd had the same thought thousands of times, but it still had the ability to snarl up her intestines like gas station sushi. Gas station hot dogs. Gas station burritos. Any hot food from a gas station.

"Are we talking about a sleepwalking episode, Mr. Simms?"

He nodded, but his eye twitched, and her hackles rose once more. "They happened more in my twenties—the episodes were bad ten years ago. Then they just stopped for nearly seven years. I had a few sporadic episodes about three years back, but I hadn't had another since... until the other night."

Three years. Between his twitchy eye and his pressured tone, it felt like a lie, but the timeline was a strange thing to alter. "Sometimes people begin sleepwalking in response to a stressful event; the body's way of processing a trauma they aren't dealing with while they're awake. Can you think of anything that fits that bill?"

He pressed his lips together so hard they went white—a tight line of suppression, as if he were physically trying to hold the explanation back. He glanced at his fingers, flexing them almost absentmindedly, then turned his hand over.

Shit. She'd been wrong; this was not just anxious finger-chewing. He had a wicked gouge along one thumb held together with butterfly bandages. His fingertips looked like they'd been torn off, as if he'd tried to remove his finger-prints with a cheese grater. Maybe he *had* tried to remove his fingerprints because of the whole "the cops are after me" persecution-delusion thing—she'd seen stranger. One thing she knew for certain: he was holding back some crit-ical piece of information. She could read it in the fine lines around his mouth. Early in her career, she might have guessed shame, but after ten years, she registered shame reliably deep in her belly. It dripped off Mannie Koch—she could practically smell it on him.

From Tristan Simms, she felt deception and fear. A spot low in her chest was vibrating, like his suppressed panic was leaping from his guts on little currents of energy to lodge inside her rib cage. But there was something else there too—recognition, not of him, but of a hidden place within him that mirrored something in her own soul.

That's stupid, Maggie. You understand pain, that's all. Regret too.

She planted her elbows on the desk and leaned toward him over clasped hands. "What was happening in your life at the time of the first episode?" she tried again. "I can't help you if I don't know the history of this problem."

He exhaled with a noise like a balloon slowly losing air. When he spoke again, his voice was soft. "Ten years ago, my father shot my mother and killed himself. That was three weeks before the episodes started." His eyes widened as if shocked that he'd said it aloud, and she could under-stand why. With that backstory, Tristan Simms was a comic book villain in the making. He ran his wounded thumb over the pale band around his wrist—he was missing a watch, one he wore religiously from the tan lines.

She squinted. From zero to explained in thirty seconds? That seemed a little too easy. "I'm sure that was difficult.

Did you have emotional support during that time?" Maybe a therapist?

He nodded. "My mother's friend, Benedict, always acted like my dad—foster father, I guess you'd call him. And Jeanna, my sister, was great. And then there was my... ex-girlfriend." He winced. "She got possessive, thought I was cheating on her when I vanished at night." He shrugged. "I'm not sure what I expected from a girl I met in a strip club."

Huh. Most strippers wouldn't go home with a guy they'd just met—that was dangerous at best. Had he been a regular at the club?

"Anyway," he continued, "we were off and on for years, but I wasn't ready for a relationship, and we broke up soon after my mom died. The sleepwalking stopped too. For nearly seven years, I didn't have an episode, even though Christine and I... reconciled."

"What happened three years ago?"

He averted his gaze. "I met someone else. Christine lost it, threatened to kill herself, and wound up in the hospital. And then I went to sleep and woke up in my backyard." He raised his head; his eyes were glassy. "Those episodes went on for a few months, then they stopped again. But now..." He shook his head. "I don't know what's happening now."

You don't? It seemed obvious—maybe too obvious—but patterns were sometimes invisible when they were happening to you. "Let me lay out what I'm hearing: You lost both of your parents in a traumatic way, just before the first episode. The sleepwalking settled for a time, but resurfaced after you nearly lost a friend to suicide?" But there was more, she realized. Unlike Mannie, Tristan Simms didn't need the right question; he needed to give voice to something he was very much aware of. "Losing your mother so traumatically would certainly explain why you'd react strongly to any threat of loss. Have you lost someone in the last few months, Mr. Simms?" She wasn't yet sure how the police fit in, but she'd have to tread carefully with that. Firmly held delusions weren't easy to tease apart from real events, and defensiveness was this man's go-to.

He stared, his jaw hard. The fine hairs along her forearms prickled. "No. I haven't had a girlfriend in over a year." But there was fire in his eyes now—*definitely lying*. "Can you just tell me how to make it stop? That's why I'm here." He raised his hands. They shook, the injured tips angry red and mottled with brown-black scabs. One of the butterfly bandages had come loose, blood weeping around the edge of the plastic strip. He frowned at his fingers then snatched them into his lap. "I don't want to hurt anyone."

Her shoulders tightened; her back was oily with sweat. The way he said it... "Mr. Simms—"

"I think this was a mistake." He shoved himself to his feet. "I'm sorry I wasted your time."

Maggie pushed her chair back and skirted the desk, but by the time she'd made it halfway across the room, he'd already thrown open the door and vanished into the hall outside her office. "When you're ready to talk, I'm here," she called after him.

He did not acknowledge her words. The last she saw of Tristan Simms was the back of his broad shoulders as he turned the corner into the waiting area. But his words were still echoing in her brain.

I don't want to hurt anyone.

Something in the way he'd said it made her add one more word to that line: *else—I don't want to hurt anyone* else.

He already thought he had.

CHAPTER
FIVE

MAGGIE LEFT her office that night feeling more than a little unsettled. Her flesh was needling and itchy like there were ants crawling over her skin, and the prickling intensified with each red streetlight. She felt the incessant buzzing of her cell phone in her marrow. She hit the button to silence the call, checked her rearview then her side-view, but the road remained clear. No matter how it felt, no one was after her, not any more than the police were after Tristan Simms. For him, it was probably the lack of sleep playing tricks on his traumatized brain.

But what if it wasn't?

She refocused on the road and pushed the pedal to the floor. Tristan Simms had caught her off guard, something that was difficult to accomplish. Killers, she understood—even psychopaths had patterns. Depression, grief, anxiety, cheating, every set of personality traits and diagnoses became predictable once you got to the root of the issue.

But with Simms there were inconsistencies, not only in his case, but in the way her body wanted her to react—a significant discrepancy between her gut and her head.

Patients almost never caused this kind of rift; she made logical decisions and she stuck to them, and that was that. It was safer that way. Had she chosen to go by the book and follow the "best practices" she knew at the time, she'd still have a brother. She'd also have that piece of her head, the spot that ached sometimes as if there were still teeth locked in the scar.

She used to imagine that piece of her scalp was out there, a little hitch of flesh and hair, burgeoning, growing into a new fully formed but slightly stupider version of her. Maggie was not okay with skull-flap Maggie being superior —talk about a shot to the ego. But she also wasn't okay with that part of her being missing. Or dead.

Maggie sighed. She was not going to end up like her parents or her brother, and she wasn't about to put herself in harm's way again. She would also not put her patient in harm's way without a concrete reason; her father would agree. The book—she had to do this by the book, even if she *felt* that Tristan Simms was lying, maybe paranoid. Would a few more *Hound Dog* jokes have made a difference? Maybe a different line of questioning—one that was less threatening.

The streetlight at the end of the block eased from green to yellow.

What about rumination, Maggie, like the whirlwind of thoughts you're entertaining now? Maybe you're the one who's obsessive—maybe you're the one who's broken.

The streetlight blinked red. Maggie squinted left then right, her heart racing—no other cars. She gunned it. The intersection blew past in a flurry of pavement and glaring side streets, but she came out the other side unscathed. She released the pressure on the gas.

She felt as if she were trying to build a Dungeons and

Dragons character sheet, with numerical scores assigned to different abilities and weaknesses. In the game, it helped when determining what a character might do, but she had no such blueprint now. And the injuries to his hands, as if he'd been buried alive and had to claw his way out, so frantic he'd lost his watch in the process...

Had he only hurt himself?

Had he hurt someone else?

And most importantly: Would he do it again?

She shook her head. *Stop obsessing, Maggie—he left, there's nothing more you can do.* He'd made his choice as Mannie had, and she had no solid reason to believe he was a danger to anyone, no legal reason to make a phone call that might ruin his life not to mention conflict with every ethical tenet she held dear. Whatever Tristan Simms had done, whatever he was struggling with, he was on his own because he didn't *want* her help.

So why did she feel like she'd failed?

But another voice whispered right back: *You know exactly why.*

Her skin was still itchy when she made the highway turn that would take her out of Fernborn, the opposite direction of the prison. Sweat had dried to sticky trails of salt along her spine, but her blood was vibrating so hard it felt as if her capillaries might explode.

Her phone buzzed again, making her jump—third time in an hour—but it jolted her out of her own head. She pulled the cell from the cupholder and glanced at the incoming call just as it stopped ringing. Alex. Again. She was settling the cell back in the console when a text came through:

"Where are you, hon? Love you, miss you, xoxo."

Maggie squinted at the highway, the engine whining, and reached over to turn the phone off. But she couldn't turn off her brain. Her neck muscles screamed with tension. Every headlight glared at her. Her rearview mirror teased her with things she could not see—prying eyes from other cars, monsters hidden in the trees at her back.

Do you work with a lot of crazy people?

No, Mr. Simms. I'm the crazy one.

Her car seemed to drive itself to her final stop of the night: four parking lots separated by an *x* of lawn just wide enough for the centuries-old shade trees the city had deemed protected. In the daytime, the thin lawn was a place for fast-food patrons from the front buildings to eat their meals. At night, the trees blocked the tall spires of floodlights from reaching the cars parked at the back of the lot.

She made her way beyond the pair of restaurants; a furniture store held vigil in front of the third lot. But the back corner was where she was going: a long, squat building in shades of brown the size of an old-fashioned saloon, and that's exactly what it used to be—an underground speakeasy. A neon sign for psychic readings glared from one of the ground-floor windows. Despite the garish pink neon, no palm reader sat inside. The flip sign on the door always read CLOSED.

She made her way over the asphalt, eyes on the building, refusing to give in to the prickle along her spine. She marched past the plate glass window to the symphony of night birds and the drone of highway, the neon coils an angry beacon. A small set of stairs at the corner of the building appeared like the entry to a storm cellar, a narrow tunnel to shelter, nothing more.

She descended into the dark.

The heavy wooden door at the bottom was equally nondescript, but inside, the world was alive, though not much brighter—lit by candles. An espresso machine perfumed the air with the hissing promise of caffeine. A sign behind the bar simply said COFFEE, the word burned into a single plane of birch. The barista behind the long stainless coffee bar nodded to her, thick lips pulling into a smile. Maggie wasn't sure what his eyes were doing; the top half of his face was covered in a Mardi-Gras style mask, a shiny white background heavily crusted in green and purple jewels. Always the same style, rarely the same mask. People who came here enjoyed novelty.

A series of glass dishes on the far end of the counter held braided bracelets in different colors—green, red, purple, yellow, white, black. She grabbed a red one, nodded to the barista, and headed for the curtained wall to the right of the coffee bar. At first glance, it appeared to be nothing more than a wall of fabric covering up the old stucco, but if you knew where to slip between—*exactly* where to go—you hit a hallway instead of plaster.

Her heart throbbed, harder, harder, and her pelvis echoed the beating of her feet against the wood floor —*thud, thud, thud*. Low walls, all covered in white curtains which made it feel as if she were traversing a cloud. The vibration on her skin remained, the tension along her spine keeping her rigid. Somewhere, a man moaned, long and loud, but that might have been the creak of a door or simply her imagination.

The hallway ended at another door, heavy and metal and locked, but she had a keycard. She let herself into a dressing room cast in muted orange light from a series of salt lamps around the perimeter. The walls here were curtained, too, and it made the room undulate, tattooing lacework patterns on her trembling flesh. Two rows of lockers ran down the middle, the fronts dressed up in carved wood.

Her suit and polka dotted blouse went into her cubby, replaced by a silk robe in richest obsidian, the fabric slipping against her skin like oil. She exchanged her sensible flats for a pair of tall black boots and tightened the laces to her thigh, her fingers hot against her skin. The moan came again—definitely a moan.

She slipped the mask over her face last, dark threads of nylon over molded ebony leather, cool against her suddenly feverish forehead. She secured the band at the back of her skull, just above her scar. The tension bled from her shoulders. Her lungs expanded.

Maggie headed for the door at the back of the room.

Into oblivion.

CHAPTER
SIX
TRISTAN

TRISTAN SIMMS LET his feet rest in the water, the edge of the pool grating against his heels. A large patio spanned the distance to the house, the pool sunk into the middle like a lake in a natural stone outcropping. His home felt very far away. No swimming today—he'd reached in to scoop a toad out of the filter, and the pad of his thumb was still stinging from the chlorine.

But the knife in his other hand helped him forget that pain. From the speakers hidden in the foliage, Elvis crooned *Hound Dog* with sticky sweet melancholy. He hadn't been able to get the King out of his head since his appointment.

He dragged the blade across the chunk of pine, careful to avoid splinters as the razor-sharp edge cleaved a tiny knot from the middle. It had been two hours since Tristan watched Maggie Connolly walk across the parking lot with his breath tight in his lungs. For those three minutes, there had been nothing else, nothing except her red curls gleaming under the streetlamps like a halo. But she was no angel, he knew that now. And the lithe way she walked, the rolling of her thighs beneath her dorky outfit. What was with that? Polka dots went out in the fifties, if they were ever in style at all. The clothes appeared to him like armor —dots instead of a metal breastplate, but equally effective at keeping most others away.

But not him.

In his mind's eye, Tristan watched her vanish into the building from his place on the other side of the parking lot, and then he was back beside the pool, the world around him alive with sounds. The wind whistled through the trees with a high-pitched whine that mimicked that of the birds. The chill in the air heaved with decay, dead leaves already skittering against the edge of the pool. The holdouts clung to the branches above him, stifling the moon.

Tristan frowned, inhaling deeply, chlorine fumes biting at his sinuses—cleaning his lungs. He wound the blade around the tiny wooden spear near his opposite pinky, carving out a savage corkscrew detail, trying to remember when he'd started doing this—creating these instruments of death. He could not remember. It seemed that he could not think at all. His brain and ears were fuzzy as if he had fallen into the pool and was unable to understand which way led to the surface. It felt like drowning.

He finished the final curve of the tiny four-pronged corkscrew and heaved himself to standing, the water sticky against his ankles. Uneasy—unsteady. He had never been a man of mystery, but he was certainly a man of privacy, mostly because he knew how easy it was to expose the things you wanted to keep quiet. And Maggie Connolly *bothered* him. Dragging words out of his mouth, forcing him to speak, to say *something* just to make it stop. His parents... a gunshot? Murder-suicide? Why had he told her that? He knew exactly what had happened to his mother—it was the fault of the cop even if he couldn't prove it.

But if Maggie could help him... might he finally be able to prove the detective guilty? It might prove Tristan guilty as well, but perhaps that was okay, so long as he didn't go down alone.

His feet ached as he slapped across the stone that surrounded the pool. She'd made him lie, he decided—forced it out of him. He'd been near the woman for ten minutes, and he'd started running his mouth like a drunk frat boy. Stupid—it was so stupid, especially because the police might have gotten to her already. And what if they had? Was she already poisoned against him? She'd certainly been looking at him as if she knew him.

Which is why he needed insurance—why he'd followed her to that club. Few others would know what was on the other side of that unassuming storefront, but he'd made millions by scrounging up things that others didn't want anyone to know.

He was in the business of secrets. Just like Maggie Connolly.

But not all secrets were easily kept. Where would she draw the line? It was impossible to tell, and he couldn't ask the person who'd sent him to Maggie for insight.

Not anymore.

He stopped near the gardens at the back of the pool's deck. Hydrangea bushes in blue and white loomed at either edge of the pool-scape, hiding the nets and pumps behind them, their boughs heavy with silken flowers, wilting as the season died. He crouched at the corner where the thick black dirt was overlaid by a skin of fine petals and discarded leaves. They crackled when he touched them—brittle as too-thin glass.

Tristan could not afford any more mistakes. He needed to make sure that Maggie wouldn't side with *them* when they finally got around to her. And if he'd screwed up this afternoon, which he had, he'd need to work carefully to hedge his bets.

He lowered the wooden spike into the dirt and scraped. Hunting.

Tristan did not have to wait long. The dirt undulated and shivered as the creatures beneath attempted to burrow deeper—attempted to escape. He pressed the wooden spike into the soil, careful not to get the filth onto his hands; the beetle beneath wiggled, then surrendered. He felt the shell crack, heard it, too, the satisfying snap of exoskeleton.

He stood carefully, squinting at his fingertips—no dirt. The stone tiles were chilly beneath his feet. The pool had changed color in the moonlight, silver-white like the dead eye of an evil giant.

Evil. The word echoed in his head. In the last few years, something had taken over his body—his brain—and he was only now realizing the extent of its malice. The medallion brightened with heat, a little circle of molten steel just above his clavicle. His mother had loved it, pious as she was, but right now it felt like a weight around his neck. Dragging him down.

Wait... no. He raised his fingers to his chest. The necklace wasn't there.

He was hallucinating. Exhaustion, surely. He hadn't slept in days, and when he did sleep... well. Who might die the next time he let fatigue drag him into bed?

Tristan ducked beneath the overhang of the porch. Angular walls of glass surrounded him as if he were already inside. His living room loomed ahead through the wall of windows; long black couches, area rugs in gray, modern art on the walls, the fireplace dark and cold. To his left, he could see his bedroom, the tall windows perfectly positioned to let in the moonlight. But that wasn't his destination either.

He turned to the right, to the glass wall that separated his home office from the outside. But that wall was not a window. A floor-to-ceiling freshwater tank stared back at him. And just in front of where he stood was a long rectangular lid—the feeding trough.

The water shimmered with movement at his approach, first one fish, then another, their silvery bodies glittering in the moonlight, the red on their bellies merging into a writhing band that appeared like a ribbon of blood. Piranhas were very old-school villain, but that was not why he liked them. He kept the fish because they'd eat anything.

The fish watched him, zipping into the middle of the tank, battling to be near the trough. He peeled the beetle from the tine of his makeshift weapon—cold and slick but it did not disgust him as the dirt did. The fish thrashed, the water turbid like the ocean's surf.

He held the bug, watching the twitch of one dying leg as it struggled above the tank's opening.

Tristan let go.

The fish set upon the bug, sparring and snapping, twisting and fighting. The water hissed and roiled, and even as he thought it, he could hear the hiss of volatile breath against his ear. He could feel teeth on his neck, the needling of fingernails on his back. He could smell the blood, cloying and metallic in the back of his throat. Something was wrong with him—very, very wrong.

I'm losing my mind.

A single rogue beetle wing floated from the fray, undulating in the writhing current before being snapped up by another fish.

In seconds, the water settled.

The horrible creature was gone.

CHAPTER
SEVEN

THE GREEN WALLS of her mother's breakfast nook made Maggie feel like she was being slowly smothered by the Jolly Green Giant.

Maggie shoved a bite of sweet potato toast into her mouth, relishing the way the jalapeños lit her tongue on fire, but it didn't drown out the stink of recently burned sage. That smell was in the carpet, marinating the fir-green curtains, locked into the very fibers of the emerald dress her mother had draped around her shoulders, maybe even soaked into the giant piece of jade she wore on her middle finger. Maggie suspected that her mother wore the jade so she could say she didn't have space for her wedding ring. Sometimes, a cigar was just a cigar, but sometimes a cigar was a convenient place to keep your wedding band while you daydreamed about being divorced.

Maggie adjusted the collar on her purple turtleneck, ribbed, nineties style—an original. A little itchy, but nothing went with her purple-and-gray striped pencil skirt quite as well.

"So how's your father?" Her mother always started

their breakfast conversations with that question, and every time, the answer was the same.

"Good days and bad days."

"Is there anything I can do?" Her mother had a sing-song way of speaking that was grating to most people—recklessly cheery—but Maggie heard the edge on her words. Sometimes she wished that wasn't true; it was easier to smile if you didn't know the people around you were suffering.

"No, Mom. There's nothing you can do to help. At least, not from here." *And you're not allowed to go anywhere else.*

Her mother forked up a piece of honeydew and raised an eyebrow. "That's unnecessarily hostile, darling."

Maggie shrugged, feeling as if she were on the stand. To be expected from her ex-lawyer mother, *ex* being the operative word. "It's a statement of fact. You can't, in fact, leave this house at will." She gestured to a space beneath the table where the ankle monitor blink-blink-blinked at the hem of her mother's dress.

"A ridiculous condition." Her mother snorted. "As if I'm going to sneak off to pass out weapons."

"You sure about that?" Her mother'd had a stash of weapons in her law office for twenty years, but Illinois required that you took safeguards before giving away a gun. No one knew about her weaponized charity gig until one of her clients stalked into her abusive ex's job and shot three others before killing her ex-husband. And Mom told the judge the entire truth: that she willingly provided weapons to vulnerable women regardless of their felony histories and without a single background check. Her honesty was as reckless as her cheerfulness.

Hence six months in jail and an ankle monitor.

Her mother looked at Maggie pointedly, a smile playing

at the corners of her lips. "Well, I suppose someone *should* take over in my stead."

Maggie suppressed an eye roll. Sure, domestic violence victims needed protection that the system was not providing, but statistics showed that women were more likely to die if there was a gun—any gun—in their house. And she was a numbers girl.

Mom glanced at Maggie's breakfast, frowned, and spooned up a bite of blobby yogurt from her plate, her chunks of honeydew slick with white. Her mother hated sweet potato toast, and she hated Maggie's choice of toppings even more, but nothing says good morning like cream cheese and pickled jalapeños.

"Speaking of taking over in my stead," her mother began, "you have a consult today, yes? One of mine?"

Maggie nodded. "I do." But Maggie's side gig was within the law. Sketchy, perhaps, but she'd looked at the data on domestic violence, examined the ethical considerations, and she'd made her decision. Make-a-choice Maggie, that's what all the cool kids called her. Kidding, kidding, they probably called her "D&D dweebie" or "that weird redhead."

Her mother was still watching her. "Do be careful with her, Maggie. Helena's husband is an absolute monster."

But Maggie did not need the reminder. She'd been dealing with monsters since she was thirteen, even if she didn't know the one who had taken her brother. "Don't worry, Mom. I'm fresh out of weapons that might escalate the situation."

Her mother's gaze darkened. It looked like she could handle a burn from the truth about as well as she handled the burn from pickled jalapeños.

"Are you still spending a lot of time at the cemetery?"

Oh, reversing the burn. *Nice.* "It helps me think."

"I wish you wouldn't do that. He's not even buried there—"

"It's the thought that counts." Maggie forced a smile. *What else should I do, shoot my way out of grief with an illegally procured weapon?* But she knew why the topic always came up. Though her mother would deny it, she still blamed Maggie for Aiden's disappearance. And she should. Even if she only knew half of the reasons.

"Have you gone to visit Kevin lately?"

His ashes were spread over a park on the far side of Fernborn. When they were children, it had been an office building, but the city had torn it down the week after she and Kevin used bricks to smash all the internal office windows. It wasn't as malicious as it sounded—the building was condemned and slated for demolition. They were just blowing off steam in an original "Rage Room"... while her brother was being kidnapped and murdered.

Yeah, she'd definitely failed enough in her life.

Mom was still watching her. Maggie shook her head. "No. I haven't been to the park."

"Good." Her mother nodded. "It's been six months since he died, dear." Six months was almost no time at all, but she wouldn't expect her mother to understand; she'd moved in with her current husband three weeks after she'd left Dad. "Maybe it's time for you to embrace the people in front of you instead of talking to the dead."

Tristan Simms's face flashed in Maggie's mind, then vanished. She couldn't shake the feeling that her mother somehow knew about her shortcomings with that patient and was twisting the knife a little deeper.

"What about Owen?" her mother asked, bringing her back. "Has he started dating yet?"

She almost laughed. "I'm not going to date Owen, Mom. He's still mad that I wanted to name our practice 'Shrink This.'" She still wished they'd gone with that instead of the most boring name ever: Lake Forest Counseling Center. "He's my business partner"—*secretary, ha-ha* —"and—"

"All the better. Your finances are already entwined. Less to worry about if you end up married."

"And if we break up?" Which they would. He didn't understand her sarcasm. *Like that matters—I don't sleep with anyone I'd actually talk to.* At this point in her life, she couldn't handle any more pain; she would not risk heartache. And dating Owen would be like... screwing her cousin. If she had a cousin.

"You'd be no worse off than you are now," her mom went on. "And the years are moving on whether you're ready or not." Her mother's eyes lit on the wall—a photo of her husband and his two teenage daughters whom Mom said were "a few bricks short of a wall." Mom's husband was attractive and good in bed, and Maggie suspected that this was why she married him. Her mother had married a smart guy once, and his mind had fallen apart. Might as well go with orgasms.

Even if she had forgone the ring.

"I'm not worried about getting older, Mom. I've got plenty of miles left on these loins." She slapped her thigh for emphasis.

"I'm not worried about your prowess, darling. I'm worried about you spending too much time with a vibrator. They can lead to de-sensitivity, you know."

Dear god.

"Speaking of prowess... how's Alex?"

"Alex is... Alex."

"Say what you will, but if you want a good time—"

"*Mom.*"

"I'm just saying, you and your friends act like children. You're in your mid-thirties, and you haven't changed since middle school."

Maggie took another bite of toast. "That's ridiculous— I've changed a lot. Owen, Sammy, and Imani all have children, and I'm *at least* a quarter inch taller than those little punks."

"And those ridiculous jokes you guys make, constantly saying you're going to see a man about a horse or some other such thing as if it makes any sense at all—"

"Pass the jalapeños, please." She glanced at her already full sweet potato, extra pepper slices scattered beside it on the plate.

Her mother shrugged one shoulder and pushed the jar her way. "I always tell you the truth, darling. Even when you don't appreciate it." She forked up a chunk of melon, green and shiny, dripping with yogurt—snotty looking.

Maggie took a bite and chewed, letting the peppers burn her lips. "Then maybe you should stop telling me the truth."

Her mother smiled. They both knew she didn't mean it. If there was one thing Maggie didn't tolerate, it was liars.

CHAPTER
EIGHT

THE SWEET POTATO and jalapeño extravaganza was still churning in her belly when she got to the office, a physical manifestation of regret at the week's mistakes. But she couldn't save everyone. All she could do was make the most logical choice and stick to it—what ifs would beat you down if you let them.

So instead of dwelling, Maggie took a breath, picked up her coffee mug, and appraised the man across the desk. Unlike Tristan Simms, this guy wanted to be here... kind of.

Elroy Hanson was shorter than she was, the thin, buttoned-down CEO of a mid-level paper company. Michael Scott, but without the hilarity or beet-farming coworkers, edged with "going to see a man about an umbrella" since he looked like he'd absorbed a thundercloud. White streaked the thick black hair at his temples and made the silver-blue of his eyes sparkle. The corner of his lip twitched up, but his mouth was not a flirty bow dripping with entitled machismo. Hanson knew why he was here, and he was more than a little bitter about it, growly like a storm.

She sipped at her chai, cinnamon burning her throat. "Cut the shit, Hanson."

The man's eyebrows hit his hairline. "Excuse me?"

She leaned back in her office chair and crossed her arms, her face mirroring the subtle smirk she'd seen on his just moments ago. Eye-to-eye, direct—unwavering. "We've gone over your motives thirty times, and you always say the same thing: that you cheated on your wife because you thought you deserved more physical attention than you were getting, and you knew that you wouldn't get caught. But that isn't why you're here."

"I'm here because my wife made me come. She thinks I'm a narcissist." He rolled his eyes, silver-gray dulling to a cloudy pewter—agitated, but sad. Narcissists knew how to play on your guilt and were usually a lot better at manipulation. Elroy wasn't good at manipulation or at faking being a good guy. He was desperate. He and his wife had already separated, and Maggie figured he had a month on the outside before his wife filed for divorce. She probably would anyway once she realized the extent of what he'd done.

"You're cocky, I'll give her that," Maggie said, "but you're not here for narcissism. You're here because you got an STD from a hooker you picked up at a hotel bar."

He crossed his arms, his shoulders stiff. "Most women expect some form of payment. Dinner, a hotel, a fancy gift —I paid for the house my wife lived in for the last fifteen years. Everyone has a price. At least the hooker was direct about it."

"That's all well and good, but it's a deflection."

"A deflection from what?" He threw his hands in the air. "I'm finally being honest here!"

"Are you? Because this hotel hooker situation isn't the same as the other incidents you described—the ones your

MEGHAN O'FLYNN

wife doesn't know about. You had sex with a woman at work, with a few women you met online, but you never paid for it. You don't *have* to pay for it. And you said yourself you were smart enough not to get caught—that it was the disease that finally outed you." She put both feet on the floor and waited until he met her eyes. "You weren't there for the sex."

"That's... I mean..." he sputtered. "What else would I be there for?"

She sniffed and recrossed her legs, feigning nonchalance. "What did you believe would happen when you picked her up?"

"I... I believed we'd have sex. What else would I think?" But his voice sounded less sure, and the spark in his eyes had dimmed.

"But you used protection with every other woman. Why not her, arguably the riskiest dalliance?"

His face fell. His eyes went tight. "I think maybe..."

She leaned closer, her gaze on Elroy's face. Her turtleneck was strangling her.

"Maybe I wanted to get caught," he whispered. And as he hung his head, she couldn't help but think that if she'd read Tristan Simms correctly, she'd have been able to help him, too, instead of scaring him off. Sometimes her best—anyone's best—just wasn't enough.

THERE WAS no room for error with her next patient—her mother's consult.

Helena was a fifty-year-old female with a traumatic history, an abusive husband, and two previous court-mandated therapists who had believed Helena was the aggressor due to her domestic violence arrest. Her probation had just lifted last week.

"Do you really think you can help me feel better?" Helena's brown eyes were tight with concern. "To be honest, I'm skeptical, but I heard... well. Things. That you help people when no one else can."

From Maggie's mother, no doubt. "You'll need a safety plan," Maggie said. "Leaving a relationship is the most dangerous part." This was all the more true since Helena's husband was a captain with the police force and had a prior girlfriend who'd died under mysterious—but ultimately deemed "accidental"—circumstances. And Helena already knew about the risks of going toe-to-toe with him. She'd called the police after he attacked her, and she was the one who ended up with a year of domestic violence counseling and an arrest record. Maggie wasn't entirely sure where her mother found these referrals, but Maggie had a system in place that was safer than a stockpile of illegal weapons.

"Leaving a relationship?" Helena's eyes filled. She ran a hand through her black hair, grabbing it into a knot at the nape of her neck—panicked. "I just want to... feel less afraid. Less depressed, you know? I can't leave; I've tried everything to get out. I've made calls to the police, but he always makes me look unstable and tries to get me locked away. If I try to get him arrested again or try to leave him, he'll kill me. I even looked at the domestic violence shelters, but he knows everyone there, and—"

"What if I told you that I have a place—a way out? Would you leave then?"

Helena dropped her hand and raised an eyebrow, but Maggie saw more than confusion in her expression. A burst of relief mingling with the heavy pallor of doubt. A justified reaction since no one had ever tried to help her before, at least not in the way she needed.

"You... do? That's why she sent me here?" Tears welled in Helena's eyes but did not fall, as if they were holding themselves in check the way Helena was holding hope in a stranglehold. Maggie had held onto a similar hope that Aiden would be found alive. Of course, she'd been severely disappointed. But if Helena ended up disappointed here, she'd also end up dead, and Maggie would be damned if she'd let that happen.

She leaned on her elbows and met Helena's watery gaze. "I'll provide what you need to get out of town safely. But you need to be sure that this is what you want. Once you're gone, there's no coming back—"

"Oh, there's nothing for me here." A single tear broke free and trailed a line over the hollow of Helena's cheek. She dropped her head and swiped at her eyes with the back of her hand. Bruises on her forearm. A scar near the elbow—a knife wound? "But it's still so fucking *scary*, and..."

"I know. But you can work on that once you're living in peace—once you're physically safe, somewhere far away from here."

By tonight, Helena would be hidden in Maggie's father's old house, and by tomorrow, she'd be on her way out of Fernborn. And then her mother's friends—Sammy's friends—in the district attorney's office could build a case against Helena's husband.

Helena's lip trembled, and this time, tears coursed down her cheeks. "I don't know what to say. What do you say to someone who's literally saving your life? It's like..." The words disintegrated into a heartrending sob that Maggie felt in the soft spot beneath her heart; her eyes burned.

Maggie passed Helena the tissues, trying to force the heat from her face, willing her voice to remain steady though her insides were trembling like a coked-out Chihuahua. "We'll make sure he can never hurt you again. You're going to be okay."

She only wished she could have made the same promise to Aiden. Or to Kevin.

CHAPTER
NINE

MAGGIE ATE A HAM, pickle, and banana pepper sandwich for dinner while completing case notes at her desk, but nothing tasted right. Her guts churned, a headache throbbing sharply as much in her ears as in her temples.

Why did she feel more impotent than a goldfish at a dog fight? Helena was already at the safe house, she hoped, and that alone should have made her week a success. She'd saved a life—what more did she want?

But Mannie wasn't going to get better, not in that prison. Elroy's wife was going to leave him regardless of whether he understood why he'd cheated. And Tristan...

Tristan Simms.

It had been three days, and she was still obsessing over the patient who had stormed out of her office. Her follow-up call had gone unanswered.

Maggie could hear her friends in her head, telling her to let it go, to stop overthinking, that she made the right decision—the only logical decision—but her own voice was louder: *Whatever he does next is on you.*

She pulled her paperwork closer. No looking back;

Tristan Simms's case was not life and death, and she had other cases that were far more pressing. Maggie snatched up her pen, gulped down the final dregs of cold chai, and flipped the first case file open.

Twenty-two-year-old Jack Olsen was serving a fourteen-year sentence for rape, but there was a catch: the guy was innocent. By the time he'd confessed, he had a shattered cheekbone and three broken molars. Now, after three years inside, Olsen's best chance was a professional to say that he wouldn't do it again, and she was prepared to stake her reputation on his intentions at tomorrow's parole hearing.

Yeah, if she could get a win for Olsen, maybe she'd feel better. Sammy would be happy too—he was the one who'd passed her Olsen's case on the down-low. He hadn't been sold on Olsen's guilt back when it went through the D.A.'s office, though the douchebag attorney who had prosecuted Olsen had disagreed.

She lowered the pen to the paper.

Bzzzzt-bzzzzt-bzzzzt.

She jumped; the pen left a long line of blue ink on the sheet. It figured that when she finally found something she could control, she got interrupted.

Ready to go back to that basement club, Maggie? You get all *the control there.*

She shoved the thought aside, fumbled the cell from the top drawer, and dropped it on the desk. She tapped the screen to answer.

"What's shakin'?"

At least Alex sounded happy. "Jell-O?"

"Rhetorical question, Mags. Are you listening to Elvis?"

Oh... yes. Alex snorted. "When did you get so weird?"

When my brain stopped working. When I started obsessing

over someone I couldn't help... again. "Isn't that the reason you hang out with me? Because you look so cool in comparison?"

Another snort. "Luckily, I'm here to save you from your lame-ass existence." From the cell came a noise that might have been the squealing of car tires.

"Where are you?"

A pause. Then: "Going to see a man about your bullshit work schedule."

Maggie glanced up at a light rap on the half-open door; Owen poked his head in. The Tiffany lampshade, once her father's, streaked his white-blond hair green—his shirt was spattered with rainbows of stained glass. It made him appear like a very tall but overwrought leprechaun who hadn't gotten the memo that his Lucky Charms had already been returned.

Maggie waved him into the office as Alex said: "Check your texts in five. We'll see you at eight o'clock sharp, and if you're late, I'm coming after you."

It was as close as Alex got to a threat. "Fine. I'll let Owen know."

"Already did," Alex said.

Of course. The line went dead. Maggie blinked at it, then turned to Owen, who was already shaking his head. "Abrupt send off?"

"You know Alex."

"Yeah." He nodded. "I'm going to grab dinner if you want to join." But his eyes remained tight at the corners. His broad shoulders were tense—knotted. He worked out daily, said it was good for stress relief, but it appeared the tactic was failing. The man needed a massage not free weights.

She pushed her phone aside. "I have a few things to

finish before I head over there, but... are you okay? If you talk for"—she glanced at the clock—"three hours, I can skip Alex's gathering. Unless Alex drags me out by the hair."

Owen shrugged. "I'm as okay as I can be. We both know how divorce goes. But thanks for being here." He flashed her a wan smile, then headed for the hall.

"Anytime." She grabbed her pen. "Hey, by the way, if you see Fluffy crawling around, let me know so I can recapture him."

Owen whipped back, ghost-pale even in her peripheral vision. "Oh god... what if it's in my office?" She looked up in time to see his gaze settle beyond her shoulder. "Maggie... he's right there." He shook his head. "That's the last time I fall for that."

Liar. But at least he was smiling—legitimately smiling.

She waved her goodbye and listened to the front door close. The elevator binged, bright punctuation like a period marking the end of Owen's work day. Then she lost herself in the scratching of ink on paper.

Maggie was putting the finishing touches on her statement when the phone rang, the sound deafening in the otherwise silent office. She nodded at the page—she had managed not to destroy it with more jagged blue lines. *Neat-o, magneet-o.* But beyond the window, the sky was thick with velvet night.

Shit, what time was it? Was she already late? *If you're late, I'm coming for you.*

She tapped the button to answer. "Hey, Alex, I—"

"Doctor Connolly?"

The voice was soft, pressured, but she recognized it. "Mr. Simms?"

"I need to see you," he whispered. "It happened again."

CHAPTER
TEN

THIS IS STUPID, Maggie. What are you doing?

But this was not some outside-the-law excursion. She was not passing out weapons or leaping in front of bullets. She was helping someone who had asked for it—who needed it.

Healing did not always come when it was convenient. She'd done therapy sessions in hospitals, at funeral homes, and once, on a boat. She'd visited the houses of agoraphobics, easing them into the office. Sometimes, healing happened in secluded strip malls, down in the dark, while wearing leather boots and face-obscuring masks.

And he'd sounded so... scared.

But it was more than that. Maggie couldn't deny the thrill in her blood—equal parts exhilaration and redemption, at least the possibility of it.

Such opportunities were few and far between. If she'd gone with Kevin the night he drove off that bridge, he'd still be alive. If she'd walked her brother home the day he vanished, he'd still be here too. With Tristan, she had done nothing so severe, just pushed a bit too hard in session, but now she could correct the error. She had the chance to fix it.

She hit her blinker and turned into the hotel lot, the sign glaring through the windshield and painting brilliant stripes across her vision. Maggie had refused to go to Tristan's home—she didn't know near enough about him for that—but at the hotel, someone would hear her scream if the session went horribly awry. She didn't anticipate a problem, though; she'd been around plenty of men who wanted to hurt her, and Simms didn't feel like one of them.

She parked in a hotel structure that reeked of fried shrimp, possibly of the gas station variety, then made her way through the lobby, her footsteps echoing hollowly against the high ceilings. The elevators were empty. So was the hall. But she could hear whispers of life from inside the rooms—laughter in one, the thudding of a headboard in another, someone having the time of their life.

Maggie paused in front of room 5478.

She raised her hand to knock, but the door swung inward before she could bring her knuckles down against the wood. Tristan Simms stood inside—jeans and a T-shirt, a wardrobe that felt out of character. Water speckled the cloth on his shoulders and dripped down one forearm; droplets shone in his close-cropped beard. And though his arms were pink, newly scrubbed, fresh gouges bloodied his fingertips. Black edged the fold beneath his tattered nails like he'd been clawing at the dirt.

Maybe he had.

He stepped back to allow her inside, and when no niggling prickle of gooseflesh warned her off, she followed. The suite was larger than her entire office, Owen's room and the waiting area included. The guy definitely had cash. The bed was mostly hidden behind a large wooden divider carved with a geometric sunrise, a partition turned modern art piece. The foreground was a living area. A full-sized desk stood against one wall; a long sofa in the center faced a flat-screen television on the wall opposite. He waved a hand at the bistro table in the far right corner—two covered trays on the top. "Are you hungry?"

She hadn't been hungry back before she'd started her paperwork, but the salty aroma of potato and rosemary made her mouth water. Maggie shook her head. "No, thank you." She sat in one of the four seats, one without a tray in front of it, and waited for him to take the seat across from her.

He appraised her for one excruciatingly long moment. Fine red lines spiderwebbed the whites around his irises; purplish bruises marred the flesh beneath his eyes. He'd had more than one sleepless night this week. Was he trying to stay awake on purpose—avoiding the sleepwalking by avoiding sleep entirely? He finally approached and lowered himself into the chair, but his foot bounced beneath the table. Agitated.

"How are you, Mr. Simms?" *Easy does it.* She'd misread him the first time, and she didn't want to do it again.

He shook his head. "I'm sorry to make you come all this way. I honestly don't know why I called you."

"Maybe you wanted someone to talk to. Someone to help you, right? For now, just think of me as... a guide. Like Gandalf."

He blinked. "Who?"

"Dumbledore?"

His darting eyes settled on her. He squinted. "Mufasa?"

"Okay, sure. We'll just skip the part where I throw you off a cliff."

THE DEAD DON'T DREAM

His brow furrowed. "I... no, in the movie, Mufasa is the one who dies."

"Spoiler alert. Next time give me a warning, eh?" But his shoulders had relaxed. *I should have led with Gandalf in the office... or the* Tiger King. *Wait, no.* Lion King. *Oh god, stop overthinking this.* "So, Mr. Simms, how did you end up in this hotel trading movie notes with a shrink?"

He glanced at her, then the room behind her, and finally dropped his eyes to the table. "I set the house alarms to go off if I tried to wander outside." His voice had the crooning yet husky quality of a lounge singer—Elvis after a screaming match with whoever'd be dumb enough to fight the King. Axl Rose? He seemed cocky. "I don't remember falling asleep, don't remember shutting the alarm off, but when I woke up, I was in my backyard, and there was dirt on my clothes—*all over* my skin." He shuddered. "There was dirt *everywhere*. So much dirt."

He spit out the word "dirt" like six-week-old lunch-meat, as if the soil was more bothersome than the wounds on his hands. That fit with the OCD-spectrum issues she'd suspected. Perhaps he'd showered twice, first at home, then here; maybe he'd do it ten more times before the night was out. She studied his face, watching his darting eyes, his pupils slightly dilated as he dragged his gaze to the window and locked it on the glass. His breath was coming much too fast; he was going to pass out if he wasn't careful.

"And there were..." he whispered. "There were flowers on me, these little purple petals."

Flowers? "Take a deep breath, Mr. Simms. In and out."

He did, but remained staring at the night beyond the window, the muscles in his jaw working—ropy. She could smell fear on him through the spicy hotel shampoo.

He finally turned back and crossed his arms, his fingertips ghost-white against his biceps where they weren't marred by clotted wounds. "Did you mean what you said about not calling the police if I had no intentions of hurting anyone?"

Not a promising start to this conversation. But she nodded.

His green eyes clouded. His cheeks were pale, as if the mere prospect of disclosure was sucking the color—the life —from his body. "I think I buried something tonight."

Ruh-roh. A body? He could have buried something else, but he wouldn't be worried if he'd buried a lunchbox unless it was full of body parts. She glanced at his hands, his bare forearms. He had no defensive wounds that she could see— if he'd attacked someone in his sleep and buried them in a shallow grave, there should be some sign of it. Was it real? It might have been a dream... or something more serious, a psychotic break. Everyone was a bit of an unreliable narrator, but potential delusions made things infinitely more tricky.

"Do you remember what you buried?"

His teeth ground together so hard she imagined she could hear them, the low grinding shriek of tooth and root. "I'm... not sure."

She was suddenly very aware of his hands, not his ragged fingertips, but the size of them—he could do some damage. But the hairs along her spine remained flat.

"Can sleepwalking make you feel like someone's watching you?" The line was a staccato burst of syllables.

Yeah, but so can a lot of things. Even she'd had moments of feeling watched in the past week, and a genetic predisposition to anxiety made that tendency all the more likely. Yet Maggie didn't think he was talking about some vague sense of being observed. He was nursing a specific, concrete fear.

"Are we talking about the police again?" And sleepwalking... it was dark now, but when had this happened? An hour ago? Two? He'd been asleep before dinner?

"It's not the whole police force, just this one detective, and..." He shook his head and leveled his gaze at her. His foot stilled beneath the table. "It's not in my head. Someone was there when I woke up, watching from the front yard. A few minutes later, I heard tires screeching up the road, but I wasn't fast enough to catch him. I wish I'd gotten it on video, but I have a long driveway, and they were too far down for the camera to see." He shifted, the edge of his bare foot poking from beneath the bistro table. Scratches ran from his toes to his heel—from chasing this unseen intruder?

Simms followed her gaze, frowned, then reached into his back pocket and retrieved a small package of alcohol wipes. Sharp astringent hit her nose as he scoured his foot with antiseptic, rubbing the already injured skin raw.

"If you think someone's following you, you should contact the police. Someone besides this detective you mentioned." But the police would be more worried about the dirt under his nails than keeping him safe from a potential stalker. It was even possible that this detective, if he existed, had a reason to watch her patient. Maybe the detective suspected that Simms was, *oh, I don't know,* burying people.

"What exactly am I going to say?" He righted himself and tossed the packet of wipes onto the table. "I don't even know where I went—my yard isn't torn up. I have no proof of a stalker on my house cameras. I look insane. I'm not even sure that whatever I did was a crime; no one found a body after my last episode."

Not that they discovered yet. But... "How do you know they didn't find a body?"

"It's my business. Technology, data management, the works. I scoured thousands of databases, including those of the police department."

"If you're hacking into the police database, don't they have a reason to watch you?"

"They don't know. I'm sure about that. *No one* knows; being discreet is part of the gig." He looked at her, suddenly calm as if talking about work had erased his other concerns from the blackboard of his mind. "I deal in secrets. Everyone has some—*everyone*." In those last lines, his tone went cold, as if he were talking directly to her, about her, and it was this that finally raised the hairs on the back of her neck. *What the heck is that about?*

"As far as the car in the road tonight," he said in his normal tired-Elvis voice, "I can't just accuse a detective of following me. I called it in before, and Rich made it look like my ex, which wasn't hard. Christine used to call my girlfriends, threaten them—got most of them to break up with me. Every time one of them stopped returning my calls, I knew it was because of her. But she'd have no reason to follow me now."

Rich... the detective? Helena's face flashed in her head —*he always makes me look unstable and tries to get me locked away*—then vanished. When Simms finally turned his face to the window once more, the prickly flesh that had popped up along her back settled. Panic? Threat? No, it didn't feel like nerves. Was it... a biological reaction? Yeah, because all girls just loved the whole I-might-be-a-murderer vibe. *He looks like your best friend turned lover, the man you almost married—the one who just died. Duh, Maggie.*

She shook the thoughts from her head, and said: "If someone's following you, a woman who calls to threaten your girlfriends might be the logical choice."

"Please don't side with him." The desperation in his voice was palpable, the calm knowing she'd seen moments ago all but gone. "Besides, Christine doesn't need to follow me. She always knows exactly where I am."

That sounded like a lot to unpack. But what were the odds that a stalker was the problem here? Why would a stalker watch him bury a body... or a lunchbox, for that matter?

He jerked his hand toward his head so fast that she startled, his fingernails close to his face as if examining them, as if he'd suddenly remembered that the dirt existed. He shuddered and snatched up the alcohol wipes once more, rubbing the edge against his fingernail. Dirt smudged the white, then blood, the red spreading over the cloth in a haphazard pattern of thick stripes like a child's drawing of a roadmap. And still, he scrubbed harder, his breath panting from his lips in tiny bursts. The still-forming scabs on his thumb opened; the butterfly bandage dislodged and stuck to the edge of his nail. Blood wept from the wound and dripped down the meat of his palm onto his wrist.

She laid a hand on his arm; his flesh was vibrating. He froze at her touch, blinked at her fingers, but she got the distinct impression he wasn't looking at her. A spot on the table, maybe. Thinking. Or trying to compose himself.

"You're safe now." Almost the same thing she'd said to Helena earlier. But Maggie couldn't be sure it was true for either. Maybe Helena's husband had shot her on the way to the safe house. Maybe a stalker was waiting for Tristan outside this very hotel so they could... what? Watch him dig around in the dirt?

She withdrew her fingers and leaned back in the seat. Was Simms delusional, dangerous, or a victim? She didn't want anyone to get hurt, but she also didn't want him to fall through the cracks, especially if he was innocent. Plus... no body, no crime. It could all be in his head. Very few had killed in their sleep—it was a statistical anomaly. And if she suggested hospital admission, she'd lose his trust, and he'd never seek help again.

Maggie squared her shoulders. "You should sleep here at the hotel tonight, Mr. Simms; maybe even for the time being. You might be able to shut off your home alarm in your sleep, but if you stay here, the hotel staff will see you if you try to meander out. We can give your car keys to the front desk with instructions to lock them up until daybreak so you can't abscond in the middle of the night. You don't want to be driving on autopilot." *Or burying bodies.* "What if you swerve to avoid hitting an imaginary Elvis and speed off a real bridge?" Like Kevin had, though she doubted the King had anything to do with Kevin's death.

He raised an eyebrow. "Does that happen often?"

"Elvis usually sticks to the prisons."

He raised one corner of his lip and finally nodded, but it looked more like defeat. "If it keeps people safe, then fine."

People—not him. "Have you had anything to drink tonight? Taken any drugs?"

His shoulders were so tight, they looked painful—the tendons in his neck were stretched like piano wires. "I usually make a vodka tonic in the evening... afternoon today. I thought I'd just take a nap, but..."

A vodka every day—that might indicate abuse. Kevin had started out with a nightly gin in high school. "I'd like you to get a full medical workup to rule out any physical factors and to ensure that you aren't taking any substances after you're asleep. We'll schedule a sleep study too." She'd read a case report of a woman who sleepwalked into a club and was none the wiser the next day; she believed she'd been roofied until video footage and a series of sleep studies proved otherwise. Actually...

If they could figure out where he had been, could they prove his fears were unfounded? Unless they *were* founded. That'd be a different kind of problem, but either way, they could make more informed decisions. "I also need you to lock up any weapons that you own, maybe pass them off to a friend."

"I don't have any weapons..." Understanding registered in his green eyes. "You think I did something wrong." Not a question.

"We have no evidence that you hurt anyone." *Yet.* "Some people get into bar fights or scuffle with neighbors while sleepwalking, so it's best not to have the means to escalate the situation. But if we can figure out where you're going while you're asleep, perhaps we can put your mind at ease."

He swallowed hard. "I'm not sure where I was. I just remember the purple flowers and... some streetlights. There was a bench, too, I think—one of those wrought iron ones."

That sounded like a park. Good—someone would notice a fresh grave in a park. But there were a lot of parks out there, dozens if he drove. "Do you have GPS on your car, tracking on your phone?"

Tristan shook his head. "I didn't have the phone with me, and I drive older muscle cars—no GPS. I appreciate the classics." He cut his eyes at her. He must have noticed her DeLorean in the office parking lot.

"It's like I'm purposefully trying to keep secrets from myself," he went on. But his breathing had steadied. For a moment, she heard a little voice whispering that he knew exactly where he had been, but she pushed that away. He'd just told her that he buried something, implied that he might have buried a body; he had no reason to hide the location. *Unless he wants to lure you out there next week the way he lured you to this hotel room.*

He winced at his bleeding thumb, then wrapped the bloodstained alcohol wipe around his hand. "Sometimes I feel like I'm an entirely different guy—someone I don't even recognize." He met her gaze. "I think you know what that's like." His voice no longer shook, and his eyes had cleared, brightened, the look almost accusatory as it had been when he'd mentioned "secrets."

Gooseflesh exploded across her back, pure instinct—threat. Her fingertips dampened. Something was very wrong. She didn't know what it was, but she was suddenly quite certain that Tristan Simms was not at all what he appeared to be.

CHAPTER
ELEVEN

THEY WENT over the safety plan four times: car keys at the front desk, door locked, straight to bed. Maggie had been one step from handcuffing him to the bedpost, but there wasn't a page in the psychologist's ethics manual for consensual non-sexual handcuffing. And while she wanted to ensure that he didn't leave again, make sure he followed the safety plan to the letter, she couldn't stay there—*shouldn't* stay. She'd seen her father become so wrapped up in his patients that he forgot to eat for weeks, and her mother's obsession had gotten her arrested and disbarred.

Maggie had no intention of ending up there, but she was walking a thin line—she could *feel it* eating at her, the barest support of tightrope wire beneath her arches, between the logical-ethical brain book and the other side—her guts. And her guts weren't reliable. She'd seen this man twice—*twice*—and she had already lost hours considering him, plus spent an evening in his hotel room. She hadn't done anything illegal, nothing ethically unsound, but it didn't look good. And he might be delusional. He might be dreaming. He needed a medical workup.

They had another appointment in a couple days, one that would hopefully clarify the issues at hand, but for tonight, she needed space to think.

Maggie's shoulders were so tight she could feel the tension in her neck when she whipped into the Sherwood's parking lot beside Alex's VW bug. She snatched her leather case off the back seat. The DeLorean's door screeeeeeeed through the night.

The September air had already taken on a crisp edge like decaying crabapple; she could smell the chilly sweet rot as she made her way through the parking lot and ducked beneath the awning. From the walkway outside the oak door, she could hear the steady *thud-thwack, thwack, thud-thwack* of metal on wood, the heavier *thonk* of wood on wood. She could feel it in her bones, too, pent-up aggression seeking escape, the pulsing of unspent energy.

Inside, the walls were papered with an expansive realistic mural—trees as far as the eye could see. It'd be like walking into a forest were it not for the lanes along either side, targets at the far end of each. Round tables sat positioned in the aisles, and the back of the building was marked by a long counter where they served refreshments. It resembled a bar turned gun range, but there were no guns here. Bows and quivers leaned against the front of some of the lanes; one man held a spear. The spear-throwers got charged extra because of the damage to the wooden targets, but the sharper weapons didn't create as much drama—they went in fast and came out smooth. *That's what she said.*

"Mags!" Alex was a large voice in a tiny body, and her words rang through Sherwood, excited as if she were pitching a high-priced lakeshore property, which was what she did for a living. Were the hollows beneath her eyes a bit darker than usual? But Alex wasn't one for sharing... or for dwelling on the past, at least not out loud or in the presence of others.

Alex skittered up to Maggie's side with the light movements of a pixie fairy. Her enormous earrings swung against her shoulders below her neat blonde bob as she linked her arm around Maggie's elbow.

Maggie knew better than to resist. She let Alex drag her past five, six, then seven wide lanes. Instead of paper targets, painted human silhouettes stared as she passed by them, all tattooed by the remnants of blades. *Thwack. Thwack.* Cheers rose from somewhere to the right, the sound of slaked bloodlust.

Owen stood near a lane at the end of the row, his face pinched. Owen Jennings-Steele, with his fancy hyphenated last name, was a testament to progressive non-violent childhoods, and even throwing blades in a controlled environment made him uncomfortable. But he always showed up. That was the kind of man he was.

Alex released her arm, and Owen handed Maggie a glass—lemonade. The tension at the corners of his eyes and in his wiry forearms had dissipated, a far cry from his demeanor at the office. Lucky duck—her own shoulders were bundles of angry knots, which made sense after being in a hotel room with a guy who might have buried someone a few hours prior.

Had he? Nah, surely not, but what were informed decisions without all the information?

"Hey, Mags! You made it!" They both turned as Sammy headed back from the lane, ax in hand. Sammy had dark skin and a shiny bald head, his polo shirt loose over his jeans. Her oldest friend, second grade to be exact. His eyes had remained excitable through years of Dungeons and

Dragons and marching band practice and law school, his grin forever infectious. Sammy's wife, Imani, was right behind him. Her tight curls smelled like lemons and courtroom when she threw her arms around Maggie and squeezed.

"Show us what you've got, big shot." Sammy tossed his hand ax in the air, caught it by the handle, and passed it over the table. But unlike Owen, his eyes were tighter than usual. Was he okay? Probably work stress. *Like me.* Or… Kevin. *Also like me.*

She shook her head. "I brought my own."

"Oh. Yeah, I forgot what a dork you are." Sammy shook his head, and Imani elbowed him, her yellow silk blouse shimmering in the light—perfectly professional despite the hour. She and Alex had tried to give Maggie a makeover exactly once, but Maggie had wrapped a silk scarf around her head and done an impression of Alex's Polish grandmother "going to see a man about a pazcki" until the store clerk kicked them out. She had not regretted it then, and she did not regret it now.

On cue, Alex strolled up to the table and set her drink on the edge. Cranberry juice, like always—they did not serve alcohol here. Whiskey and weapons were a terrible combination, of course, but they'd started coming here because of Kevin; he'd been in recovery since his twenties. "Leave her alone, Sammy. Mags would be bored with that little ax of yours."

Sammy reared back with fake shock, his fingertips against his chest. "This ax has crushed many a board, I'll have you know."

"If you say so, honey," Imani said.

Maggie chuckled and set her lemonade down. Her axes, a birthday gift from Alex, were still sheathed in their leather case, and as she made her way to the line, she pulled one free. The weight against her palm centered her, but her skin was still prickly like she had insects marching along her spine.

She stepped to the tape line. Maggie raised her arm, back singing, fingertips melting into the cool leather of the handle, her vision tunneling on the target. She whipped the ax, listening to the whistle of the weapon cutting air. The blade went wide, thunking into the wood beside the target's head.

"You suuuuuuck!" Sammy boomed.

Brothers. She took a deep breath, but found that her hand was already steadier. Maggie raised her arm again.

This one caught the target square in the neck. *That one's for Mannie—for the X that marks the spot.*

Alex hooted. "Get 'im, Mags! Hit him in the dick!"

Maggie retrieved the blades. Sweat prickled between her shoulders; the ants on her skin remained. She went again. *Thwack, thwack.* Retrieve.

For the hours spent behind the desk—for Helena.

Thwack, thwack. Retrieve.

Tristan, the gouges on his hands. Tristan Simms panicked about going to sleep.

Thwack, thwack. Retrieve.

Tristan with his soft skin and his piercing eyes, sitting in the hotel room all alone, trying not to bury another human beneath the ground—*I heard you're good at keeping secrets.*

Thwack, thwack. Retrieve.

Again. Again. Again.

It wasn't enough. Not nearly enough. She threw the last ax—it flew to the left of the target, hit the metal bar at the corner, and ricocheted back toward the group, but buried itself in the rubber mats before it got too far. Imani was no longer standing at the table behind her, Alex either—gone to get food? Hopefully, they'd bring back nachos… and extra jalapeños. Maybe she should have eaten those rosemary potatoes at the hotel.

"Nice shot!" Owen called from his spot behind the table.

She raised her brows in his direction. "You sure? I was aiming for you."

Owen laughed, but it didn't reach his eyes; he looked hurt. *Ah, Owen.* The rest of them had leaned into sarcasm in high school, like any D&D-loving band geeks should. Get funny or get hurt. All except Alex. She had been popular, but a freak cancer diagnosis and a radical middle-school mastectomy had made her re-evaluate her group of shallow socialites. And when Maggie's brother vanished, she'd ended up being the one hugging her in the school bathroom while she cried, a surgical drain sticking out below her right armpit. Alex hadn't let go since. When she'd had reconstructive surgery in high school, Maggie had stayed in the hospital room with her.

Maggie collected her blades and gestured to Owen —*your turn*—then headed for the stool beside Sammy. But despite being the only one at the table, Sammy did not look up when she eased onto the chair beside him. He was too busy frowning at his ice cubes like they'd wronged him somehow.

She patted him on the shoulder. "What's wrong, dorkus?"

He shook his head. "Just work stuff."

"Is it protected?" Attorney-client privilege was as rigid as doctor-patient confidentiality. She glanced at Owen, already at the tape line, readying himself to throw... badly. His form was all wrong.

Sammy shook his head, but finally drew his eyes from the glass to meet hers. "No, we don't have anyone to charge yet, but there's going to be a lot of shit coming down the pipeline. They're pulling out old missing persons cases, trying to make connections between the victims."

The room stilled; Maggie could no longer hear the thudding of Owen's blades in the wood. Actually... Owen wasn't throwing. He stood with his back to them, fiddling in his front pocket—his phone. She tried to keep her voice steady as she said: "So you're worried they won't catch the... criminal?" Missing persons meant kidnapper. Or murderer.

"I'm worried they'll end up with another unsolved." He sighed. "The latest woman went missing late last week, but she matches a known profile from three years ago. Unless they catch this guy, and I lock him away for good, this week's disappearance won't be the last."

This week... Three years ago... There wasn't enough air.

Tristan's first episode had been after his mother died, but the sleepwalking had calmed then started again three years ago... right around the time Sammy's first victim went missing. And the episode that drove him to therapy had occurred late last week, which matched Sammy's timeline, and...

I think I buried something tonight.

And she'd just left him in that hotel room.

"Mags!"

She jumped at Owen's voice—pressured. His eyes were tight, too, infused with concern, his knuckles white around his cell. "We have to go."

"We just got here!" And she really needed to talk to Sammy

about this missing-woman thing. The pit in her guts was burning, worry tugging at the chasm beneath her heart. She had a million questions she needed answers to, not the least of which was: *Is my patient a kidnapping, body-burying murderer?*

"There's an issue at the office. The police are already there." Owen slipped his jacket over his shoulders, his voice strained, his eyes bright with panic. "We need to hurry."

CHAPTER
TWELVE

THE AIR on the ride back to the office felt exceptionally heavy, like she was driving toward her own murder, though it didn't sound like the issue at the office was dead-body related. Yet, her brain would not calm. Her guts were a twisted nest of briars.

Was Sammy's case related to her patient? Tristan was sleepwalking, but he had no defensive wounds. He hadn't kidnapped someone—killed someone—had he? Maybe if the victim was drugged... or charmed. Sleepwalkers could appear totally normal, spitting game better than half the men who had hit on her over the years. At least Tristan hadn't likely used the "Did you fall from heaven?" line.

Shit. He'd said he didn't want to hurt anyone. She'd filled in *anyone else.* Then Sammy. And now... this thing at the office.

She needed to talk to Sammy again—she needed to fill in some blanks. Because if her patient really was a killer... she'd have to do something about it.

A police car sat in the office lot where she usually parked—lights off. Not an emergency, not anymore. She squeezed her DeLorean next to Owen's Mitsubishi Outlander and hustled through the front doors and up the stairs. The thought of being stuck in an elevator right now made her want to scream, and every hollow thunk that echoed through the stairwell made her heart beat faster and intensified the throbbing in her temples. Her turtleneck smelled of rosemary and salt, which made her stomach roll. She liked the feeling at the top of the roller coaster hill, the exhilaration before the fall, but she didn't usually tumble down the track like an overripe cantaloupe.

She burst from the stairwell on the third floor and hustled down the hallway. The door to the suite was ajar, the doorjamb smashed. Owen and the policewoman at his side turned her direction as she skirted the waiting area chairs and the reception desk that was only for show—they currently used an answering service. No guard downstairs either; bare-bones, which was by design. Many clients disliked signing in with a uniformed stranger for privacy reasons, and they'd never had a security issue... until now.

"Are you Magma Connolly?" the officer asked.

Magma, ugh. A name chosen by her parents because of her fiery red hair, but they hadn't kept up the hippie-dippy trend when they'd named Aiden. Her working theory was that they'd liked him better. "Depends. Am I hot enough?" *What are you doing, Mags?* But it was a knee-jerk reaction—she'd had to brush off enough jabs about her name in elementary school. And middle school. High school. College. *Get funny or get hurt.*

The policewoman raised a thick dark eyebrow. It made the bindi in the center of her forehead rise like a literal third eye, vaguely suspicious. Maggie couldn't help recalling the way officers had interrogated her parents after Aiden went missing, barking questions, asking why they hadn't kept a closer eye on him. They'd questioned Maggie for hours, too, though she'd appeared more suspect. Her hair had covered the gruesome bite taken out of her head, but she hadn't been able to hide the bruises on her knuckles.

Maggie scanned the room. Behind the cop, the door to Owen's inner office was ajar, but unlike that of the front door, the frame and the knob appeared intact. The wood around her doorframe was a splintered mess. Had the police arrived before the intruder could ransack the rest of the place? Or was she just special?

The officer was still watching her. "Yes, I'm Maggie Connolly," she said, sidling toward her door. The officer lowered her eyes to the pad in her hand, maybe checking boxes for her report. Maggie toed the door open, wanting to race in, but also dreading to see what lay beyond. "What happened?" she said to no one in particular—whoever knew the answer should respond.

Maggie stepped across the threshold.

Her brother's baseball mitt was undisturbed, a little league game ball snugly inside. A photo of the two of them that many believed were Maggie's children still sat beneath the window. The chairs in front of her desk were intact. Her water bottle lay on its side on the desktop, butting against her paperweight, but both were unbroken. That was where the normalcy ended. Papers—blank assessments, case notes, intake forms—were scattered over the seats, on the desk, on the floor. The canvas that usually hung behind the desk lay cockeyed on the carpet —TRUTH.

Fluffy was fine, thank goodness, crouched in his makeshift cave behind the desk. The only witness, all those eyes, all those legs, and he couldn't help. Didn't that just figure. At least she was no longer hungry. *Ain't no diet like the office break-in diet because the office break-in diet makes you want to hurl.*

"Tenants across the street saw a flashlight in the window about an hour ago," the officer said from the doorway. "Do you know of anyone who might want something from you? The rest of this place was untouched, so whoever broke in was after something in your office."

It was her mother's voice that answered inside Maggie's head: *Do be careful with her, Maggie. Helena's husband is an absolute monster.*

Maggie finally let her gaze rest on the area she'd been avoiding: the antique filing cabinets, the ones her father had proudly displayed in his office until he'd been unable to practice. Her blood boiled. This was worse than a smashed doorframe or a toppled painting. Her secrets—*their* secrets.

She headed that way and crouched beside the lower drawer. The back of her desk appeared fine, but the locks on the filing cabinet were shredded, the latch carved apart— had someone come in here with a chisel? A section of files near the middle of the drawer was missing, hanging folders scattered haphazardly on the floor in front of the cabinet, pages fluttering in the wispy air from the heating ducts. She frowned into the void, mentally checking off current clients in her head. Today's intakes were there. Mannie's case file was too. She didn't have a file on Helena, so if the culprit was Helena's soon-to-be-ex-husband cop, he'd have found nothing. But Elroy Hanson's file was missing and...

Tristan's file wasn't in its assigned alphabetical space either—whoever had broken in had definitely taken those two... or tossed them around. But why?

Elroy's wife wouldn't show up to look at what he'd said about her. Tristan had no reason to peek, not that it would matter if he did. She'd only managed to finish one progress note on Simms, and she kept such notes purposefully vague so that if they were subpoenaed they would be of little use to a prosecutor—*Alert, oriented x3, no suicidal/homicidal ideation, family history discussed as part of biopsycholosocial assessment.*

She frowned. What the hell? Were there other files missing? Anyone who was court-mandated wouldn't break in here and risk taking a file when they needed those notes to go to their probation officers. Some of her current patients came in with their partners, and none had the personality traits you'd expect for a crime like this. And if it was a previous patient, someone discharged in months or years past, they'd have broken in back then, when they were still under her care.

No, you couldn't always predict what people might do. But you definitely needed a reason, rational or not.

"Anything missing?" the officer asked from the doorway. Her voice was like syrup—sticky and slow enough that it hurt Maggie's teeth.

Yes. She let her eyes slip to the carpet where orange progress notes crinkled with her footsteps. "Not that I can tell." The lie hurt her chest, but she couldn't disclose the names of the patients who had missing files. She would tell her patients what had happened directly and go from there.

She abandoned the filing cabinets and bent, gingerly lifting the painting—dented, a small tear in the canvas near the corner, the wood frame showing through. Papers back here, too, Elroy's name on the ones behind the painting. Tristan's name graced the cardboard cover of the file at the baseboard. Her shoulders relaxed. It looked like she hadn't lied after all. She retrieved Tristan's folder and flipped it open, but inside the cardboard cover...

Nothing. The progress note, however vague, was gone.

The referral page was gone too. She didn't see his assessment forms. *Dammit.* Maggie scanned the floor quickly, looking for the pages from Elroy's file—those were definitely here, intact, covered in her familiar blue scrawl. But nothing from Tristan Simms's file remained in her office.

She lifted the painting with shaking hands and gently repositioned it on the wall—TRUTH, TRUTH, TRUTH. Unless you needed to LIE, LIE, LIE to the cops, apparently.

Owen was talking to the policewoman, something about cameras, but she couldn't focus on his words. In all her years of practice, she'd never met a single psychologist who'd had their files vandalized. A professor in graduate school had been killed by his patient's jealous boyfriend—the jury was still out on whether he was sleeping with her —but she could think of no one who might want to make her files vanish. Though Tristan Simms had a unique set of complications, he hadn't stolen his own file. He'd been with her when this had happened, right? An hour ago, the officer had said.

Maggie glanced at the clock. She was with him an hour and a half ago. It had taken her thirty-three minutes to get to the office just now, and she wasn't known for her conservative driving speeds. If he'd come here when she'd been driving to Sherwood... he would not have made it. That window was too narrow. Plus, she'd given his car keys to the front desk herself. Was he dumb enough to take a lead-footed Hytch to a crime scene? No way.

"Maggie?"

She jumped at the sound of Owen's voice. Her friend was holding his cell, his arm stretched her way. Surveillance footage on the screen—footage of the parking lot.

Maggie stepped closer to examine the grainy video of someone, presumably the intruder, stalking across the lot wearing a baseball cap and a large camouflage coat. It was impossible to see the intruder's face as he walked up to the building, but it wasn't Tristan Simms. It was in the stride—too confident, that march. Almost angry. And Tristan Simms was a cautious man, someone well-versed in video cameras and surveillance. An expert. If he'd broken in, they wouldn't have caught him on video, which wasn't exactly comforting.

She shrugged at Owen—*I don't know him.* But as she did it, an uneasy prickling began on the back of her neck and spread over the wings of her shoulder blades. She turned, half convinced that she'd catch the glimpse of someone in the window, but there was only the oppressive black of night and her patient's words echoing in her brain: *It's not in my head. Someone was there when I woke up.*

What if he was right? Though she had no idea how this break-in might be connected to his sleepwalking or whether he was being pursued by the detective he'd mentioned, it seemed that he *was* a target. Someone really was watching him.

But that wasn't what was making the flesh crawl along her spine. She often kept strange hours—she was usually still at work now. Whoever had been here had known exactly when to break into her office. When she'd be gone.

They were watching her too.

CHAPTER
THIRTEEN
TRISTAN

THE HOTEL ROOM door eased closed with a hiss, the latching mechanism so quiet he almost didn't hear it. Tristan kicked off his shoes.

"Took you long enough."

Tristan blinked his bleary eyes. He'd had a few drinks since the good doctor left, and his world was hazy and discombobulated. The room was dark, steeped in shadow, but that voice had to come from somewhere. It was not coming from the uneaten potatoes still resting on the bistro table. It was not coming from the sofa. He walked past the divider that separated the living area from the bed and flicked the light on.

Christine rose like an apparition from the mattress, her blonde hair wisping back from her throat, her bare toes sickly pale against her brilliant red toenail polish. Red like blood.

His belly rolled, sick and oily. "I thought you weren't coming," he said. Did he really think that? Was he drunk? Maybe. Or it was the sleeping pill he'd swallowed. It was harder to run around if you were drugged to the gills… or so he hoped. "How'd you get in?"

"The people at the front desk know me by now, the same way they know you." Christine moved toward him, but her feet were silent, completely silent—that was weird, wasn't it? She stepped over the black duffel bag, and all he could hear was the shh-ing of her silk pants against the floor and the blood whooshing in his ears. "I told them I forgot the keycard."

Of course—that made sense. His regular patronage of the hotel was something he'd neglected to mention to the doctor.

Christine frowned suddenly, her glittering sapphire eyes sharp with agitation, and when she spoke, the words were low and dangerous. "Where were you, Tristan?"

"Just taking a walk. I needed some air. It's been a… really long night." The words caught in his throat. "A… bad night. And—"

"I'm not here to talk." She stepped closer. "I'm here to figure out why you called me and then vanished. Why you'd keep me waiting."

"I'm here now."

"Yeah." She smiled. "You are." But her gaze remained suspicious. "Were you with someone else?"

The world pulsed black—Christine vanished. But though he could no longer see her, he still felt compelled to answer. "Not just now."

"Earlier?"

He stayed silent. But he had been with someone else, in a manner of speaking.

The world was still dark, his eyes screwed shut; amorphous gray shapes scurried behind his eyelids. But he felt her when she raised her lips nearer to his ear, could imagine her blonde hair brushing his shoulder.

"You're such a piece of shit." Her breath was damp against his neck—so hot.

"I know."

She slid her palms up his biceps and wrapped her fingers over his shoulders like talons. They served as talons, too, clutching at him, as much his mind as his meat. The first time she'd grabbed him like this, he'd still been stripping; she was the club's bartender. She'd used that grip to pull him out of a dark place, and she hadn't let go since. For a while, he thought they'd finally split for good, back when he'd thought Tonya was the one. But Tonya was gone now.

They were all gone now.

Only Christine ever stuck. Like briars in his flesh. Like nails in a coffin.

"You don't deserve me," she whispered.

"No. I don't." But she was here anyway. He was cemented to her as if she'd stapled their skin together, and the rending pain each time he tried to rip himself away was more than he could bear. But he hadn't thought about her when he was watching the doctor walk into that club.

His heart throbbed in his temples. His stomach churned.

Her nails scratched harder, sharp and pointed, digging into the soft spots around his shoulder blades. He could feel the corners scoring his flesh, the sweet agony where she broke the skin. She cut her nails that way on purpose, filed them to razor's-edge precision. He was certain.

"Why do you treat me like this, Tristan?"

"You already said why."

Her tongue swiped at the side of his neck—he wished

she'd just bite him, tear his throat out already. "I want to hear you say it."

He inhaled sharply as her nails dug deeper into his skin. "Because I'm a piece of shit."

She released him. His shoulder was wet, his shirt sticky where she'd scratched him. "I've had it with you, Tristan," she snarled. "I have really fucking had it."

He nodded. "I know." He kept his eyes closed and turned slowly, showing her his back. Tristan hung his head. He was trying to breathe, but the pressure in his chest was too intense, his heart fluttering like a trapped sparrow. He could hear her behind him, a scraping sound like rats in the walls, but he made no move to investigate, the duvet before him a blank void of nothing. Oh, what he'd give to feel empty—to give in to the numbness.

But he did not feel numb when she returned to him. Her palms pressed hard against the fresh wounds, tugging the pulsing ache in his shoulders to a barbed crescendo. She massaged his injuries, angrily—meanly—then slid her fingertips higher over his neck, the flats of her palms tight against his throat. Blood rushed to his head. His temples throbbed. His face burned as if with fever. For a single excruciating moment, he wondered what it might be like to let her keep going—to let her choke him out of existence.

But then she released him, her fingers creeping down over his clavicle, then past his abdominal muscles to tug at the hem of his shirt. She jerked the garment up over his head and tossed it to the floor. Then nothing. He waited. The frantic zzzzz of the zipper on her duffel bag vibrated his eardrums.

He bent forward and put his palms flat on the bed.

Tristan heard the whip a split second before he felt it, a

high-pitched whistling as it sliced the air. It cracked against his spine; a terrible sharp sting lit his nerves. Again. Again.

He deserved it, as terrible as he was. But as the flesh on his back split, all he thought about was Doctor Magma Connolly.

CHAPTER
FOURTEEN

THE NEXT DAY dawned with a thickness in the air, a heady vibration that prickled over her skin like infected gooseflesh. Clearly, someone wanted to know what Tristan had told her. They cared enough to come after her and violate her sanctuary—her patients' sanctuary.

She had scoured Google Earth the night before looking for local parks with the bench Tristan had mentioned, looking for purple flowers, but none had both, and too many had one or the other. Trying to figure out where he was going at night was impractical anyway. The break-in, along with Sammy's revelation about an unidentified kidnapper, had changed the equation from "maybe we'll uncover a logical non-murdery reason for your sleepwalking" to "I need to figure out why someone broke in to my office and is maybe killing women."

But she had other patients. Other life-and-death situations.

Jack Olsen was top of the list when she started her day. Now, sitting at her desk in her office, she could still smell the prison, that cold, clammy room where Jack waited before the men who would decide his fate.

She'd told them her clinical opinion: that Jack was unlikely to harm anyone. Yet, even as she spoke, she'd known what their answer would be, and she had wished she could projectile vomit *The Exorcist* style, give those men the farewell they deserved.

Denied. Denied. Denied. Only one parole board member, a twitchy *Night-Before-Christmas* skeleton of a man who looked on the verge of a full-blown panic attack, blinked before he followed suit. Jack had just stared; only one of his cheeks was wet, as if only half of him was crying.

Half of her still was.

She set her mug on her desk, slopping chai over the rim, narrowly missing her laptop. Maggie soaked it up with a napkin and leaned back in the seat. She'd visit Jack next week, see if an appeal was possible, but for now, she had to work on the things she could change. Even if she didn't know what the right course of action was... yet.

So, what *did* she know?

Someone had broken into her office and stolen Tristan's file. *Only* his file—she'd verified that last night. And she'd been feeling eyes on her back since Friday; since the day Tristan Simms first came to see her. Maggie didn't believe that was a coincidence.

But if Tristan was kidnapping women, and subsequently burying them, a stalker was unlikely to watch him do it without calling the authorities—a detective definitely wouldn't. If the goal was blackmail, they only needed one such event, and this had been going on for years. Even a romantic stalker would have used that information before now as a way to build trust with their desired conquest. Tristan would have asked that person for help with preventing his homicidal sleepwalking instead of seeking out a shrink to guess at things he already knew. Involving Maggie was an unnecessary risk for a killer.

And the burglary certainly indicated another malevolent force at play—another guilty party.

A thought had occurred to her overnight, hooked into her brain like a barb, and it had only been driven in more deeply by Jack's desperate eyes: What if, instead of being the culprit, Tristan Simms was a victim as he'd said? He'd been having these episodes for years, since his mother was murdered—shot by his father. What if he'd witnessed an unrelated crime during a sleepwalking episode in the aftermath? What if he'd seen the kidnapper that Sammy had mentioned? What if the real culprit was now watching Tristan to figure out what he knew? That person wouldn't tell a soul about Tristan digging in the dirt. That could also explain the timing of his sleepwalking episodes —just hearing about the crimes might have triggered a relapse.

She frowned at her tea, but the mug offered no consolation and even fewer ideas. There weren't many reasons to steal a therapy file, and the most likely motivation was that the thief believed Tristan Simms might have told her a secret—something they didn't want anyone to know. Heck, his sleepwalking episodes could be him trying to unearth a body he'd seen someone else bury. Maybe he couldn't remember where he'd seen it, and his traumatized brain was waking his limbs each night to go searching.

Crazy? Possibly. But that was the thing about being a shrink—you've almost always seen stranger. It made even the most far-fetched possibilities seem... well, possible.

She sipped her spicy chai tea—extra black pepper in this blend, her third mug of the day—and wrote her notes.

But as morning bled into afternoon, every session dragged her thoughts back to Tristan Simms.

Her eleven o'clock was Eric Small, a court-mandated patient with two DUIs, seeing Maggie to complete alcohol abuse counseling. As he described all the reasons why he shouldn't have to be there, why it was really the system's fault, she heard Tristan's voice: *I don't know what I do when I'm asleep.* And then Sammy's words: *Unless we catch this guy, this week's disappearance won't be the last.* And Kevin—poor Kevin—the night she'd turned him down, when she'd said, "I love you, I just don't know if I'm ready to get married, if I'll ever be—"

"Doctor Connolly?" Eric Small blinked at her. He had finished complaining and was surely waiting for her to ask questions. Sometimes silence was an opportunity for patients to direct the session, but here... she needed to pull herself together.

Maggie refocused as best she could, redirecting him to what his behavior had done to his family—if he thought he had any role in the conviction. No, of course he didn't, which meant he'd be here for the long haul. The case that had been punted twice already, through two different mental health professionals. She was supposed to be good at "tricky patients," but his smug, insolent face made her jaw clench. He needed help, but he didn't *want* help. He was mandated to be here, and even then, he couldn't bring himself to cooperate. She never took such things personally, but today it felt like a slap in the face.

Today, it felt like a waste of a life.

CHAPTER
FIFTEEN

MAGGIE MANAGED to push Tristan out of her head the rest of the afternoon—she had come to think of him as Tristan and not Mr. Simms despite her best efforts, probably something to do with spending an evening in his hotel room. But when her four o'clock patient was a no-show, the minutes ticked past in slow motion, and the flood of thoughts came rushing back. The way his face looked sitting at the hotel table last night. The way he'd smelled of antiseptic and fear, his hands covered in slowly clotting blood.

What did it all mean? She reached into her top desk drawer and brought out her "emergency" bobblehead doll: Bert from Sesame Street. Kevin had given it to her in middle school—an O.G. fidget spinner—and it still helped her to focus. Kevin'd had the matching Ernie bobblehead in his car. She hoped that sarcastic orange bastard was the last thing Kevin saw—that he remembered how much she loved him before he closed his eyes forever.

Maggie set the toy on the desk and stroked Bert's spikes gently, making his head waggle. She liked to be decisive, but she was having a hard time connecting the information in a way that made sense. All she had was speculation and way too many ideas, which was not a new phenomenon. Overthinking was basically her superpower. Might as well lean into it.

She hit the toy again. Bobble, bobble, bobble, Bert saying: "Go for it, Mags, spin that web of racing thoughts no matter how crazy they sound." *Fine, Bert. Fine.*

Option one: Tristan was a kidnapper, a killer, and he didn't remember because he had been sleepwalking at the time. Though the sleep study for verification was a week out, she believed that he was sleepwalking; it made no logical sense for him to see a psychologist if he knew what he'd been doing. That disclosure was an unnecessary risk. And there certainly wasn't a detective following Tristan if he was a murderer. If a cop had watched him bury a body, Tristan would have been in handcuffs, not that hotel. Tristan might have been wrong about who the stalker was, but she no longer believed he was delusional.

Option two: He witnessed something while sleepwalking, and his subsequent episodes were his brain's attempt at consolidating it. Now, the actual kidnapper-killer was stalking Tristan, trying to figure out what he knew... or shut him up for good.

Option three: None of this was connected at all. Tristan was a sleepwalker doing weird but not illegal stuff at night, Sammy's kidnapper was someone else altogether, and the person who stole Tristan's file was after him for another reason.

Was the file-stealer unconnected to the rest? If someone was watching him—and her—the most likely culprit was a romantic stalker, either an ex-lover or someone who wished they could get it on with the delectably complicated Tristan Simms.

THE DEAD DON'T DREAM

She glowered at her cold chai, then at Bert—silent and still now, not so much as a singular nod to encourage her. *Kevin would have encouraged me... because he loved me, probably even more than a stalker.*

Maggie sighed. When Tristan had reported being followed, the police had seen his ex-girlfriend as the most logical culprit. The ex seemed logical to Maggie too— Tristan himself had admitted that Christine *always* knew where he was. And if she could prove that the burglar was a jealous lover, she would at least know she wasn't being stalked by a kidnapper... or a killer.

But it's still possible you're treating a kidnapper, Maggie. Another woman could have gone missing last night, and the police might not even know yet. She had more questions than a virgin at an orgy.

The sunlight from the window beat against her right arm, the fine blonde hairs shimmering. There was no way that everything was unconnected; that would be far too coincidental. And if she assumed that her patient was connected to Sammy's missing women, someone else getting hurt outweighed the ethical considerations of poking around the public profiles of a client. The hotel's added layer of security between Tristan and the dirty, dirty nighttime world would only help for so long. Listening was not enough when you were dealing with wounded men in hotel rooms and shattered locks on your filing cabinets.

The only real question was where to start with her research.

Perhaps the detective, the one Tristan had mentioned. If there was valid suspicion of criminal activity, the whole police force should be watching him. A single officer as Tristan described sounded more like a personal vendetta.

So though it felt like a gross invasion of privacy, she

opened the laptop and typed: Detective, Rich, Fernborn Police Department.

No results, at least not for that name. Just links to the main site. There were a few news articles with the names of other detectives—media coverage for convictions was what she had been counting on, since police department websites didn't list their full roster of employees. But... nothing.

Was he with another department? If so, he wouldn't have jurisdiction here, but vendettas tended to stretch beyond arbitrary manmade boundaries. Maybe he was just bad at his job—spent all his time harassing Tristan instead of closing other cases.

She tried again without the city name, but again, came up empty. A detective three hours from Fernborn had the last name of Rich, and there were two Richards, but both lived too far away to be watching Tristan Simms.

She grabbed her phone from the drawer and texted Sammy:

"Is there a Detective Rich with the Fernborn P.D.?"

The reply came immediately:

"Not that I know of. Is he cute?"

Bert glared at her.

Tristan was likely wrong about the detective being a stalker—she had expected that. But she had not expected that the detective was a figment of Tristan's imagination. Maybe this Detective Rich was new, maybe he was there consulting on some cold case and Sammy had never met him, but it felt wrong. There was something strange going on—break-ins didn't happen for no reason—but that did not mean she could rule out Tristan being delusional.

Bert watched, his beady eyes brimming with judgment, as she opened a new tab and typed in: Tristan Simms.

Unlike the elusive Detective Rich, her patient was definitely real. Tristan Simms was a ghost on social media, not that she would have relied on it—her social accounts just had pictures of things her friends hated and the occasional jump scare to keep them on their toes. But the search engine had a ton to say about Tristan. Maggie's guts squeezed tighter with every article she read, her index finger stroking Bert's judgy face.

Her patient was the CEO and owner of a successful technology start-up, specializing in privacy considerations —security. Ah... he did have access to data. And he'd told her that even the police didn't know he was hacking into their databases, so it was unlikely that some stranger would suspect he'd uncovered their secrets and come after him. This stalker had to be after something more concrete. Was it related to his work?

She sighed, frustrated. What did she have, really? A nonexistent detective and suspicions about the missing women Sammy mentioned. She'd poked around on the kidnappings last night after googling parks, but she couldn't find a single news story—they were obviously keeping the case reports close because it was an active investigation, which meant that involving Sammy might put him in a compromising position. Even asking him about Rich was straddling an ethical line that she did not want to cross.

Her fingers paused over the keyboard. The only other, and perhaps most likely, suspect she had was the ex Tristan had mentioned. The jealous woman with obsessive tendencies, the one who'd called his girlfriends in an attempt to break them up—who had made many a woman leave him. What was her name?

Christine.

Maggie clicked off the articles and scrolled through the search engine images of Tristan Simms. Tristan shaking hands with other suited men in front of one gray building or another. Tristan at large V.I.P. parties: him with the mayor, him with... was that the governor? In every photo, he had a different beautiful woman on his arm. A playboy, huh? That fit. He seemed to have trouble with relationships as evidenced by his ongoing connection to a woman he knew was bad for him. He'd said Christine was jealous and obsessive, and yet she didn't have to stalk him because she always knew where he was, which implied he shared this information freely. Codependent?

She scrolled. Most of the professional photos had captions complete with names, but no Christines. It wasn't until the fourth page of results that she found a shot of Tristan at a gala, a tall blonde on his arm wearing a glittery gown and dangly earrings like the ones Alex always wore— she could almost imagine she'd seen them before. Maggie narrowed her eyes at the caption, her heart racing. *Christine Archer.*

She opened a new tab and typed Christine's first and last name into the search bar.

Unlike Tristan, Christine had a significant social media presence—pictures of her food, shots of new outfits clinging to her lithe frame, a whole series with her face shining and sweaty after a workout, the kind of post that made men imagine how she'd look after sex. One photo in particular made Maggie pause: a different set of dangly earrings, but that wasn't what stopped her. They were

THE DEAD DON'T DREAM

unusual, with carved bluebirds along one side of each spiral hoop. Maggie was positive that she'd seen them before.

She shook it off—she wasn't here for jewelry. And more interesting than the earrings was that there were no other people in any of Christine's social media shots, not even Tristan. Maybe he'd told her not to post about him.

But Maggie frowned at the dates on Christine's social pages. The woman posted religiously five to ten times a day, sometimes more. But over the last four days... nothing. She hadn't posted anything since the day Tristan had awoken with dirt on his hands and blood under his nails.

Maggie pulled up a few other social sites, looking for any sign of the woman, but every site Christine usually frequented was a blank void after the night of Tristan's sleepwalking episode.

Her heart vibrated in a panicked frenzy. Sweat popped up along the back of her neck.

Was Christine really missing? Had she simply realized that social media was a destructive force and opted out? That was about as likely as gremlins flying out of her butt, an event Christine would surely have live streamed for the enjoyment of her followers.

Shit. It might be nothing... but it might be something. And Maggie's muscles were aching to find out which.

She closed the laptop slowly. Her gut didn't like the idea, and her brain was on the fence. Even Bert appeared to have a strong opinion, his black eyebrows seemingly more closely knit than they'd been just minutes ago. She was obviously crossing lines, but the other alternative was calling the police. Calling Sammy to ask if anyone had reported this particular woman missing would put him in a compromising position and force him to ask questions that she couldn't answer without breaking confidentiality.

Maggie plucked the bobblehead from the desktop and returned it to the top drawer, finally shielding her from Bert's critical gaze. Before she did anything else, she had to be sure that Christine was even missing. Right now, Christine could as easily be Tristan's stalker.

Maggie didn't want to wind up like her father who had a bullet lodged in his rib from trying to protect a suicidal patient from the police. She didn't want to be like her mother, locked up in her house, unable to help anyone else.

But she also didn't want to make a mistake that cost someone their life.

Not again.

CHAPTER
SIXTEEN

THE ADDRESS LISTED for Christine Archer was a tan brick single story located at the end of a long cul-de-sac. The squeal of her DeLorean's door hinge cut through the silence at the curb.

A tall spire of streetlamp rose in front of the home; a few hours and it'd click on as the sky faded with twilight, but Maggie planned to be gone well before then. Low wrought iron fences revealed a bench in the back—a garden. *A bench, the streetlight...* Was this where Tristan had spent his night digging? His ex's backyard? He should have recognized this place, but sleepwalking was an area of study that was still emerging, and it was difficult to tell what he might have experienced—what he'd seen in his brain while his eyes were peering at the real world.

The little oh-so-indecisive and overactive voice in her head whispered: *What are you doing, Maggie? You could lose your license for this. You can't just go to a patient's home!*

But she wasn't. She was going to a patient's *friend's* home to see whether this woman was missing or dead or a violent crazy stalker. What could go wrong?

The truck in the driveway had a rusted rear wheel and only one taillight. Not what social media followers would expect sweaty-sexy Christine Archer to drive.

As she crossed the lawn, she could hear Owen's voice above the cawing of the birds: "This is reckless, dangerous, you need to be safe, Maggie!" But it was her father's off-key whistling that filled her ears as she climbed onto the porch. He'd whistled to keep calm after he'd taken that bullet to the side; it had sent him to the ground so the police could shoot his suicidal patient center mass. Pulling out a knife was an unexpected twist, but you never knew what a desperate person might do, and the very presence of police tended to intensify that desperation. Dad once told her the fact that he'd tried to shield his patient was the only reason he could sleep at night. And she knew what it felt like to stop sleeping—to feel that guilt. The police had to be a last resort.

Like the truck in the drive, the paint on the front door was past its prime—peeling. The woman's perfectionistic social media accounts suggested she'd be out here with a piece of sandpaper and a paintbrush at the first sign of wear, but social media showed life without blemishes. A falsehood.

Maggie raised her hand. For a moment the world vibrated with the lingering echo of knuckles on wood, the notes growing softer and softer like ripples on a pond. A scuffling came from inside, then the *shhhht-clink* of a chain lock.

The door swung open.

Christine stood in the doorway, staring from beneath a fringe of glossy blonde hair, same as in the online pictures, sans the giant glittering earrings. She wasn't missing—*she's not dead*. Maggie realized that she'd half expected to discover the woman buried next to that bench, which was probably why she had the sudden impulse to hug her in a weird-o celebratory way. From the look in the woman's eyes, that would not be a welcome intrusion—her mouth was set in an irritated scowl. Christine would probably punch her square in the ovary at the slightest provocation.

Christine crossed her arms and cocked her head, eyes narrowed at Maggie's face. "Who the hell are you?"

I'm you, from the future! Eighty-eight miles per hour, baby, didn't you see the car? Thankfully, she didn't have a chance to respond before Christine finished: "Are you one of Tristan's skanks?"

Ruh-roh. But maybe this would work to her advantage. Maggie crossed her arms, mirroring Christine's stance, hoping she looked every bit the jealous lover Christine apparently expected. "I haven't seen him around in a few days, and I figured you'd know better than anyone where he might be. You were always so close." *If she's not a victim, she's a stalker, a file-stealer, Maggie, what are you doing?*

Christine's nostrils flared. "He's with the police. He's not a guy you want to cross. Just ask Tonya."

Tonya? And... the police? Was he telling them about the sleepwalking episodes? Her heart sank, but it felt more like relief than concern. If the police were already with Tristan, if he'd turned himself in, she didn't have to intervene. But the flaring of Christine's nostrils, the upturned outer corner of her eye... *Is she lying?* Maybe she only intended to scare yet another of "Tristan's skanks" off. He had said that she had a habit of making threatening calls to his girlfriends, so that was within the realm of possibility.

Tread carefully, Maggie. Make her think she's the most important person in the world. "I don't know any Tonya," Maggie said. "Tristan only ever talks about you." But the name—Tonya—was familiar, *so familiar*, just as Tristan's had been the day they'd met. He hadn't mentioned a Tonya, had he? No, she was sure he hadn't.

"He dated Tonya before me." Christine frowned. "She vanished into thin air. I'm not sure why he'd keep such an *important* thing from you, but you should watch yourself around him if you want to make it to next month, girl." The word *girl* was sharp with pure spite, but that wasn't what made her chest constrict. *Vanished, vanished, vanished.*

"They never found her?" Maggie heard herself asking. It was the question Christine wanted her to reply with, but it felt bitter on her tongue.

"Nope." The corner of Christine's mouth curved into a smile that might have appeared sultry on her Instagram feed. The spark in her eyes was brighter now too. She was delighted that the woman had vanished. Exactly what Maggie would expect from a stalker... or from a woman who'd make her rivals disappear.

The hairs on Maggie's spine prickled angrily. Maggie took a step backward off the porch.

"I'm sure Tristan's just pulling away like he always does," Christine called. "He doesn't do well with relationships." She followed Maggie down the first step. "I'm the only one who sticks. The boy can't stay away." Christine glared at her, fingertips white against her upper arms.

Jealous? Yes. High stalker probability? Absolutely. But could Christine have been the burglar in her office surveillance video? The angle of the camera and the ballcap had hidden the face of the perpetrator, and the intruder had been wearing a big coat—it obscured defining characteristics.

But Maggie could see her taking those files—breaking in. The savagery done to her cabinets indicated a rage beyond a simple fact-finding mission. And she was certainly looking at Maggie like she knew her.

Maggie swallowed hard. The important part was that this woman was fine. There was no evidence that Tristan had hurt anyone. He bore no defensive wounds. Someone else had gone to Maggie's office and stolen his file. Maybe Christine herself.

So what to do about it now? She had to talk to Tristan... no, not Tristan. *Mr. Simms.* Her *patient.*

But as she backed toward the driveway, she couldn't drag her gaze from Christine. Her square shoulders. Her angry mouth. Something about her... ears? Devoid of earrings. But then Maggie blinked, and the world around her slowed to a crawl.

Maggie could suddenly see the jewelry as if it really existed, the earrings she'd seen on social media. Familiar— so familiar. And when the sun peeked from behind the clouds and glinted off Christine's cheekbone, something clicked in her head. Yes, she could see those earrings clear as day, dangling against Christine's shoulders. But the face was no longer Christine Archer's.

Now she knew why those earrings had looked so familiar. She'd seen them on Tonya herself. In person.

Tonya, the woman Christine mentioned, Tristan's ex-girlfriend... she'd been Maggie's patient too.

CHAPTER
SEVENTEEN

THE EARRINGS. Christine had been wearing her patient's earrings.

Maggie blinked at the road, the trees whizzing by on either side of the DeLorean, her foot smashed to the floor, her heart in her throat. Was she wrong? Memory was fallible; ideas changed constantly to accommodate new pieces of information. Imagining that she'd seen a pair of earrings before might fit the bill.

But the jewelry was distinctive, and she'd felt it the moment she'd seen them in Christine's social media posts. Maggie wasn't perfect, but she had a pretty good memory, unless that was just her brain trying to talk itself up. But if that cocky lump of electrified Jell-O inside her skull was right...

Was the jewelry Tonya's, and Tristan regifted it to Christine after she vanished? But she couldn't see Tristan doing that. From those shiny shoes, the perfect lines in his suit pants, his considerable resources, he had no issue spending money on pretty things.

Christine could have stolen Tonya's earrings—with the

break-in at her office, this was logical. But now Tonya was missing. Had Christine made Tonya vanish when she couldn't scare her off with a phone call? Had she hurt other women too? And what did that have to do with Tristan's current sleepwalking issue? Perhaps Tristan knew Christine was responsible for Tonya's disappearance, and the guilt was driving him from his bed while he slept.

She hooked a right, the tires shrieking, spraying bits of stone and asphalt. A car horn blared, and she relaxed pressure on the gas without looking in her rearview.

Christine could certainly be lying about Tonya, but the knot in Maggie's chest refused to ease. She'd gone too far. Maggie felt it in her bones, a sharp heaviness under her ribs. She had alerted Christine—possibly a stalker, a thief, a kidnapper, a killer—to the fact that Maggie knew about her. And though it had made sense, she'd gone to see a patient's ex-girlfriend... or current girlfriend. She'd already screwed up in the eyes of the licensing board. And it had happened *so fast*.

How had it happened so fast?

But sometimes it just did. Her father had decided on the spot to jump in front of a bullet. Her mother began providing weapons to domestic violence victims early in her career, but it had only taken two hours for one of those women to kill four people once she had that steel in her hand. Even the scarred bite on Maggie's own head, the series of events that had led there...

This is why you go by the book, Maggie. This isn't even close to the book. And a more subtle whisper in the back of her mind: *Tristan is not Kevin. And he's not your brother. You can't protect him as if he's family.*

Maggie hooked a left into the office parking lot, the wheel gripped so tightly that her palms ached. Maggie'd had reasons for going to that house, good reasons. She'd gone too far, but she did not regret it, even if she should. The act, no matter how ill-advised in hindsight, had paid off—she'd learned something vital.

Tonya.

Tonya. Tonya. Tonya.

She slammed the car into park and practically ran up the stairs to the office, but unlocking the office door was as much a punch to the gut as it had been this morning. She'd cleaned up the scattered papers on her desk, the picture was back on the wall, but the deep gouges on the filing cabinet glared, the raw wood like deep, bloodless scars.

She jerked the top drawer open and flipped until she found the folder she was after. Tonya's file was still tucked neatly inside. She opened the chart to the intake forms, then further into the meat of the file, as much reading the sparse notes as recalling what wasn't written down. Her patient notes would be useless to anyone except her, and if her memory ever gave up the way her father's had, there'd be no one who could use them.

Alert, oriented x3, she'd written, but she'd drawn three dots in the corner of the page, her personal shorthand for grief, beside the number two and a diagnostic billing code. That was enough to jog her memory. Tonya had come in seeking treatment after the death of her grandfather and her dog, both in the same week—the last of her living family members. She'd been experiencing panic attacks, a passing phenomenon. She responded well to therapy, and over the course of six months, the panic attacks eased.

No suicidal/homicidal ideation, read the second to last note, something she'd written on each. But the little plus sign she'd added to the corner... Tonya had started going out socially again near the end of her treatment and reported having a boyfriend—her *plus* one. Thrilled and in love. She'd said her significant other was kind to her, and she had noted that he was very supportive of his sister, which she'd seen as a good sign. Maggie frowned. Had his sister been raped, gotten pregnant? She was almost certain that was the case. And he had taken care of her the way a brother should. A good man, according to Tonya. The pièce de résistance had been a large pair of custom-made earrings—a gift.

Maggie could see the jewelry in her mind's eye just reading her sparse scribble-scrabble writing, the same earrings Christine had been wearing in her social media post. Tristan had been Tonya's boyfriend. That also explained where Tristan had gotten Maggie's name.

Maggie read on—*well-dressed, affect stable, mood positive* —remembering Tonya's face, the way she'd glowed when she talked about Tristan; the first smiles she'd seen in months. Had he, even then, been a gentleman during the day and a sleepwalking monster? Had he, not Christine, made Tonya vanish? Maybe Tristan knew exactly what he'd done, and his main motivation for making the appointment was to get a peek at these files and figure out what Tonya might have said about him.

Maggie paused with her finger resting near the end of the page. That didn't make sense. If she were going to tell someone about Tonya's sessions, implicate him in a crime against her patient, he'd have come after her three years ago, when whatever she knew might have mattered, not now when Tonya's case was long cold. Besides, if the intruder had wanted to know about Tonya, they'd have taken Tonya's file, too.

No, the burglar had come here to learn about Tristan.

And the one person who had absolutely no reason to steal that file was Tristan himself.

She flipped to the final note, Tonya's last session. *Patient initiated scheduling for next week.*

Her chest constricted. Tonya had ended their sessions abruptly over three years ago. But Tonya hadn't just ended the sessions, had she? She'd just... stopped coming. Patients stopped showing for all kinds of reasons, but for Tonya, it was unusual. She glanced back through the file, but didn't see a single missed session, not until that final appointment.

Maggie was quite sure the woman had intended to return.

Tonya hadn't come back because she couldn't.

CHAPTER
EIGHTEEN

TRISTAN EYEBALLED HER COOLLY, his gaze clear. Even the wounds on his hands seemed calmer, all wrapped up in clean gauze. But Maggie didn't imagine he'd stay so nonchalant once she told him why she'd called him in.

"Do psychologists usually tell patients to skip dinner for a session?"

Only if they or their associates might be burying bodies for funsies. "There are extenuating circumstances." She tried to keep her face a mask of calm support, but her heart was humming like an agitated cricket in her chest. "Someone broke into this office last night, Mr. Simms. Your file was torn apart, and the intake page was stolen." *You ready to explore who's really after you?* Maggie wasn't buying the detective as the culprit now that she knew he didn't exist, though she still wasn't sure whether "Rich" was a delusion of persecution, an incorrect assumption, or mistaken identity—Tristan could be wrong about the name of the cop. Rich could also be a bald-faced lie.

Tristan crossed one ankle over the opposite knee and blinked as if she'd just told him that she disliked cantaloupe, but thought honeydew was the bee's knees. Near complete non-reaction, which made no sense given what she'd just said. "What is your office doing to locate this stolen intake page?"

Yeah, he was far too calm, though it was possible that he wasn't really worried. He'd said he was sleepwalking during their first session, but nothing that would give him issues in court even if she had written it all down. Which she hadn't.

"Unfortunately, there's nothing I *can* do."

He balked, but recovered quickly. "For a woman who values privacy—"

"That's why you're here: so I can protect your privacy. Your file was the only one taken. Despite this, I have not released your name to the police, which would reveal that you're a patient here. But this also means I'm in the dark and unprotected. Whoever had a motive to break in here may have insidious motivations that I'm not privy to. So either we need to figure out why someone might come after you, and by proxy me, or I have to inform the police so they can ensure our safety."

He leaned forward, his eyes clear, brighter and more interested than they had been when he arrived—almost excited. "So... you *know* I'm telling the truth about someone being after me. You know about Rich."

"I don't know anything, Mr. Simms." She didn't even know whether Tonya was on Sammy's list of missing women; one-off disappearances still happened during kidnapping sprees. "Perhaps you can help me figure out what this intruder wants from you. You're certainly a man of means."

His gaze darkened—angry, but not surprised at the

assessment. He laced his fingers, a ball of knuckles. "You researched me? You're going to get yourself hurt."

Was that a threat? The hairs along her spine bristled, but she squared her shoulders and kept her eyes locked on his. "The choice was between telling the police that your file was taken and risking an investigation that I would have no ability to keep private, or looking you up to ensure that I was safe in my interactions with you. I think you'll agree that I made the right decision." She crossed her legs; her chest was on fire. "I'm a psychologist, Mr. Simms, not a cop, and I don't appreciate being put in harm's way. So who would want your file?"

"I don't have any idea."

"Christine? You mentioned her last time." *And I saw her today.* The woman was at the top of her list for file-thief stalker. But was she a killer? Had she made Tonya vanish?

"Like I said, Christine has no reason to stalk me or to break in here, and..." He shook his head. "I don't think Rich would be stupid enough to break in. But I might be wrong." He squinted. "Has he come to see you yet?"

No, because there's no Rich working with the police department. But if he was under the spell of a full-blown delusion, he'd react strongly to her refuting it outright. Instead, she shook her head to answer the question, then said: "What about another ex-lover, someone jealous enough to pry into your current life?"

"No." Another lie—from what she'd seen online, he went through women like water, which meant there were plenty of people out there with a reason to be jealous.

He still wanted to play games, and she'd had enough of it. He was as bad as Eric Small, denying that he was part of the problem. At least Kevin had known when he needed help, though it hadn't kept him from giving up after she'd broken his heart.

Her guts twisted; her shoulders went rigid. Everyone got second chances to make things right except the people she loved. It wasn't *fair*. "Who told you to come here, Mr. Simms?"

His eyes sharpened with understanding. "Do all shrinks pry into their patients' lives if they don't get the answers they want?"

Even now, he was trying to keep her in the dark—threatened by this line of questioning. But she had no intention of backing down. She could practically feel the holes in the damaged file cabinets glaring at her.

"If Christine really knows everything about you, she surely knows you came here." And Christine had been wearing Tonya's earrings mere weeks after the woman vanished—she had photo proof. Unless Tristan gave the same earrings to every girlfriend he had. But that felt a little too tacky, like giving your wife and girlfriend the same perfume so you could cheat in peace. "And you were at a gala with Christine the month after Tonya's death," she finished.

"Tonya isn't dead," he said softly. "She just... left."

She'd used the terminology on purpose, to gauge his reaction. His eyes revealed no panic at her assertion, but his shoulders slumped. *Huh.* Tristan did not seem concerned that she'd uncovered some closely held secret, nor did he have hope that Tonya would ever be found. No matter what he'd said, he did not believe that Tonya was still alive. And neither did Maggie.

Maggie leveled her gaze at him and waited. Finally, he sighed.

"Christine and I have been off and on since college. I

don't even know what we are right now, but she knows when I go out or when I sleep with other women. She doesn't have to break in here to find out what I'm doing."

Hmm. So Christine was an unstable woman that he consistently shared his life with, and he was hurting her over and over again, rubbing his conquests in her face? Of course she'd have some feelings about that.

"How did Christine feel about Tonya?"

"She... didn't like her. Wanted me back. I resisted harder that time; Tonya was the first woman I really thought I had a future with."

Which was absolutely a reason for Christine to kill her. And if Christine thought Tristan knew she'd hurt Tonya, it was a motive to steal his file. Had he really not made the connection?

Tristan was watching her strangely, distress mixed with an unabashed curiosity that made gooseflesh prickle on her arms. "I looked for her, you know. Tonya. But she was just gone. And it was my fault."

The words hung in the air like a bough full of poisoned apples. She stiffened, her palms hot against her knees. "That sounds... difficult." Was he about to confess to helping Tonya vanish? But Maggie could have said the same about her brother. Aiden was just gone—and it was her fault.

"Christine isn't blameless," he went on. "She told Tonya that I'd been arrested for stalking her, which was ridiculous. Telling people that I've been arrested or that I'm in jail is a shtick she pulls whenever she feels threatened. She even went to see my foster father—made a huge scene at Eden, his jewelry store."

Perhaps that explained Christine's statement that

Tristan was with the police this morning. Was that the same thing she'd said to Tonya?

"Anyway, Tonya and I got into a huge fight about it, she got out of the car, said she was going to walk home. I figured she'd call a Hytch." He sniffed. "I never saw her again." His eyes had gone glassy. He appeared to feel genuinely guilty, but was it guilt that he'd let her walk alone, guilt that he'd actually hurt the woman, or, alternatively, because he suspected that Christine had killed Tonya? Either way, his pain tugged her own to the surface, fresh as new razor burn. She'd let her brother walk home alone for selfish, irresponsible reasons. Aiden had never come home either.

This is not the same, Maggie. But her heart didn't quite believe it. "I'm not here to assign blame, Mr. Simms," she said, trying to keep her voice from shaking despite the trembling deep inside her chest. She recrossed her legs; her hands had left damp spots on her pants. "Did you tell the police about Tonya? How she intended to walk home that night?"

He nodded. "I did. The police suspected foul play, of course, interrogated me for hours."

Made sense. The story he'd just told her would have been suspicious. But there remained several unexplained pieces—the detective for one. Paranoid or delusional? "Is Detective Rich the one who interrogated you about Tonya?"

His nostrils flared. "You need to watch out for him."

That certainly sounded delusional—exaggerated. "What precinct does he work out of again?"

The silence stretched. His eyes locked on Fluffy. "If I didn't know better, I'd think you didn't believe me." His eyes glittered darkly, and it ratcheted her heart into overdrive in a way that didn't quite feel like anxiety... or at least not only anxiety. *Just stress—just the stress, Maggie.*

"But you of all people know that sometimes the most unbelievable things are true," he went on. "Between your work at the prison, and people like Helena..."

He was still talking, his mouth moving, but she could no longer hear his words. She tried to speak, but her heart had lodged itself in her throat—she could barely breathe. *Helena.* She didn't even have a file on Helena. The only way for him to know about the woman was if he had been keeping tabs on Maggie... and on her patients. And for someone like Helena, that could easily prove deadly. Not only was Helena's husband a threat, but Tristan might be as well, and Maggie would have no way to know if Helena had vanished as they'd planned, or if she was hidden in a shallow grave.

I think I buried something tonight.

Maggie narrowed her eyes at him, willing her voice not to shake. "You need to understand that my options are limited, Mr. Simms. My job is to protect the innocent."

"And you're not sure whether I'm one of them?" He grinned, but it was all teeth, lips skinned back—wolfish. "Is this my last chance, Doctor Connolly? Is this when you decide whether to turn me over to the cops?"

She might have said yes had it not been for Helena. And... *That's why he mentioned her.* If she turned him in, he'd expose Helena, or any of the dozens of women she'd helped over the years. *Shit.*

Maggie cleared her throat. "I'm the last line of defense between people's history and their future. And I have no intention of putting anyone in harm's way. As for you..." She pushed herself to her feet. "It's my job to help you do better." *Or to make sure you go down once I can guarantee my patients' safety.*

His gaze tightened; his nostrils flared. "Listen—"

"Our session is over, Mr. Simms." She'd figure this out for herself, rules and books be damned. She was in too deep now. And she would not allow another of her patients to vanish at the hands of a monster.

CHAPTER
NINETEEN
TRISTAN

The darkness was like pitch in front of Maggie's house, thick and sticky. Her house was dark, too, now that he'd cut the external lights, every window a black eye gaping from the brick.

Tristan tugged his leather gloves tighter, then popped the hood on her car—so weird that the engine was in the back. Five hours since their session, and his chest was still hot. He'd gone too far by bringing up Helena, he'd seen it in the set of the doctor's jaw.

But he'd had every reason to go on the defensive. Christine had called him before Maggie's DeLorean had made it off the curb. All that talk about confidentiality, and Maggie Connolly had *investigated* him. Peeled back layers of his life without his permission.

Rage clawed at his throat, a liquid burning that rivaled the slashing wounds on his back. An unfortunate turn of events. Yes, he'd need to be extra careful. She was playing a horrifically violent game, and he wasn't even sure that she believed it.

Tristan reached into the bowels of the car, seeking what

he needed by feel. The hairs on the back of his neck prickled. He turned, expecting to see a pair of prying eyes from the trees; Rich watching from his car or from an empty home across the way. But the world remained solitary and deep, a velvety stillness that he felt inside him. Perhaps the prying eyes were inside him, too, his conscience glaring at him, whispering in his ear, *Do you have to do this, Tristan?*

He turned back to the car and ducked beneath the hood. The item in his hand vibrated, accusing him with its presence. *Is this necessary?* it whispered. *Do we have to?* Yes; of course the answer was yes.

Maggie Connolly kept your name from the police, the other side of his brain argued. *She tried to protect you.* Despite everything she knew about him—despite his dirty hands and his questionable evening activities—she'd kept his confidences. No smart person would see him as trustworthy, but she'd done right by him... almost.

But though she'd held his name back in relation to the break-in, there was no telling whether she'd continue to maintain his privacy. And the moment she outed herself as being involved with him... well. Hopefully Helena would be enough to hedge his bets. The doctor would surely protect a vulnerable woman who would most *certainly* die at the hands of her abusive husband even if he *might* be dangerous. It was the logical choice. And she seemed to lean heavily on such things—the rationality of her decisions.

Kicking him out of her office, though... He did not like that, or what it meant. Which was why he was here.

He squinted in the dark and moved his hand just a bit to the right and finally found what he needed. He leaned over, the edge of the bumper digging into his hip as he maneuvered his hand around the engine block.

How many hours did he have until Richie showed up

here? Even with a warrant, the doctor should keep her mouth shut about him—she'd protect Helena. She wouldn't tell Rich anything.

Would she?

He righted himself, frowned at the engine, then eased the hood closed and secured it with the barest of clicks.

Rich would come here, he was certain. He would also stop at Christine's. Richie went to see her every time something bad happened in Tristan's life; he used any excuse he could to see the woman.

And who knew what Christine might say to the detective this time.

Tristan slunk down the drive, the sharp pressure in his throat easing the farther he got from the house, but his ribs stayed tight.

He made the sign of the cross—forehead, chest, shoulder, shoulder—as he headed up the street to his own car.

He had to get to Christine now. Before Richie did.

CHAPTER
TWENTY

THE ROOM FELT black more than appeared so, a heavy, impenetrable void that weighted her shoulders and pinned her to the bed. But she could see by the hazy silver light of the moon.

She could see him.

Tristan Simms emerged from the shadows at the corner of the room and stepped in front of the window. His hair appeared lighter in the moonlight, the tips stained a silvery white, the whiskers around his mouth sparkling. His eyes were black. Deep. And when he fixed them on her, she felt like she was drowning.

She couldn't move. She couldn't breathe. Her wrists were locked above her head though she could see no chains. Her legs were stuck to the mattress. Even her head felt too heavy to lift.

And then he was there. He loomed over her, those eyes boring into hers. He reached for her, the tips of his fingers brushing her clavicle. She wanted to shrink back, but all she could do was watch, her skin on fire, her flesh tingling as he moved his hand lower between her breasts over the top of her T-shirt.

His ruined fingertips reached her bare thigh, scratching, scraping her flesh in a delicious way, his eyes still on her face. "Do you think I'm dangerous?"

"Yes." The word was a whisper that seemed to come from somewhere outside of her.

"Do you want me to be dangerous?"

Yes. But this time she couldn't say it; her voice was gone, her breath was gone. All that existed was the pressure of his hand as he slipped his fingers between her legs. And then he was inside her, his knuckle massaging the sensitive place at her center, her body quivering around him.

He climbed onto the bed and straddled her hips, drawing his face down toward hers, closer, closer, closer, his fingers working her. He wrapped his other hand around her throat, rough as sandpaper against her skin.

"Do you want me to be dangerous, Maggie?"

"Yes," she hissed.

"We're both dangerous," he said. "Killers have to stick together. No one else can understand what we are." And then he squeezed, the pressure on her throat intensifying as he increased the speed of his fingers between her legs, the heat in her abdomen building...

She woke with a start, her heart hammering, trying to burst free from her chest. There were no fingers around her throat, but she could not find the air.

What the hell was that? A dream, just a dream. *It's okay, Maggie. It's okay.*

She kicked the covers to the foot of the bed more forcefully than necessary. It made sense to dream about the guy she'd been focused on at work, but holy crap. No, this was not okay.

She'd never cross that line with a patient. Not ever.

But you've thought about it, Maggie, don't lie to yourself.
Isn't that why you went to the club the other night? Before you
met him, you hadn't gone to that club in three months.

Maggie heaved herself from the mattress, her shirt
sticking to her back. She undressed in the bathroom while
the shower heated. Her perspiration-soaked clothes went
into the hamper. Finally, she stepped beneath the spray—
much too hot.

She squeezed shampoo into her hair. Tristan. His
fingers. His hands. She scrubbed at her skin until it burned,
scraping at the scar beneath her hairline, letting the pain
center her thoughts. She had patients to see today, her dad,
the prison. That would keep her occupied. It would also
keep her from going to visit any more of Tristan's exes
while she figured out what to do. While she figured out
what was... real.

Was Tristan a sleepwalking murderer? He'd basically
blackmailed her into keeping quiet, though she didn't have
any concrete evidence against him. Knowing that someone
sleepwalked was not the same as having proof of a crime,
and any prosecutor would laugh her out of court if he had
to convict based on her circumstantial assumptions. And
Tristan was smart enough to know that.

Why weren't these pieces fitting together? Was his
motivation in mentioning Helena just a slice of the paranoid pie? Maybe he assumed she was working with "Rich"
now and had to make sure she didn't expose him, though
again... she had zero actual evidence of wrongdoing.

Her mind kept wandering back to those earrings,
dangling against Christine's throat. And Tristan didn't have
a reason to steal his own file. But he clearly had access to
things he shouldn't—he was spying on her other patients.

She sighed and rinsed the conditioner from her curls, wishing she could rinse the rest of this nonsense away too. What to do about Helena? Maggie had no idea where Helena was now, and that was by design. Everyone from her mother to those in charge of Helena's end destination was just a step in the chain—any one of them would be no help to a crazed abuser with a taste for revenge. And trying to tease apart the rest of the network, especially when she was being watched, put not only Helena, but other women in danger. No, seeking Helena out was not an option.

She threw the shower knob into the off position and grabbed her robe.

The sun was kissing the horizon line when she made her way to the kitchen to put on water for tea. The air in the living room was sweetened with the mildly astringent scent of eucalyptus from the clay vase on her table—a giant psychedelic-looking mushroom. The eighth weirdest thing in the house, according to Owen.

Alex liked the mushroom, but they all hated Maggie's framed photos. Alex's least favorite was the one that contained a pair of shoes, perfectly clean but with one of the laces poked through the wrong hole—just a bit askew and immensely frustrating. Imani's Achilles heel was a photo of a man standing on a high ledge, toes off the side, the sky beyond dropping down to a street with cars the size of ants. The painting over the couch always made Owen shudder: a giant spider superimposed over a cityscape. Sammy refused to go into the downstairs bathroom—he worried the sharp-toothed clown over the toilet might haul itself from the frame and swallow him whole while he did his business.

Exposure therapy was a useful tool. Sure, her friends hadn't consented, but if your best buddies weren't a little uncomfortable, you weren't really trying. Her gaze lingered on the picture beside the mantel—a pair of glittering eyes peering from the blackness, the silvered bark of trees visible in the foreground. It had never been the dark that Kevin was afraid of, not precisely, but he knew better than most about the monsters who lurked within it. Had he not returned to that abandoned building, her attacker would have torn out more than just a piece of her head. She should have reported it, but the police were already suspicious that she'd done something to her brother. And the attack had happened while she and Kevin were vandalizing a building. No thirteen-year-old would willingly get into trouble for the sake of some anonymous teenager with a drive to bite smaller children, but it was more than that—she'd stabbed the guy in the face. Between the stabbing and the vandalizing, she had figured she'd be the one in handcuffs if anyone found out.

The kettle screamed. She retrieved her tea, then stalked to the couch and snatched up the remote, her gaze on the spider. Her heart had slowed, but the pressure at her throat remained, like Tristan's hands were still around her neck, squeezing the way they had in her dream.

Why didn't you call it a nightmare, Maggie?

She punched the button on the remote hard enough to make her thumb hurt. The screen blinked on: a pair of anchors discussing the weather, rain later this week. Maggie rarely watched television in the morning, but her brain was gibbering more than a flock of angry seagulls fighting over a strawberry Pop-Tart. The chaos in her head did not abate while the newscasters blathered on about some fluff piece—a surfboarding dog who would surely rather be chasing Pop-Tart-eating seagulls. But the voices in her head went silent when the newsroom feed changed from the surfing canine to crime tape stretched between two trees, the rough bark pulsing with red and blue lights.

Oh no. She lowered the cup and grappled with the remote to raise the volume, but she could barely hear it over the rushing of blood in her ears. Loud again. Always so loud inside her head.

"A grisly discovery in one local neighborhood has many residents asking whether they need to take extra precautions." The newsfeed cut to a video that appeared to be taken by a smartphone—nighttime. A field, the wispy tops of gone-to-seed grass trampled by first responders. No benches or other cars, just a singular streetlight glazing the grass in yellow haze. Near the back of the field, tiny against the crime-taped foreground, a short man rolled out a trash bag... no. A body bag. The lookie-loos that surrounded the crime tape pointed and chattered.

Her chest constricted. The newscaster droned on: "The body of a young woman was discovered yesterday evening in a field off Plumdale Road..."

Maggie couldn't pull her eyes away from the video feed. It was not the flashing lights that held her attention, not the horror of the body bag in the distance. On her television screen, Tristan stood at the edge of the field behind the crime tape, watching the officers from the cover of shadows.

The screen shifted to a tall burly man, his suit sharp, yellow pocket square too fancy for grave digging, his jaw hard even from a distance. Detective Reid Hanlon, according to the stripe at the bottom of the screen. She turned the sound up, but she could not drown out the shouting in her brain.

Tristan was there! Had he been sleepwalking? But that did not ring true, not after Helena. No, he had been

127

loitering at the scene of the crime, watching them unearth the victim like a serial killer. He knew exactly where he'd gone, where he'd been digging with his chewed up fingers —what he buried. He'd only pretended to be unsure. Was it part of an insanity defense?

Shit. She'd tried to make logical decisions, and she'd screwed up anyway. No matter what she chose, she was destined to be wrong. Was that how her parents felt in the aftermath of their choices? And now there was as much of a risk that Helena would die if she turned Tristan in as that Tristan would hurt someone else if he remained free.

But why would he cement his guilt by showing up to watch them dig a body from the earth? Maybe he couldn't help it. Many killers were compelled to watch the aftermath... and the police knew it. Which made this stunt extra stupid.

The field vanished, replaced with a close up of a woman, presumably the dead woman: pretty, dark-haired, wide blue eyes. The scrolling words beneath the picture identified the victim as Lillian Mace, though it provided no other details—nothing useful to Maggie. Was she one of Sammy's missing victims?

The screen flashed back to a wider view of the scene, and Maggie hit pause, squinting at the back of Tristan's head. The police routinely watched crime scenes for perpetrators. No matter what she did next, no matter what choice she made, this was almost over. But if Tristan told the police about Helena, especially with Helena's husband being a cop—

Bang! Bang! Bang!

Maggie jumped and fumbled her mug, chai sloshing, the handle slippery—too slippery to hold on. She raised her knee, trying to catch it, but she was too late. The cup tumbled toward the earth in slow motion and shattered against the floor. Chai splashed onto her bare toes and painted a Rorschach test on the wood. *Smooth*, like that time in gym class when she broke Mrs. Scottdale's nose— making a band geek play kickball was just asking for trouble.

Bang! Bang! Bang! Bang!

Shit. She had major problems to solve and she was thinking about kickball? With a final glare at the tea, she headed for the door and flung it open, brushing at the stains on her shirt because breadcrumbs and tea were basically the same, *duh.* But her hand froze when she looked at the visitor.

The man on the other side was tall and burly, his jaw working overtime. He smelled of cinnamon gum. And he was familiar.

The detective from the television. The one who'd just last night been standing over a corpse.

CHAPTER
TWENTY-ONE

"Magma Connolly?" The man raised an eyebrow and waited until she nodded to go on: "I'm Detective Reid Hanlon. I understand you had a burglary the other night?"

Wait, he was here about the burglary? *At least his name isn't Rich.* Although... maybe that would have been better. At least then, Tristan's detective was real. "I... yes. At my office."

The September breeze ruffled his hair, then settled. His suit was just as crisp as the one he'd worn last night, deep blue with a robin's egg tie and matching pocket square— more high-priced lawyer than detective. *A pocket square for a square.* Did people still use the word *square* as an insult?

"We came up with some additional security footage taken across the street from your office. I thought I'd swing by and see if it meant anything to you." He pulled his cell from his front pocket and tapped the screen, then extended it toward her. She stepped nearer, though her muscles were tense, yearning to slam the door and run. But going full-on meerkat seemed unwarranted based on the photo: a thick-shouldered shadow in front of her building. Nearly the same shot they'd gotten from the parking lot surveillance, but the angle of this camera made the chest and lower face visible; she could more easily tell height and girth. This person was not Christine. A man, almost certainly a man, and a rather strong one from the looks of it.

"Does he look familiar?" the detective asked.

She frowned at the phone. "He looks like you." *Not Tristan. And not Christine. Christine is not the one after me, not the one who took Tristan's file.* So what other suspects were there? It was ridiculous to think the break-in was unconnected to the bodies, to the sleepwalking, but she didn't understand the link. *Yet.*

"Ms. Connolly?"

"Doctor."

His lips curved into a half smile. He took his cell back, but did not put it in his pocket. "My sincerest apologies, *Doctor* Connolly. Are you... okay?" He glanced down. She followed his gaze to... ah. Her tea-splattered feet. One of her toes was bleeding, sliced by a shard of glass. It didn't even sting.

"Just a little chai mishap."

"Are you quite certain? You seem upset."

It seemed she wasn't the only one good at reading body language. She resisted the urge to cross her arms, which he'd surely read as defensive—and he'd be right. "You were on the television this morning, weren't you? On that homicide?"

"Most civilians call it murder." He cocked his head. "Then again, most civilians don't routinely work with convicted killers—don't spend their lives protecting the honor of thugs and thieves."

Well, he knew more about her than he should for a routine B&E follow-up. The hairs bristled along her spine.

Her phone jangled distantly—from the kitchen. "Everyone deserves respect, Detective. Even you."

His eyes widened. "Ah, yes. Even detectives who look like burglars." He chuckled. "So... are you going to invite me in?"

She'd forgotten that cops were like vampires. They couldn't enter unless you asked them... or unless you were in imminent danger, which was basically the opposite of vampires. Quite the brain-buster. Her cell chimed again. "I already told you that I don't recognize the intruder," she said, glancing at the entry to the kitchen. The phone—that stupid phone.

"I have a more pressing matter to discuss with you."

He wants to talk about the body they found last night. He saw Tristan there, and he somehow knows he's my patient. She was not inclined to tell him anything, not yet, but she needed all the information she could get to protect Helena.

She forced a smile that she was certain looked fake, exactly the way she intended it. "Where are my manners?" The words were so saccharine that they hurt her teeth. She opened the door wider and stepped back. "Won't you come in?"

He followed her over the threshold but stopped at the arch that led to the living room, his eyes on the television. She'd paused it on a shot of the crime scene—on Tristan. *That's what happens when you think about kickball instead of murder.* She skirted the shattered mug, snatched the remote from the couch cushion, and when the television went black, it felt as if a weight had lifted.

The detective smiled, amused, though she couldn't imagine that he actually felt jovial. What was wrong with this guy? "Starting the day with a little light storytelling?" he said.

She ignored the question. "You're welcome to have a seat, but I need to sweep up."

Maggie left him standing in the hall and escaped into the kitchen. The moment she was beyond of his line of sight, she released a pent-up breath, though it did nothing to assuage the tightness in her shoulders.

She hadn't killed anyone, so why did she feel like he was there to arrest her? *Probably because you feel guilty. If you had turned Tristan in, maybe Lillian would still be alive.* But they hadn't said when Lillian was killed; she might have been missing for weeks. Maybe the detective himself was making her anxious. Reid *did* bear a striking resemblance to the intruder at her office—the exact same build.

Ridiculous. She was as paranoid as her patient. Maggie stooped to dab at her bleeding toe—almost stopped now. Did she need a bandage? Peroxide? She suddenly felt inept to make any choice at all, especially one that might have consequences.

The hallway floor creaked; the detective was moving around out there. She needed to give herself time to figure out her next move. *Be smarter than your parents, Maggie. Don't be impulsive. No leaping in front of bullets; no tossing illegal guns at people. Just listen—that's your job.*

Maggie grabbed the broom and stalked back to the living area, but despite the creaking she'd heard, the detective had not moved from the hall. He turned his phone toward her again as she passed, but this time, the image was not frozen on a security screen grab. A photo. Of Tristan.

"Do you recognize this man?"

Of course I do, he's my patient, a man I've been obsessing about for a week... even in my sleep. Plus, Tristan had just been on the television. Maggie was certain the detective had seen that much. She inhaled softly and turned away, heading for the glass, hoping that he couldn't see in the set of her shoulders what was surely visible on her face—the lie. *Don't talk, just listen.*

She needed guarantees about Helena's safety before she could say anything that might put the woman in danger. And even without the threat to Helena, the detective needed a warrant before she could tell him whether Tristan was a patient, at least until she was certain that Tristan was guilty. And... she *wasn't* sure, she realized. His innocence was a gut feeling, perhaps borne of his resemblance to Kevin—an innocent if ever there was one, someone else hurt by her actions—but there were also logical inconsistencies. Tristan hadn't stolen his own file. Christine was the one wearing Tonya's earrings. Yes, Tristan had blackmailed her—he was a desperate man. But he also came to her for help. If he was guilty, telling her anything at all, especially "I bury things in my sleep," was a terrible idea.

"No, I don't know him," she said. She lowered the broom to the floor in front of the glass.

"You sure that's the way you want to go?" he said to her back.

The glass made a tinkling noise that mingled with the scraping of the raw edges against the wood—the scratching of fingernails on a basement door.

"Fine," he said. "How about this: We need to speak about one of your patients." He stepped into the living room, and though she did not turn, she felt him there, looming large at her back. That kind of behavior probably made most people shy away, but other people did not spend a portion of every week locked inside barred cells with killers twice their size. *What a putz.* She kept her shoulders rigid, the broom moving as he went on: "Should we do this here, or at the station?"

She kept her gaze on the floor, but her hackles rose; the officers had said something similar after her brother vanished too.

"When you have an arrest warrant with my name on it, you let me know." She detached the dustpan and stooped to collect the shattered bits of mug, one her father had given her. *Keep Calm, I'm a Psychologist.* Figured. "For now, I can neither confirm nor deny that I have any patients at all."

"Lillian's mother doesn't care about patient privacy. She cares about justice."

"What she wants is none of my business." *Scratch, scratch* went the glass into the dustpan. "I'm a psychologist, Detective."

"So you keep secrets."

Almost the same thing Tristan had said. "I do what I must to help those who need it. There are no other considerations." But there were. She just needed time to gather enough data so that she could make an *informed* choice and move forward with a clear conscience. She'd made enough mistakes in her life—Aiden and Kevin were only the most glaring. The cost of impulsivity was far too high.

"Fine." He sniffed. "Let's call this a consultation, since you don't give a shit about keeping people alive or punishing the guilty. Just send your bill to the department."

A consultation. She *could* do that without it being a conflict of interest—she need not mention any patient. It was not the first time she'd been asked for a psychological profile, and this might give her an inside track with the details of the case. So why would the detective offer it up? Did he think she'd see whatever evidence he was about to share and presume her patient guilty? That was most likely —a ploy.

"I'll send the bill to your attention, Detective." She finally pushed herself to her feet and glanced over. He already had his phone out in front of him... again. Did he live in that pose, one arm out, cell held aloft forever? He probably had epic forearm strength in that one limb, a real *Popeye* situation.

"Does this symbol mean anything to you?"

Maggie blinked. She knew a crime scene photo when she saw one; pale dead flesh had a certain wax-like quality to it. A single round blistered burn marred the skin—red and purple, the edges seared black. A tiny band ran just below the upper rim of the circular mark... lettering? But there was too much blistering on the flesh to know for sure.

"What exactly am I looking at?" she asked. She could not pull her eyes from the screen. Was this Lillian's body, or was it older—was it Tonya's?

Her phone rang again. Damn. She should have turned it off when she was in the kitchen.

"Do you need to get that?"

She shook her head. They both listened to it ring again, again, again.

When the phone went silent, he said: "Pay careful attention to the negative space—the places where the burns aren't."

I know what negative space is, dude. She swallowed hard and blinked at the patches of irritated but unblistered flesh that ran along either side of a central oval shape, almost like an eye inside a larger circle.

He cleared his throat. "For me, it's like seeing the Virgin Mary on a piece of toast—I see the differences in the burn, but I still have no idea what it means. I think it's a medallion of some kind," he said. "Definitely metal, probably ritualistic. If I had to guess, I'd say it's religious, but that's just a gut feeling. Maybe a psychologist known for dealing with the worst of the worst might have some insight into what would make such a mark."

She had to admit there was some relief in his theory. Ritualistic killers had specific patterns, and Tristan did not seem to fit that particular profile. Unless he was turning into a different man while he slept.

"It could be anything," she said. "A necklace, a swimming medal connected to a high school rivalry gone wrong—"

"Mean girls turn into Mike Meyers in their thirties, eh?"

She nodded. "Something like that. Though they were probably worse than Mike Meyers in high school." With that, Maggie had direct experience.

He appraised her with eyes of steel. "And what about young men? What do they turn into?" When she just stared, he lowered the cell. "The implement is about this big, too small for a medal." He touched his thumb to the tip of his forefinger. About the size of a watch face.

The air thinned. The band around Tristan's wrist—the tan lines. Was that what they were from? A medallion, not a watch? Did it match this specific murder token?

"The victims in this case were drugged, branded, and finally asphyxiated," he went on. "I think he likes them alive when he burns this symbol into their flesh. But as you can see, the injury didn't sear in evenly. From the positioning, it appears he was holding the object while heating it with a flame, maybe a torch lighter." His gaze bore into her own. "Do any of your patients have injuries on their fingertips?"

Her knuckles throbbed around the dustpan; the broom

handle was slick with sweat from her palm. The detective blinked as if trying to see into her head.

She hadn't seen any burns on Tristan, no blisters, just the cheese grater aesthetic of road rash, but perhaps those injuries looked similar. Yet even if Tristan was guilty, legitimately guilty, she didn't have privileged information that might help them connect Tristan to the crimes. They wouldn't care that he was sleepwalking; they'd see it as a defense tactic before she finished the sentence. Anyone could see his hands. And Helena...

Helena.

"Are the victims killed in the same place they're dumped?" She had not recognized her intent to speak until the words were in the air.

He cocked his head. "Yes." One corner of his mouth turned up. "Your turn to answer a question."

Maggie squared her shoulders. "I can't talk about anything except what you've contracted me for—a profile."

"But you know who he is. You know exactly who I suspect. I've been after him for some time, but he's always one step ahead. I need your help."

Been after him for some time? But this man's name was Reid. Did Tristan believe his name was Rich? Lying about his name would be a good plan—if Detective Rich didn't exist, it would serve to make Tristan look delusional if he called the police... which he had. *I've made calls to the police, but he always makes me look unstable.* And that surveillance photo outside her office, the one that looked so much like the man in front of her...

Ice prickled along her spine. "I can't help you," she said, her voice cold.

He replaced his cell in his suit pocket. "We found traces of linen embedded in the burns, too," he went on as if he hadn't heard her. "The killer wraps the wound just after the burning ceremony and then asphyxiates them. Lillian is only the most recent victim we've found with this very specific M.O.—it's been almost two years since she was killed."

Wait, Tristan was at a two-year-old crime scene? Was he... unburying the victims? Had he witnessed Lillian's burial while sleepwalking, or had he killed her and was only now beginning to remember? Way too many options —far too much speculation.

"Tonya Rupert is another of his victims. I'm positive that you know her, even if you won't admit it."

Her throat went hot. Welp, that answered that. Her patient was officially connected to at least two missing women: Tristan was Tonya's boyfriend, and he was at Lillian's burial site last night. But if Lillian was the latest... "Are you telling me that the most recent victim was taken two years ago?"

He nodded, but he was lying. Sammy had told her they had a recent victim—a woman kidnapped just last week, right? Were they still trying to keep the newest victim under wraps, or had they just not found her body yet to confirm the connection?

"We're not reopening this case because these women are being taken now," Reid went on. "We're investigating because we're finally finding the bodies."

She frowned. The dustpan was too heavy; her wrist ached. "The picture you just showed me wasn't of two-year-old flesh. That was a fresh burn."

"I suppose I can keep secrets too." He smiled, but there was nothing friendly in the gesture. "Watch your back, Doctor Connolly. The man who killed these women is after you now. The recent break-in at your place is not a coincidence. And from your behavior, I can't tell if you're protecting someone, or if you're doing something uncouth yourself."

Uncouth? Strange language for a homicide detective. But all she heard were the officers asking after Aiden: *You expect me to believe you didn't see him all evening? That you were supposed to walk him home like you do every day, and you just left him in the woods? What happened to your wrist?*

She stiffened. "Fortunately, you have a picture of the person who broke into my office. That man is not my patient, and he clearly isn't me." *Though he might be you.* And she did believe that this detective was a liar—a sneak. She did not yet know what he was hiding, but he was all kinds of wrong.

"Things aren't always what they seem, Doctor." He slid a business card from his jacket and extended it her way— no, not a business card. A scrap of paper with his number. That wasn't right, wasn't professional, not at all, and it was completely at odds with his fresh-pressed suit and fancy pocket square. Had she even seen his badge? She'd seen him on the television, but...

Maggie stared at him—level, unwavering. When she did not take the scrap, he dropped it into the dustpan on top of the glass. "If you'd like to revise your statement, you know where to find me." He turned for the door. "If you make it that long."

CHAPTER
TWENTY-TWO

MAGGIE WATCHED the detective stalk out, dumped the shattered glass into the trash, and grabbed a new coffee cup, trying to ignore the way her knuckles still ached. Did the detective just threaten her? *If you make it that long?* And passing around scraps of paper like they were business cards? What the heck was up with that?

She glanced at the digital numbers on the microwave—two hours until she had to be in the office. Not even nine o'clock, and she was already fried. Just another day of leaping from one crisis to another, *Suspicious Minds* straight to *Jailhouse Rock* and back to... *Don't?* Maybe *Devil in Disguise.* Elvis sang far too many love songs to actually apply to this crazy life of hers, but maybe the titles were enough if you had the imagination.

You're deflecting, Maggie. Distracting yourself.

Tristan had called four times while the detective had been in her house, left a message that he'd had to leave the hotel. But she already knew he'd left the hotel—she'd seen him on the news. As if a hotel could contain a fully awake tech wizard intent on wandering around a crime scene.

She shoved the phone into the pocket of her robe; she wasn't ready to call him back. What was she going to say? "Hey, caught you on the morning news! Are you a serial killer, or what?" Even if he knew the answer, he wouldn't tell her—he'd made that much clear. Maggie wasn't even sure how he'd gotten her private number. The same way he knew about Helena, she supposed.

Maggie was done playing puppet, doing what people wanted or expected her to do. By the book, which was supposed to be the set of logical, legal choices, had not helped her here—she'd put Helena in danger, albeit accidentally. The detective had threatened her. And the gall of that Tristan Simms, the audacity to blackmail her and her patient and expect that she'd keep playing his game...

She'd have to figure this out herself, *Scooby-Doo* style. She'd make a good Velma. It'd be nice to catch a killer, help an innocent man, and protect Helena at the same time, but she wasn't sure she'd get that lucky. Even if she just managed to keep Helena safe and get a murderer locked away, two out of three wasn't bad. Maggie ran her fingers through her hair, and immediately got her thumb tangled in her curls, as if the universe had decided that she needed a side of scalp pain to shock her brain into gear. She ripped her fingers free. The scar on her head throbbed, then settled. *Think, Maggie. Overthink it—that's your jam.*

Tristan had been at a crime scene. He had known Tonya. It'd be so easy to believe that he was guilty, a purely black-and-white situation, but there were too many inconsistencies. Too many pieces that didn't fit.

In the beginning, Maggie had assumed that the idea of someone following Tristan was a delusion or a function of his dreaming brain, but she no longer believed that. A flesh-and-blood *someone* had broken into her office while she was with him—someone who had known Tristan was seeing her. That information was not public. And if you knew you were a killer, why the hell would you go to a shrink and tell her you're sleepwalking, that you were burying unknown items in the dirt? She'd briefly considered that he was padding an insanity defense, but most didn't try that until they were arrested. No reason to figure out a plea deal and risk blowing your cover if you weren't sure you'd be caught in the first place.

She believed that Tristan was telling the truth about the detective too—wrong name or not, Reid Hanlon had admitted to being "after him for some time," and had given her a slip of paper instead of a business card as if daring her to call the station.

And the earrings—Christine had *those fucking earrings*. Tristan Simms would not take earrings off his girlfriend's dead body and give them to a woman who posted everything she did on social media.

The earrings were bothering her most of all. Wearing them was cocky—stupid too, unless you didn't know where they'd come from. But giving them away was just as stupid, and despite his presence at the crime scene, Tristan didn't strike her as dumb. A sleepwalker might behave more erratically, but...

She resisted the urge to bang her head on the kitchen table and tapped computer keys instead, looking up Detective—*if you make it that long*—Hanlon. He'd smelled like cinnamon and looked like a man "off to scam those old ladies out of their retirement." Smarmy—devious. And it did not *feel* as if Reid was following a routine lead. He had not interrogated her using open-ended questions as if searching for the truth. He had tried to get her to vilify a suspect he'd already deemed guilty. This was a dog-with-a-bone situation. A vendetta.

The screen coughed up a list of website hits. Maggie had expected to find "no results" as she had for her "Rich" search, or a different face staring back at her from the screen, but the man was legit—a series of arrests, his name linked to criminals he had brought to justice, praise from the brass. She didn't see any news articles on him for anything "uncouth," but he could be a dirty cop. The very worst of them were the best at hiding it, and smart criminals with badges were often the most dangerous. In her years spent hiding domestic violence victims, she'd seen far too many with a partner in law enforcement. There was nothing like unchecked power to get a psychopath off. Those guys gave good cops a bad name.

She hit the search bar again and typed: Lillian Mace. While the detective had said she was dead, Maggie was not sure about the timeline. He'd shown her a picture of newly dead flesh, so either he was lying about when Lillian was taken, or he was lying about who the most recent victim was.

She didn't have to search long. Lillian Mace's family had been active on social media following her disappearance... two years ago, as Reid had said. All page posts after that consisted of friends sharing stories, missing her—a virtual group therapy session.

But one post made the world tighten around her: Tristan and Lillian at a beach, his lips on her cheek, the woman grinning ear to ear. Lillian had captioned it "Me and Tris," but he was not tagged in the image, had not liked it or commented. To be expected since he didn't have a profile on the platform.

Maggie leaned back in her chair. Tristan had been intimately connected to Lillian, just as he was connected to Tonya. If Tristan himself wasn't the killer, it had to be someone choosing victims based on his relationships... or his movements. If Tristan knew where Helena was, if he'd followed her, then his stalker—the killer—might also know Helena's location.

Too many loose ends—too many potential suspects. A giant poop sandwich.

Tonya's face flashed in her head. Her bright smile. Those glittering hoops. Again, with the earrings—they felt so critical.

She needed to start whittling down her suspect list. And Tristan wasn't the one wearing Tonya's earrings. He wasn't the one who'd broken into her office. He didn't appear jealous, didn't seem to have the rage issues she'd expect of the person she was looking for. And off the top of her head, she could definitely think of a few people who'd seen what Christine was capable of.

Maybe the easiest way to protect Helena was to investigate the people around Tristan Simms. At the very least, she could verify whether one of them took Tonya's earrings off her corpse.

CHAPTER
TWENTY-THREE

Maggie's skin vibrated as she locked her front door behind her. The car seemed miles away, her feet heavy like she had a pair of chubby raccoons clinging to her legs.

Did Christine get a different set of earrings made, or did she take Tonya's, which would make her far more suspicious? If nothing else, Tristan had called the jeweler his "foster father," so the man was close to Tristan himself and would have information about Christine's dramatic scene at his store. Perhaps he could offer insight into both. Plus, "Benedict, Eden" had pulled up a search engine hit immediately, as if Google was encouraging her to move ahead.

The air inside the DeLorean smelled stale, like dust and day-old French bread. *This is crazy. This is his family.*

But it didn't matter. She didn't see another viable path. There were no good options that guaranteed Helena's protection from her husband—none that ensured Tristan Simms would keep his mouth shut about Helena's location if the police picked him up.

The detective was already investigating Tristan. She'd investigate everyone else. Someone had to explore the other

THE DEAD DON'T DREAM

options, including the shifty detective himself. Someone had to care about the truth.

The car door shrieked. Her keys rattled like wind chimes as she shoved them into the ignition. Maggie turned the key.

Rrrrr-rrrrr-rrrrr—click!

She frowned. Today of all days.

Rrrrr-rrrrr-rrrrr—click!

Maggie turned the key again. This time it didn't even try to turn over. Was the battery dead? *Dammit.*

She should call a tow truck, get the car in to be fixed, but she could do that later. She had less than two hours before she was supposed to be at work—closer to one and a half now.

Maggie left the car sitting in her driveway, called a Hytch, and managed to make it to the rental car place before she crawled out of her skin. She picked a Toyota that looked shiny enough, but smelled like sadness. Most people believed sadness didn't have a smell, but she knew better. It was salty—musky. Like nearly rotten spuds, by far the worst kind of potato.

She was down to an hour by the time she got onto the highway. She gripped the Toyota's wheel and pressed harder on the gas.

The strip mall was not hard to find, nor was it crowded —good. She didn't want an audience. She parked in the front of the lot and made her way under an awning embossed with silver leaves on gilded vines. Emeralds of Eden, one of twenty independent jewelry stores in the area, and the only one owned by a Benedict, which is what Tristan had called his foster father during their first session.

The front door was made of oak, and there was no bell

to announce her presence. That made the place feel quaint, but the glittering pieces on display erased that perception. As in most jewelry stores, glass cases formed a large U-shape around the outer perimeter of the shop, glowing white lights aimed at the sparkling goods beneath. No fluorescents here, only a series of lamps in each corner and goosenecks behind the counter for those who wanted to examine their jewelry more closely. Two dark doorways stood along the back wall, the left marked by an enormous golden cross off the right side of the frame: three feet tall, the messiah's eyes a blue stone that might have been sapphire, a glittering crown of thorns perched atop the poor sap's gilded curls. Catholic torture porn was next level.

She wanted to cringe, but instead she put on her shrink face and stepped up to the counter. Maggie tapped the bell, half expecting a black-capped attendant to appear and ask if she needed help with her bags.

"They'll be right out for you."

Maggie jumped. An elderly woman with crepe-paper skin sat in a chair against the far left wall, hidden from the front door by the counter, her white hair streaked with black, a hint of receding hairline above her widow's peak. Short and squat and weirdly lumpy, like an owl in a person suit. Tristan's foster... grandmother?

Maggie opened her mouth to reply, but a young woman with long dark hair was already emerging from the back room, a little girl plastered against her side. Was this Tristan's sister, Jeanna? She believed so. With a child in tow, she appeared to be family and not an employee.

"Hey there!" The woman smiled with straight white teeth—genuine. "What can I help you with?"

The old woman snorted. Maggie wasn't sure where to

look. She picked the less owly of the two. "I have an unusual request. A friend of mine got a pair of earrings from you around three years back." She pulled out her cell and rested it on the glass. "Do you recognize these?" Maggie tapped the screen and turned the phone to show Jeanna a close-up social media screenshot of Christine's earrings. No face in the picture, just the little birds flying in different directions. "I'd love to buy a pair."

Jeanna's smile faltered, and the child at her hip looked up—wide, moon face, chubby cheeks. Three years old or so. "Well, my father never makes the same pair more than once; we specialize in custom jewelry. But I'm sure we can make you something equally beautiful." There was a hope-fulness in her gaze, but it was edged with desperation. From the state of the empty store, the tiny chip in the glass case near Jeanna's pinky... money issues?

The child blinked at Maggie as if begging her to hurry up.

"It's a shame that you don't make duplicates. I really love these earrings." She sounded like a broken record, but she needed to verify that the custom-piece thing was accu-rate. If only one pair of earrings existed, then they were evidence that linked Christine to the dead woman.

"Sorry, my dear," a much lower voice boomed. The man who emerged from the door beside the glittering crucifix wore a beard of tight gray curls to his clavicle and eyebrows that were just as unruly—very Santa Claus. Benedict Rose, presumably. He grinned, but she could only tell from the way the balls of his cheeks moved; she couldn't see his mouth at all. "They aren't special if anyone can get the same."

"Amen!" said the woman in the chair.

Maggie suddenly felt outnumbered. But she had what

she'd come for. If they never made the same pair twice, that meant Christine was wearing stolen earrings—Tonya wouldn't have given them away. And shifty though he seemed, it's not like the detective had taken the jewelry off Tonya's corpse and given them to Tristan's off-and-on girl-friend. That would make her a witness.

Benedict approached, exchanged a smile with the child, then squinted at Maggie's cell, still resting on the counter. His face changed; his gaze darkened. Rage, but well-suppressed rage, the kind you read in the jaw muscles. A Proud Boy in a Walmart as opposed to at a Klan rally.

Her mouth went dry—tacky. The cross glowered at her from the wall, and the detective's voice whispered in her ear: *If I had to guess, I'd say it's religious, but that's just a gut feeling.* The child shifted harder against her mother... three years old. From Tonya's file, Jeanna had been attacked around the time this child was conceived.

"I think I know why you're asking," Benedict said, and she swallowed hard, trying to refocus as he nodded toward the phone. "Are you friends with that girl?" There was malice in his words, she could feel it like briars in the flesh of her arms. "If you're associated with her, you might as well leave now. We don't need any more trouble, and Tristan brought enough of that in here."

"Dad..." Jeanna shook her head. "Leave Tris alone. It wasn't his fault."

"Mind your mouth, Jeanna," the old woman said, finally pushing herself to her feet. Jeanna stiffened, her lips pressed into a thin white line, and said nothing more. *Blessed are the meek.*

Benedict glanced back at the owl woman, stroked the child's hair—protective—then refocused on Maggie. "That woman terrified my granddaughter. All that yelling and

150

carrying on. And from her crass language, it seems Tristan knew her"—he sniffed—"biblically."

Biblically, huh? So they'd spent time painting doors in lamb's blood? Burning bushes? Taking fruit from serpents? Ah, college. They'd all been there.

Maggie's fingers clenched around the phone. This was a family business. It was time she started acting like she cared about the family if she wanted additional insight. "I'm not friends with Christine. I was friends with Tonya." Tonya had been sweet, even went to church if she remembered correctly—precisely the kind of girl that they might like as a match for Tristan. "Those earrings were Tonya's favorite, but I couldn't find them after she vanished."

Benedict's face softened; Jeanna's shoulders relaxed. Only the elderly woman's eyes remained tight. Suspicious.

"Tonya was really nice," Jeanna said, but her smile was forced. "We had dinner with her a few times. Robin really liked her." At the sound of her name, the child looked at her mother. She tugged on Jeanna's hand, and Jeanna squeezed but stayed focused on Maggie.

"Tonya seemed like a good girl." Benedict nodded his agreement. "I'm sorry for my suspicion, dear. But that Christine… she's got the devil in her. Like Tristan's own mama did, God rest her poor, confused soul." Benedict raised a hand to his chest and rubbed in a small circle, like he was massaging his heart back to life. It seemed that just speaking of Tristan's late mother hurt his chest. He was close enough to be considered a foster father, so it wasn't a shock that the man still missed her. It was called heartache for a reason.

But the devil bit was a strong statement coming from a guy with a three-foot crucifix watching his every move. She waited for lightning to strike him, and when it didn't, she said, "I understand. I guess I'm a little confused about why you assumed the photo was Christine." It was, of course, but he'd known immediately, without any distinguishing characteristics. "How did Christine come to be wearing Tonya's earrings if you never make the same pair twice?"

Benedict rubbed at his chest again. "She came in here, cursing up a storm over those earrings. Demanded a pair like the ones I made for Tonya, I assume to rub them in the poor girl's face."

All that fit with jealousy. Had she stolen the earrings because Benedict had refused her request? Because Tristan hadn't given her what she wanted? And most importantly, was jealousy a reason to kill Tonya, to kill Lillian—to kill any of Tristan's exes?

Of course. Of course it was.

"I'm so sorry," Maggie said. "You didn't deserve that. And I'm not here to open old wounds."

Robin tugged her mother's hand again, and this time Jeanna looked down and ruffled her hair. "I believe Nana Eden has apple juice in the back for you."

Robin's eyes widened. She looked at her grandmother hopefully—Eden. But the old woman shook her head. "After lunch, and not a moment before, child." *My way, not your mother's way.* Ouch. "But you go on back there now. This is grown people business."

Robin's face fell, but she did as she was told—minded her elders the way Jeanna appeared to. Eden was a formidable woman to have a three-year-old under her thumb like that. Those little punks rarely listened to anyone.

They watched the girl leave, then Benedict said, "I got Christine out of here by giving her a damaged pair. One of them was twisted up." No wonder he'd known it was

Christine in the picture. "Sometimes creating art takes a false start or two, especially at my age." He raised his hands. The small fingers on each had bulbous knuckles, but the others appeared functional. It probably took a lot more time and patience these days to make his creations. "I was going to melt the gold down, but it was worth the lost materials to get her gone—maybe even worth my reputation if she showed them around. Which she obviously did."

That made sense. He'd wanted to protect his granddaughter from the godless woman's temper tantrum.

But... huh. That meant Christine didn't have to take Tonya's earrings. Maybe that didn't matter. The jewelry was a symptom, not the cause, and jealousy was a hell of a motive if Christine thought Tristan was moving on—that he might leave her for good.

"She stole Tristan's Saint Benedict too," Eden said. Even her words sounded owly with rounded edges *this close* to a hoot. "That medallion has been his since the day he was baptized, and there it was on her wretched neck while she carried on with her nonsense." She shook her head.

Medallion... "Was it round? About this big?" Maggie showed them with her thumb and forefinger, the way the detective had done.

Benedict nodded, but his eyes had sharpened. "She's still got it, eh? I hoped she'd do the right thing and give it back to Tristan once they split. Unless she's still sniffing around him." He blinked at Maggie as if expecting an answer, but she could barely manage to swallow. The earrings might not be relevant since there were two pairs, but that medallion certainly was. And Christine had it. *Christine.*

Maggie was right about Tristan's ex... if the medallion

was a match. But she wouldn't be able to verify that on her own.

"Do you know Tristan well?" Benedict asked. "My daughter's been calling him for days about his broken watch."

Her shoulders relaxed—she hadn't even realized they were tight. A watch; that's what had been around his wrist where those tan lines were. Everything they'd said had reinforced the notion that her patient was innocent, and she'd only been here five minutes. Surely the detective could have refuted Tristan's connection to that medallion if he'd tried. She still needed to explain Tristan's presence at the crime scene, but things were not as cut and dried as Reid Hanlon had made them out to be. And this should have been the first place the detective came. He was trying to make Tristan look guilty because he *wanted* him to be guilty. But why?

"I'm sure he's just busy," Jeanna said, and Maggie glanced her way—what had they been talking about? "But maybe you can tell him that we have his stuff... if you talk to him before we do." She bit her lip. "Is he okay?"

Careful. While she was coloring outside the lines like a manic five-year-old all hopped up on Red Bull, she was not prepared to break confidentiality, especially now that it looked like Tristan was actually innocent. "He's as well as can be expected." *That should be vague enough to work.*

But Benedict's eyes narrowed. It seemed that was the wrong thing to say, either too vague or because he did not expect Tristan to be well.

Maggie tapped the screen on her cell and turned the phone to Benedict one last time, willing her hand not to shake as she showed him a screenshot of Reid Hanlon. "What about this—"

"Why do you have a picture of Richie?" Eden barked, her voice less owly and more like the sharp caw of a crow.

Richie—*Rich*. He'd been poking around the jewelry store as well. And he'd given everyone the wrong name... everyone except for Maggie.

Six eyes focused on her. Maggie's sweater suddenly felt as if it had shrunk two sizes, the wrists and neck constricting with strangling pressure. *Strangling you like a handsome patient in your dark bedroom who just happens to remind you of your recently deceased lover.*

Maggie cleared her throat and forced out: "He came to see me about an issue at my office. He said he was a friend of Tristan's."

Benedict shook his head. "Richie's worse than Christine."

Eden's eyes sparkled with malice, and when she spoke again, her tone was hard. "Richie's the one who brought that girl into Tristan's life in the first place. Dated that jezebel, talking about marrying her..." She glared at Maggie. "I don't want so much as his photo in my store."

Maggie repocketed the phone in slow motion. The detective knew Christine. Had been romantically involved with her, serious enough to discuss marriage.

"Richie was wild," Benedict went on. "He was always getting Tristan into trouble. And he certainly isn't a friend, never has been." Benedict's eyes narrowed, blood pulsing in his temples. "Richie is Tristan's brother."

CHAPTER
TWENTY-FOUR

Maggie was itchy by the time she left the jewelry store, the gooseflesh on her arms more like a rash. Her muscles vibrated with unspent tension. She clenched the wheel until her knuckles ached.

The detective was Tristan's brother, he knew Christine intimately, and he was doing his damndest to put Benedict's quasi-adopted son behind bars. But Christine had the necklace—the medallion. A jealous woman like that had a reason to break into the office... perhaps to kill. Christine was her top suspect, but how did the detective fit? Were they in it together?

Reid Hanlon certainly seemed to be on Christine's side. And it sounded like Reid had plenty of reasons to hate Tristan; the family drama was obvious. Tristan was involved with Christine, a woman Reid had wanted to marry. Maybe the detective was the jealous one. Even Benedict Rose hated Reid—"Richie"—Hanlon as much as Tristan did, though Benedict's reasons were paternal. He seemed to think "Rich" was a bad influence on Tristan, had been since they were kids. The detective had tried to make Maggie feel guilty, acting like she was the one at fault for protecting her patient, had given her that stupid little scrap of paper, threatening her however vaguely—*if you make it that long...* To Benedict, Reid was the bad guy. And it sure felt true.

Her patient had been telling the truth. About being followed, about Rich—he was not delusional.

Rich. What a weird nickname. Even Benedict hadn't known where it had come from. That was the last question he'd answered before Eden remembered they had a pressing engagement and escorted Maggie to the door.

She had twenty-five minutes before her first client of the day, but the thought of going to work like this, of Owen seeing her biting her lip and clenching her fists, made her stomach sour. Maggie checked her rearview and hooked a U-turn. Her cell buzzed. She glanced at it, expecting Owen or maybe Alex, but it wasn't: her mom.

Maggie hit *Decline* and pushed the pedal to the floor. She couldn't deal with her mother right now. Her head was a water balloon—filled to bursting, one wrong move and, *Boom!* All the children in the vicinity would scream if her head exploded. Maybe the adults too. But not the person she was going to see.

The cemetery where Aiden's tombstone was located sat on the road between her home and her office. She stopped on the side of the highway and picked wildflowers, a bushel of Queen Anne's Lace and something yellow that made her sneeze. But it was worth it. Yellow was Aiden's favorite color—*used to be* Aiden's favorite color.

She parked on one of the many winding roads and made her way over the sloping green lawn that was still hanging onto the last dregs of summer. Unseasonably warm today. Sweat popped up along her clavicle and slid between her breasts like oil.

Her brother's grave sat near the middle of the cemetery, a headstone in gray marble, fistfuls of crabgrass adorning either corner, which was fitting—crabgrass was the only thing she'd ever been able to grow. She'd once bought a lily and she'd sworn she'd heard it crying on the way back to her house. It was dead within the week.

Maggie laid the flowers at the foot of the stone and sat cross-legged in front of them.

"Hey, dude," she said. The granite did not reply. The cell buzzed again.

Her chest was so tight, she half expected to look down and see a multitude of rubber bands squeezing her like a YouTube watermelon experiment. She turned the phone off and tossed it into the grass. *Here—just be here, Maggie.* But the trees around the perimeter of the cemetery felt as if they were edging nearer. She lowered her face. The headstone was cool and smooth against her forehead.

"It's been a rough week, Aid. Dad's out of it, like usual these days. And I have this patient... a really tough case. But I think I'm upset right now because it all seems so critical— so life and death. And death... well, that always makes me think of you. Of the mistakes I made. How if I had done things differently, you'd be here."

The wind whistled through the trees and hissed along the fine bones in her ears. A deep pit in her guts churned and pulsed like a poisonous slug preparing to give birth.

"I'm sorry, Aiden. I'm sorry I let you walk home alone. That I went off with Kevin just because he was cute." She could see the abandoned building in her mind's eye, the freedom of hurling bricks through interior office windows coursing through her veins. She could feel Kevin's hand on her lower back, the first warm tickle of young love. "I paid for it—I ended up with a wicked scar from some older kid who snuck in when Kevin left to pee. But you paid a far higher price. You never came back at all. It's not fucking fair."

Kevin's warm hand vanished. She could suddenly feel the dirt the way she had that day, the dust in her eyes, the broken glass in the knees of her jeans. The stranger had smelled like copper—even before he'd touched her, he'd smelled of blood.

But that monster hadn't taken her brother. He'd been with her when Aiden had vanished, and in short order, he'd been bleeding himself, a shard of glass protruding from his left cheek. If she squinted, she could still see it glittering beneath his eye, his lips forced open with the sharp pressure of it, the jagged edge piercing his tongue.

Her eyes burned. "I can't say the best is yet to come. You're gone, Kevin drove his car off a bridge—relapse is a bitch. Dad's going too. Maybe not physically, but he's mentally gone much more often than he's there with me. I try to force myself to fix the things I can fix—to tackle the problems I have some modicum of control over. But this case... I don't know if I can fix it. I don't know what to change. I don't know which path is the right one."

She didn't. She really didn't.

"I just know I don't want to wind up like our renegade parents who named me after a river of molten stone like they wanted me to get punched in the face. I sometimes think about how it might be if you were here. How we might live up the road from each other. Maybe we'd get together for cookouts. Maybe Kevin and I would be married and your children could play tag with ours, the way we did as kids." She laughed, but it was a bitter sound. "I like to think that maybe you'd be a shrink, too, and then you could help me with this patient instead of the boy scout I'm stuck with."

Her chest was hot, a fire burgeoning in her guts. She loved Owen. She loved her friends. But she couldn't tell a single one of them what was going on. They had their own issues—they missed Kevin too. And they'd done far too much for her already.

Plus, if she told them too much about this case, they might get hurt. She could not put the people she loved in harm's way—she'd already failed Helena. She'd failed Kevin and Aiden. She was so fucking *tired* of failing.

That's why she was here. She needed one place where she could say it, all of it, out loud to someone, even if that someone wasn't really there. It was as close as she could get to him. She had no idea where Aiden's killer had left his bones.

The leaves around her rustled, the breeze whipping its fingers through her hair. Maggie winced against the chill on her back and the heat behind her eyelids. "I miss you. And as much as things suck right now, at least we have each other, right?" Her eyes smarted; this time, she let the tears fall.

"Thanks for listening, Aid."

Tears ran freely down her face. Her chin was wet. She laid her palm against the tombstone, pressed her cheek to the cold stone, and wept.

CHAPTER
TWENTY-FIVE

BY THE TIME she got to work, the pressure in her chest had eased to a tolerable level. Maggie lowered herself into her desk chair and pulled out the case files she needed for the day, trying to clear her head. But the thoughts kept coming, as one might expect from the Overlord of Overthinking, the Ruler of Rumination, the... Oligarch of Obsession.

She sighed. The victims were connected romantically to Tristan. Christine had the medallion. But Christine was menacing, aggressive—unstable. The type of person Maggie would expect to commit a crime of passion, the type of woman who would call and threaten Tristan's love interests... and she had. But was she organized enough to kill those women in such a ritualistic way? And what of the tension between brothers?

Her pen tap-tap-tapped against the stack of files, leaving tiny dents in her folders.

Maybe Christine had played things to make Reid suspect Tristan—her patsy. Or Christine's lover detective was her partner in crime. Either of them might have broken into Maggie's office to see what Tristan knew—whether he suspected them. And if Reid really was guilty, she'd have to go up against the police force. She wanted to do that about as much as she wanted to blow her nose with a cactus.

She shoved her curls off her face. Velma needed her Scooby to navigate this—*zoinks!*

Sammy was in court all afternoon, but she snatched her phone before she could change her mind and left a message on his cell. She'd be careful not to tell him anything that might put him in danger, but Sammy was already involved in the case. And he had access to information that she didn't: timelines, alibis, forensics, details on that medallion if she was lucky. Maybe he'd even have insight about Reid. Sammy worked closely with the department and was on a first-name basis with most of the detectives—Sammy was friends with everyone. But he was *best* friends with Maggie. *Suck it, Hanlon, ya square.*

In the meantime, she worked. She needed something she could fix.

Sally Winchester was her two o'clock. Grieving the loss of her daughter, the thick timbre of her helplessness kept Maggie engaged through the forty-five minute session. The death of a child imprinted on your soul, leaving a lacy pattern of raw pain that brightened at inopportune times. Maggie had strived to make her own mother smile after Aiden vanished, but it turned out that goofiness couldn't resurrect a lost kid. Who knew?

Sally's appointment eased into another session with Elroy, then a new sexual addiction intake at four-thirty. But when the patients were gone and the talking was over, the chatter in her brain started in once more. She couldn't even harass Owen—he'd left at four to have dinner with his kids.

Maggie plunked her elbows on the desk and lowered her head to rest in her hands. Tristan's case was bleeding into every area of her life. And she still had no idea how to fix it. It had only been a couple days, it had all happened *so damn fast*... but still.

The phone buzzed in her desk drawer—*Sammy, it's about time!* She fumbled it out, but it wasn't Sammy. Mom. Again. She'd sent a text, which usually meant bad news... or an emergency. Maggie hit the button, but she didn't have time to read the message before another sound cut the air from the direction of the waiting room.

Bing!

She glanced at her door; her last patient had left it open a crack. Normally, this wouldn't matter, she wasn't doing anything weird in here all alone—probably a missed opportunity. But she paused with her fingers poised over the cell screen. Was that sound... the elevator?

The outer office door opened, then the *thunk*, *thunk*, *thunk* of footsteps approached her room. Maggie stiffened. She didn't have another intake today—there was nothing else on her schedule. Owen often spent his solitary evenings in his office, but he wouldn't come back here on a night when he had the girls.

But that marching beat of footsteps... too purposeful for a janitor. They possessed the tense energy of a caffeine-infused bulldog sporting an American flag bandana.

She dropped the cell back into the drawer and spread her palms on the desk, ready to get to her feet. She didn't make it to standing.

The door swung wide, the knob smashing into the wall behind it.

Not Tristan. Not Owen. Not a new patient either.

His shoulders were as broad as her doorframe. Even without the baseball cap, she recognized him: the man from the video footage the detective had shown her this morning.

And boy, did he look pissed.

CHAPTER
TWENTY-SIX

THE GIANT MAN stalked into the room, one step over the threshold. Maggie's muscles screamed, trying to force her to move, to run, but letting him believe he was in charge was a better option. Show them that you're submissive, as you might with a rabid raccoon, or a particularly aggressive squirrel. Ultra "macho men" tended to have squirrel-sized genitalia, according to Sammy, and she had no reason to disbelieve him.

She swallowed hard, her peripheral vision scanning the desk. Pen. Letter opener. A paperweight in the shape of a coiled snake. A file folder that would leave a nasty paper cut —that should stop anyone in their tracks.

Not the time for jokes, Maggie's brain!

For a moment, the man came no closer. He stood just inside the office, shoulders heaving, jaw set, blocking the light from the hall. "Where's Christine?"

She kept her gaze level, her shoulders set, but her brain was yelling—*Christine knows the man who broke in here, every single thing is connected to her!*

The man took a heaving step forward, body listing to the left like an unsteady Ferris wheel. Drunk?

"She isn't here, but perhaps we can—"

"But you know where she is, right?" He paused behind the chairs, fingers wrapped over the top of one of them as if trying to hold himself upright, or perhaps trying to hold himself back. His knuckles were pale with the force of his grip. "You have to know where she is!"

Why would she know where Christine was? *Maybe out killing some other innocent woman?* Maggie's head was swimming. This was the man who had broken into her office, but he was here to find Christine. Not what she'd expect if they were working together. He was clearly angry, yet from the inflection in his words, his wrath was aimed at Christine herself. Did he think Christine was the culprit in these crimes the way Maggie did, and broke in to see if Tristan had confessed to her involvement? Was he a loved one of Lillian Russell? Someone who knew Tonya? *What am I missing?*

Maggie gestured to the chair in front of the desk. "If you'll have a seat, I'm sure we can discuss—"

"Don't lie to me!" he bellowed and dropped his hands, fists clenching and unclenching at his sides. "I saw you at my house! I have you clear as day on my doorbell cam, so don't even try to deny it."

Wait, *his* house? Spittle clung to the left corner of his lip, a rabid kind of fury. This was bad. This was really bad. Her pinky finger was nearly touching the paperweight—heavy enough to make a good weapon. Her water bottle might, too, but it was a bit farther down the desk; he'd see her reach for it. "I understand your concern, Mr...?"

He balked—he appeared thrown by the half question. "Archer! Gordon Archer, Christine's husband."

Her fingertip froze against the cold glass snake. Tristan's off-and-on girlfriend was married? Realization snapped the pieces into place, her sweaty palms leaving smudges on the desktop.

Gordon Archer wasn't here because he thought his wife was a killer. He was the one who was jealous. The bright gleam in his eyes was evidence enough of that—a gleam she'd taken as rage. Her belief that Christine was guilty had clouded her judgment. *This is why you can't get too involved with patients, Maggie.*

She cleared her throat. "I went to your home to speak to—"

"I know exactly why you were there—Christine told me. It was about Tristan." He skirted the chairs and approached the desk. Her spine hardened into a steel rod. This man had broken into her office; he had access to the medallion if Christine was in possession of it. But why attack those women? Who had killed them? Him or his wife or the detective?

Stop asking yourself questions, Maggie, ask the goober across the desk! Dammit. Where was Scooby-Doo when you needed him? She'd even take that dimwit Shaggy right about now.

Archer put his palms on her desktop, parallel to her own hands, and leaned toward her. She remained still, holding her ground.

"Everyone has a soft spot for that bastard," he hissed, "but not me. I see right through him." His breath was a frantic wheezing. He smelled of cheap beer.

"You strike me as an insightful individual," she said slowly—*careful*. It would do no good to further agitate an unstable and intoxicated man, and, as Christine's husband, he was probably carrying years' worth of pain. *She likes to mess with people.* Maybe this wasn't about the missing women at all. It took control to kill and hide those bodies, and this man was anything but controlled. The jealousy though... that was clear and very real. What other options were there? Why did he break in?

"Did you come here to check up on your wife?" He stole Tristan's file to see whether his wife was cheating, right? That made the most sense. But even now, she wouldn't use Tristan's name; she would not give Archer more ammunition. And though her mouth was dry, though her muscles twitched, she met his gaze, cool and direct. "I can understand wanting to find out more about your wife's friends. But coming here, coming after me... this won't fix your marriage. Maybe we can talk about it before someone gets hurt."

He reared back as if she'd slapped him, his eyes wide. "Oh, god, no, that's not... You don't understand!" Archer slammed his heavy palms back down against her desk and leaned over them, the stink of his sweat like acid in her nose. "Christine..." His voice cracked. "She's gone."

CHAPTER
TWENTY-SEVEN
TRISTAN

THE DRIVEWAY LOOMED behind his guest, her hair shining in the glare from the porch light. *Why are you here, Jeanna?*

But he already knew what had driven her into his neighborhood, and it wasn't the package in her hands. He stepped backward into the foyer. She followed, smiling at him the way she used to at church when he was screwing around—getting her into trouble had always been his strong suit.

"Where were you when I pulled up?" she asked, pushing past him into the living room. "I waited for like an hour."

She always worried about him. It surely hadn't helped that he'd been dodging her calls. So why did her blue eyes look so damn bright?

"Just... out. Driving around." It was a lie, but she wouldn't notice. His sister was a sweet girl, but he could tell her that he'd met Elvis in person tonight, and she'd believe him.

Jeanna's eyes narrowed as if thinking, but she seemed to accept the excuse. She plopped herself down on the couch, tucked a strand of dark hair behind her ear, and passed him the box as he sat across from her. "Here you go. Good as new."

Tristan opened the lid. The watch inside was unrecognizable as the one he'd dropped off at the shop. The spiderweb cracks along the front were gone, the glass replaced. "Dad added a lot of diamonds," he said, but his voice sounded hollow and strained. His focus was not on the box. In his head, he heard sirens. In his mind's eye, he saw the body bag.

She bit her lip. "I mean, you said you wanted it a little fancier..."

"Of course. You know I pay for greatness." He was always looking for an excuse to pass the shop a little extra cash, but his back still stung, the lash marks a persistent reminder of his place in the world. No matter how he tried to help his foster father, he was not a good man.

"I'm glad you're happy, because I already ran your card, moneybags." Jeanna winked.

He forced a smile and set the package aside, his eyes cast down on the closed lid as if it might solve his problems —as if it might make the women he had once cared for less dead.

"Tris?"

He raised his head.

Jeanna's elbow was resting on his glass end table, smudging the shiny surface. His fingers twitched with the desire to wipe it down. *Dammit, Jeanna.* Why did she always do that?

Because she doesn't know better. Benedict was a detail-oriented man, but his artistic side often edged out the practical. That was why Eden was always at the shop, making the big decisions and cleaning the glass—someone had to.

"I know you're not okay," she said. "I don't know why, but I know you're not."

He cleared his throat and forced his eyes away from the furniture. "I'm fine. You've got more on your plate than I do. Like that kid of yours."

"Robin's amazing," she said, grinning. Any mention of her daughter always made Jeanna's face light up despite the rather awful way she'd come into the world. "She's having fun hanging out with Nana Eden while I'm working at the shop." Benedict still seemed agitated about the child, sometimes side-eyed Tristan like he, as a man, was in charge of who his sister was banging. But Jeanna hadn't gotten pregnant by choice—they all knew that much.

"You should be working in college instead of at the shop. Taking classes. Eden could still watch Robin." Gullible, maybe, but the girl was a whiz at science. She'd planned to be a pharmacist like her mother had been. Until the rape.

Jeanna's gaze clouded; it was the wrong thing to say. "This is my home. I have family, a job... What more could I possibly want?"

Maybe a life beyond the family business? She'd dropped out of college the week she found out she was pregnant. Tristan suspected she was having flashbacks walking around campus, but Benedict hadn't asked a single question about that, only what kind of refreshments she'd like for the baptism—it was always assumed there would be one. There was no other choice. For Tristan there were many choices, and if she'd told him the name of the man who'd raped her, God help him, he'd have killed the asshole himself instead of picking out finger sandwiches.

Yeah... he was not a good guy. That much was obvious

from the angst on his sister's face. "I'm sorry, Jeanna, I didn't mean—"

"Can I ask you something?"

Thank goodness for interruptions. "Shoot, sis."

She winced as if the forthcoming question physically pained her. "How did that watch get so dirty? I don't think I've ever seen something of yours be dirty."

My end table is a mess now. But the mention of dirt, just the word itself, dragged an image to the forefront of his mind: Lillian's body being wrenched from the ground. He'd tried to trace his overnight movements as the doctor had suggested and ended up at a crime scene.

Was Richie right about him being a killer? Was he revisiting his past crimes while he slept, uncovering those bodies out of guilt? Or had Richie followed him and buried those women in places Tristan happened to go?

Either way, the doctor might be in danger. And that thought frightened him far more than he had anticipated.

"Did you hear me?"

He glanced over. "Sorry."

"Talk to me, Tris. Please." Jeanna was staring at him, her eyebrows knitted in concern.

"I'm fine," he said. "I just have a long day of work yet to go."

"Work? Yeah, right. It's late." She frowned. "You went back to Christine again, didn't you? Is that where you were tonight?" When he did not immediately respond, Jeanna said: "Why are men *so stupid?*" She rolled her eyes in true sisterly fashion. "Can't you find another girlfriend? Maybe one who isn't absolutely insane?"

Insane. *Or a normal person in an abnormal situation.* But if he was normal, why couldn't he stop staring at the smudged end table? "Nice girls are hard to find."

"What about your new friend? Should we make something for her? Dad has some amazing ideas for a new piece."

Friend? He raised an eyebrow. "Who?"

"The redhead. She came to the shop earlier today. She seems nice, Tris." Her eyes locked on his, questioning, worrying, but her words faded in his ears.

The redhead.

Helena had not dissuaded her. Perhaps nothing would dissuade Maggie until she was gone and buried. The only question was whether he'd be the one to put Maggie in her grave.

CHAPTER
TWENTY-EIGHT

"So you just happened to go to this woman's house right before she vanished?" Detective Reid Hanlon glowered at her over the desk nearly the same way Gordon Archer had, but she liked the detective less. At least she understood Gordon's motives.

Christine's husband had gone willingly to the patrol car, hadn't put up a fight despite his aggressive conduct when he'd arrived at the office. He'd merely nodded when she suggested calling the police to file a report about Christine.

But she hadn't expected Reid to show up to take the report. In hindsight, she should have. The man had been all over the case, and, according to Tristan, Reid—aka Rich—had been stalking him for years. And the detective already knew the burglary and his homicides were connected or he wouldn't have come to her home this morning.

Maggie cleared her throat. "Christine wasn't missing when I was at her house."

"Why were you there in the first place? Mr. Archer says she was pretty upset by your visit. He's got video footage

THE DEAD DON'T DREAM

too. Maybe you can tell me what I'm going to see before I watch it."

"You'll see me standing on a porch, talking." She shrugged and flattened her palms against the desk, ensuring that her hands remained steady. "But I don't have to justify that to you. I can visit whomever I want. I don't have a tether."

"Unlike your mother, right?"

Her spine bristled. He'd done his research. And her family history—her mother or her father—would not look good to the police. Reid would certainly frown on her helping women like Helena... but she didn't think he knew about that. Unlike Tristan.

The detective's muddy eyes appraised her, his mouth set in a twitchy line that was far more judgmental than Bert the bobblehead's could ever be. She remained still at the desk, refusing to react as she had with Gordon Archer. *He's just a squirrel, just another aggressive squirrel.* "Glorified 'Yo Mama' jokes aren't going to help us here. We all have family members that we'd rather not discuss." *Like your brother, Tristan. The one you're trying to lock away.*

As expected, the barb hit home. His nostrils flared. "Fine. But it seems to me that Gordon Archer had every reason to come here."

"He broke into my office, Detective. Are you suggesting that vigilante justice is now endorsed by the Fernborn P.D.?"

"I'm sure you'd love that, but no. I'm suggesting that he had a reason. He broke in because he was worried about his wife. And it appears that he was right to be concerned. You had concerns too—you went to her home because you knew she was in danger *before* she was taken." His gaze darkened, and when he spoke again, his voice was lower,

175

growly—dangerous. "Did your patient inform you of his intent to harm Mrs. Archer?"

"I can neither confirm nor deny that I have patients, but I was not informed of an intent to harm anyone, Mrs. Archer or otherwise. And just because she's not home doesn't mean she's missing." You couldn't even file a missing persons report until the forty-eight hour mark, and Christine was known for messing with people.

"But you can see why this whole thing would look suspicious." Even his pocket square looked mad, the edges sharp enough to cut. "A duty to warn does extend to the police."

"Sometimes."

"Sometimes? Are you..." He inhaled deeply through his nose and let it out slowly, trying to keep his cool like a man three bran muffins deep stuck in rush-hour traffic. "I know you feel justified not telling me about your patient without a warrant—which is in the works, by the way. But you have a chance to do good here, if you can admit to yourself that you're wrong about Tristan Simms. That you're wrong about your patient."

"I never said he was my patient." *Just like you never said he was your brother.* But she didn't want to alert him to what she knew, not yet. She had a lot of pieces to put together before she could figure out what to do with them. She definitely needed to know whether the detective was romantically involved with Christine. If so, he was as likely a culprit as Christine herself.

His eyes flashed, his neck pink. "Stop playing these stupid mind games with me! Mr. Archer is convinced that your patient kidnapped his wife. I'm convinced that your patient is a murderer. So play the semantics card all you want, but this is going to get you killed."

THE DEAD DON'T DREAM

"I had someone break into my office, Detective. That's a far cry from someone trying to kill me."

"Not when we're digging bodies out of the ground."

"I don't match the profile of the missing women."

"It seems to me that you're a perfect match. Smart, strong-willed, beautiful—"

"If I didn't know better, I'd think you were hitting on me, Detective." She cocked her head and appraised him from under hooded eyes. "That's your game? Come here, flirt with the victim of a burglary, scare me into sleeping with you?" That most definitely wasn't his goal, the assertion was absolutely ridiculous, but she could think of no better way to make him leave—talk about mind games. "Maybe I should call your supervisor." That would be the last thing he wanted. That was why he gave her the scrap of paper, wasn't it? He'd be off the case if his superiors knew he was Tristan's brother.

His cheeks flushed. "Tristan murders his love interests before they get too close to what he really is. I'd hate to see what he might do to his shrink."

"It makes more sense for a jealous woman to go after the love interests of a man she cares about. And if I were that jealous woman and realized that a body had been discovered, especially if someone came around asking questions..." She shrugged, but her gaze was locked on his face, gauging his reaction. "Perhaps I'd run too."

"Ah, I see. So Christine killed those women because she was jealous, then took off because we found the bodies?" No notable change in posture, no discernible difference in affect—no change in the flush above his shirt collar or deepening redness in his ears. If the two of them were involved, either he didn't care much about what happened to her, or he was happy to have someone else to pin the crimes on.

He raised his hand and rubbed at his temple. "Answer me this, then: If Christine is the culprit, why would she leave you alive? Doesn't she think you're honing in on her territory?"

Maggie shrugged. "She has no reason to think that. Because I'm not."

"But you wouldn't tell me if you were." The silence stretched. "Have you talked to Mr. Simms lately?"

She pressed her lips together.

"You didn't even bother to call your partner about what happened in this office tonight, did you?"

No. Owen was with his children tonight. What was he going to do anyway, come in here and fawn over her? Worry until his head exploded? "Why? Do you think he'd be better at vigilante justice? That he'd race in here and help us track this woman down?"

"Do you have a gun?"

Huh? She raised an eyebrow. "A gun?"

"I strongly recommend you get one. Because while you think you're safe, you might be the target of a killer who's been working this city for a long time. Four victims in the last three years. But it all links back to an old case of mine. My first investigation, to be exact, even if it was cold by the time I made detective." He met her eyes, his gaze solemn but pointed. "Tristan's mother was murdered ten years ago, an outline of that medallion seared into her flesh then scored deeply enough with some burning implement to char the bone beneath—same as the more recent victims. That was never released to the press. The photo I showed you was a re-creation, what we've been able to piece together from combining the evidence on all the bodies.

The only difference with Tristan's mother was the bugs. It took us three days to identify her because some kind of flesh-eating beetle had been left to chow down on her face."

He backed away from the desk. "I've done all I can. This one's on you, Doctor. You better hope we find Christine in time."

CHAPTER
TWENTY-NINE

TRISTAN LIED ABOUT HIS MOTHER.

But what did that mean? From the evidence, the burns, the scoring, they were dealing with a single killer—his mom, then the current victims. Reid seemed to think Tristan was responsible, but he could be covering his own ass... or Christine's ass. They were all in their twenties by the time Tristan's mother died. A seven-year hiatus was unusual for a serial killer, but it wasn't impossible, and this one clearly knew how to hide a body.

She forced a breath to fill her lungs, but it made her chest hurt. Her stomach rolled, bile burning her esophagus. It was like all her organs were angry at her, and the din inside her head was worse. Questions throbbed painfully in her brain.

Was Christine actually missing, or had she run off because she had something to do with the murders? The latter seemed more likely. She'd been close to Tristan for years, closer than any other girlfriend, so if their killer was going after the people he cared about, Christine should have been a victim well before now.

Their killer. It had become her case as much as the detective's. The world of homicide and clue-seeking had bled into her psychology practice. It wasn't only that she had the roller-coaster sensation in her blood, the excitement before the drop no matter how awful this drop might be—she had a stake in this. She'd suffer guilt if more people died.

Especially if the detective was right about Tristan Simms.

Maggie collected her things. The office was far too small, the stairwell smaller. Even the dark expanse of parking lot felt constrictive. But she felt no eyes on her back as she made her way toward the rental car, her thoughts running circles inside her skull.

Though Gordon Archer had broken into her office, she did not think he was a murderer. He was jealous, yes, but Archer had no reason to attack Tristan's mother or any woman who might distract Tristan *away* from Christine. In cases of sexual jealousy, the target was usually the threat to the relationship—Tristan himself. And Gordon wouldn't have shown up at her office if he was the one who had taken his wife. While it was possible that he'd come to the office to cover his true intentions, possible that he was furious enough at his wife to torture other women by proxy, it just didn't *feel* right.

And the detective... *Get a gun?* Was that real advice? She popped the car door and climbed inside, irritated that it wasn't her DeLorean, missing the squeaking hinge. Missing the normalcy—anything normal.

She collapsed into the seat and started the engine. If Tristan was innocent, the detective was as suspicious as anyone. If his goal was to frame his brother, Maggie shooting Tristan would solve his problems. Make her afraid of her patient, tell her to protect herself, tell her he's a killer, then wait for her to finish the job for him. He'd cared for Christine enough to consider marriage. And he'd been following Tristan around, making him look unstable, like any abuser might. He was unethically working a case that involved his own brother, and more than that, trying to prove that his blood was the culprit in these crimes. Either he firmly believed Tristan was guilty, or he was involved in the killings and hated his brother enough to frame him. Families were complicated.

X marks the spot.

She drove. The night outside her car felt heavy and oppressive. Maggie kept her hands on the wheel, but her skin was tight around her muscles and twitchy, itchy, unseen things crawling just beneath her flesh. What wasn't she seeing? The *World's Most* tagline whispered in her head: "With your help, these riddles might finally be solved." Oh... and Sammy. She'd called Sammy. Hopefully he'd called back by now.

She fumbled for her cell in the dark and pulled it onto the steering wheel. A quick glance told her that Sammy had not yet called. But her mother had. Twice. She read the text message she'd missed earlier:

"Need to talk to you, have a referral."

Her stomach sank. She dropped the cell into the console. Another referral. Another woman like Helena. But she couldn't help everyone—couldn't help *anyone* right now, not with Tristan prying into the lives of her most vulnerable clients.

Was the detective guilty? Was Christine? Was Tristan a killer?

Was she wrong? Really, completely wrong about every-thing? It wouldn't be the first time. The stress, the obses-sion, were eroding her ability to think clearly.

Her fingers cramped around the wheel, but Maggie could not seem to loosen her grip. She had to find a way to relieve this pressure before she exploded.

CHAPTER
THIRTY

THE BARISTA WAS WEARING A SPARKLY purple mask, the edges drawn up into eagle's wings of yellow and silver. He nodded to her. She didn't need an invitation or an introduction. All members went through a rigorous vetting process that included physician's notes, medical tests, and non-disclosure agreements.

It still boggled her mind that Owen had been the one to tell her about this place—not that he'd ever gone. One of his wife's friend's had enlightened him years back, and he'd laughed about it—*scandalized*—but she had never heard of anything more liberating. This place was far less complicated than the dating scene and safer, statistically. In a bar, the man you met might have an STD. Everyone here got tested regularly. In a bar, men got pissed if you refused a drink or tried to end the evening with a good night handshake. Here, consent was the top priority. For most people, that's all bondage was—safety. Absolute control.

Maggie came here to forget.

Thick white drapes gave way to the dressing room. Empty now. It was likely that the playrooms would hold fewer people tonight as well—weeknights were often less crowded—but that didn't matter. She wasn't here for the others, at least no particular other. She had never chosen the same man twice.

Her clothes went into the locker. Silk robes brushed her flesh, her skin already singing with anticipation. The leather boots tightened around her thighs. Her brain was on fire, too, but not in the way of release—in the way of roller coasters. She was falling. Falling.

Falling.

Maggie slipped the red bracelet around her wrist and donned her mask. The leather stifled the thoughts inside her brain, dulling them to a low roar.

The tension in her chest shuddered, but less intensely than before, and it dissipated further still as she strode into the playroom. The doors around the perimeter of the main space housed private rooms complete with everything your heart might desire. Some had leather swings attached to the rafters. Some held walls full of whips; some held feathers. The main area boasted long modern couches, chairs in comfortable fabrics, and stools with holes in just the right places. The entire room glowed with undulating yellow light from the candelabra chandeliers.

There were four others in the room tonight. One woman and two men were already spread out on the far couch, writhing in one another's arms. The leather chair in the front of the room was free, the back in a permanently reclined position.

From the chair in the opposite corner of the room, a tall man watched her as she lowered herself onto the seat. Broad shoulders, the light flickering against his shaved chest. Thick legs. Brilliant white mask with ruby feathers that covered all but his lips and chin.

Was Christine dead or was she out there right now looking for another victim? Was she responsible for killing Tristan's mother, Tonya, Lillian, and two others? She had that medallion—was it the same one used in the crimes? How was the detective involved?

Maggie kept her eyes on the man in the corner as she leaned back in the seat and widened her legs. He cocked his head. He watched. She let him, heat rising in her chest, less of a falling-tumbling sensation and more like the climb toward the top—anticipatory.

But her mind was still racing. With the similar scoring patterns, not released to the public, it had to be the same killer. Was it Tristan? Matricide was usually borne of an abusive household, often with strong religious and moral motivations... that fit.

She was so wrapped up in her thoughts she barely registered that the man in the corner had stood, but when she blinked, he was there, standing over her. Green bracelet. She opened her legs wider and drew her fingers beneath the edge of her panties. She used her other hand to point at the floor.

He knelt.

She rarely let others touch her—she often did not feel the need. The control was enough. But her brain would not stop barking at her, and there was something in the set of his shoulders that felt safe, felt right. Felt... familiar.

He's not Kevin. He's not. But could she pretend, just for a little while? Of course she could. She'd done the same every other night she'd come here... until last week.

He crawled nearer. He smelled of spices, something sharply aromatic. It reminded her of Christmas, of Kevin... again, that familiarity. Did she actually, legitimately, know him? She ignored that thought—a trick of the mind, a desire to be known. But anonymous was better; safer and easier when you had no intention of taking them home.

She couldn't control life outside these walls—she was not inclined to try. But here, she could make him do whatever she wanted.

He was still watching her face. Waiting for instructions.

Maggie pointed him where she wanted him.

His hands were electric against her feverish skin. His fingertips trailed sensation over her flesh, leaving her tingling, aching as he slid her underwear past her hips.

Then he lowered his head between her legs, his breath hot. His tongue flicked out, once, twice—testing. Maggie watched the rippling of his shoulders as he drew his fingers to the apex of her thighs, inhaling the spicy scent of him until her mind finally went blank.

CHAPTER
THIRTY-ONE

Maggie's skin had cooled by the time she left the strip mall, the breeze a kiss against her shoulders. Her flesh was no longer vibrating. Her brain wasn't a gnarled mass of nerves and prickly barbs. The tension she'd been carrying had eased enough that her lungs did not feel like smashed balloons, the worst of all party-clown balloon creations.

The streetlights still bothered her eyes, though, and by the time she'd traversed the miles between the club and her neighborhood, a headache had crept up. So had the thoughts.

Was her patient a killer or a victim? How close was Christine to the detective? She sighed. Things might become clearer once she spoke to Sammy. If they didn't... well, she'd cross that bridge when she got there, and hopefully she'd still have time to avoid careening over the side.

She made a right into her neighborhood. A few miles through the quiet streets, and she'd be home where she could think or at least get some sleep. She didn't want to get too overtired and become a nighttime body burier herself—*Hey-o!*

But any serenity she'd found quickly vanished as she made her way up the first block. The air was hazy-looking here, the sky tinged orange. She reached over to crack the window, but Maggie didn't need to open it to smell the harsh acridity of smoke.

The smoke was thicker on her road, the air brilliant with flashing red and blue lights, everything as bright as if it were daytime.

The night was no match for the fire.

Her heart was a burning stone lodged tightly beneath her ribs, every beat a pulsing flame that seemed to match the flickering reflected in the windshield. She could not get near her home—officers and caution tape marked off a wide barrier. She pulled to the curb in slow motion and got out on rubbery legs.

Maggie stared at the blaze, flames like the tongues of angry serpents, blue and white and orange all licking the sky. Her useless DeLorean—*Dammit, not my car!*—taunted her from the driveway, as if, had she managed to get it started, she'd have been able to reverse time, start the day over and prevent this from happening. The front end of the vehicle was dark, blistering with heat.

But she felt very little about it. Her insides had gone numb. Shock—had to be shock. What was she supposed to do now?

Her feet decided for her, moving nearer, drawn to the inferno. She ducked past the people around the outer perimeter, the lookie-loos from the neighborhood that had formed a wall of bustling annoyance. They weren't here out of some sense of concern. She only knew her neighbors in passing, and not one of them had noticed her walking up the road.

It seemed the detective hadn't seen her either. Reid

Hanlon, of course it was him, stood in the middle of the street, a hundred yards from her, but she could hear him yelling even over the roaring flames: "Did you find her? Goddamnit, where is she?"

Her. *Me?* Did he think she was inside?

Maggie raised a hand, trying to flag him down, but he was already running toward two firefighters in full gear as they made their way across the lawn, removing their helmets as they went. The one on the left shook his head, his face smeared with soot. "Can't get in there," he yelled, "the structure's ready to—"

On cue, an enormous roar split the night, the grinding crunch of splintering wood floors and collapsing support beams. The home seemed to sag near the center, shaking, though that might have been her eyes, tricked by the waves of heat rolling off the building.

Her house. Everything she owned. Pictures of her and Aiden. Kevin's clothes, ticket stubs from their first date.

Reid ran a hand through his thick hair, shaking his head, face aimed away from her—watching the blaze.

She went to duck beneath the crime tape, but a stocky female officer with long black braids raised a hand and shook her head. "Behind the line, ma'am."

"This is my house, and I think the detective—"

"Jesus Christ! Hey! Move!" Both she and the officer looked over to see Reid running across the sidewalk, waving her inside the boundary. The officer backed up, nodding to her and the detective in turn. A few of her neighbors nudged each other. Someone patted her shoulder. She did not look to see who.

"Thanks," Maggie told the officer as she passed, but it sounded hollow in her ears, barely audible beneath the roar of the fire. Those who have not been near a house fire cannot understand the brilliant aching throb of super-heated foundations, the wheezy crack of thousands of pounds of lumber whistling away moisture before splintering apart. The snap and shriek of brick and glass and metal. All the things that make a life, screaming their farewells.

The detective stopped with their toes mere feet apart. Sweat glistened on his forehead and dripped off his nose. His shirt was wet, too, his tie spotted with sweat and soot. His pocket square was gone. "What do you know, Doctor?" he snapped. "You ready to tell me now?"

No preamble, eh? "I'm in the process of losing every possession I have, so maybe you could stop being an asshole for five minutes."

"I'm not here to hold your hand. I'm here to save your life. Right now, you're either a target or a suspect, and I'm not sure which."

A suspect? Why would she burn down her own house? But still, she felt very little about the exchange. Her muscles were slack, her heart no more than a muted drubbing pressure inside her chest.

"Do you have an alibi for this evening?"

Yeah, I was with a stranger in a secret sex club trying to forget my life. "I was just driving around."

"I can check traffic cameras. Where did you go?"

She stared. "I don't remember."

"Well, that's suspicious." He leveled his gaze at her; the whites of his eyes were spiderwebbed with red. "Let's pretend I believe you. No accidental blaze starts this quickly, so whoever did this wanted to make sure you were dead."

But this didn't fit the profile of their killer. A house fire was a far cry from burial, although... there was the burning with the medallion, right? And whatever implement the killer used to score the bones. "Well, it appears they failed."

"They'll try again." He shook his head, glittering droplets of perspiration flying off his face into the night, onto the road. "You say you're not involved, but you clearly know something you're not supposed to."

She saw the silent accusation in his eyes: *You almost died for your secrets.* But then he shifted his gaze to a spot at her back. She turned. Sammy was bulldozing his way through the crowd, his eyes locked on Reid as if the detective himself had burned the home down. Misplaced rage, maybe, but when she turned back, Reid had already squared his shoulders, bracing for confrontation. They... knew each other. And it seemed they were not friends. If Sammy didn't like the man, that was all she needed to know.

Sammy laid one huge palm on her shoulder and extended his other hand—her keys. The keys from the rental car. Had she left it running?

She blinked at the keys, for a moment unable to grasp what she was supposed to do with them. Sammy patted her shoulder, stuck the keys into his own jacket pocket, then wrapped his arm around her and pulled her away from the detective and against his chest.

The moment her head hit his shoulder, tears smarted in her eyes and her ribs released like a dam breaking. Her chest heated in a way that felt as sharp and bright as the flames. "I got your voicemail," he whispered into her hair. "Sorry it took so long, but you didn't have to burn the place down."

Brothers. She clung to him for dear life, her lungs tight with smoke and grief. Sammy stroked her hair. "What happened here, Reid?"

"Someone tried to kill your friend. If she wants to stay alive, she needs to tell me what she knows." Sammy stiffened and held her tighter.

Maggie watched Reid from the corner of her eye as he turned to the house, peering at the car, then back. "Maybe we should talk at the station."

Sammy shook his head. "No. You ask what you need here, then I'm taking her with me."

"She has a patient who's involved in some very bad things—your office knows about it already, Sam. Another of her patients, Tonya Rupert, is already dead. Either she's covering for a killer or she's involved. I like to think it's the former, but we'll find out if it's the latter."

Sammy stopped breathing. He was as shocked as she was, though for different reasons.

Reid was still talking. "Someone just tried to kill you, Doctor," he repeated. The detective stepped nearer, and though he wasn't close enough, Maggie was suddenly convinced that he could smell her over the stink of burning wood. "What reason could you possibly have to protect him? Maybe I need to be looking harder at your involvement in all this."

Sammy pulled his head back so he could see her face. There was no accusation in his gaze, just worry; sweat glistened on his forehead. Was she sweaty too? "Mags?"

She stepped away from him and shook her head, her lips tight. "When he puts it like that, I'd rather peel my own skin off than speak to him." Immature, certainly, but he was goading her on purpose.

"Fine, Sam, you ask her. Ask her why she was at Christine Archer's home the day before she went missing. Why her patient, Tonya Rupert, ended up dead the same way as Lillian Mace. Ask her why she's treating my top suspect in a series of homicides like he's a goddamn saint while he keeps snatching up innocent women."

Sammy's jaw dropped.

Maggie went still, but her lips skinned back—she was snarling at the detective, and she didn't give a single shit.

Sammy's voice came to her at a distance: "Maggie, if your patient is hurting people, you're well within your ethical right to disclose."

She squared her shoulders. "I think the detective is wrong. Or lying. Which means that anything I disclose might hurt a patient instead of helping anyone." And Helena... Helena might be in danger. For once in her life, that poor woman deserved to have someone watching her back.

Reid snorted. Sammy turned the detective's way, shaking his head. "How sure are you that it's this patient, Reid? You don't have enough forensics, or you'd have made an arrest and kicked it to the D.A.'s office."

"Oh, I'm sure. But I can't find him at the moment. He wasn't home earlier this evening when I went to peek at his fingertips. Convenient." The glance he aimed at her was made of needles, sharp and steely, and it did not soften when he turned back to Sammy. "Our case has to be airtight before I kick it your way, especially with a rich guy like that. I brought him in before, and it didn't stick."

"What makes you think it'll stick this time?" Maggie said.

Reid's eyes were run through with rivets of ice that chilled her blood despite the heat of the fire. "If I'm wrong, why would someone do this to you, Doctor? If it's not your patient, please share your vast insights into this killer."

She frowned, her gaze on the flames. Was he telling the truth about not being able to find Tristan? Was Tristan

THE DEAD DON'T DREAM

gone, too, running with Christine? Truth or lie? But that icy gleam around the iris... *Lie*. At least partially.

But she could start with telling the truth—Maggie could write a profile in her sleep. She'd leave out any suspicions about Reid himself. And she didn't have to admit to treating Tristan. Reid had brought him up as a connecting factor between victims, so she'd know his name now even if she hadn't met him in a hotel room.

"You're looking for someone with transportation," she said. "They have a vehicle of their own for stalking the victims. Your suspect is not a jealous boyfriend, or he'd have gone after the male he believed was in his way: Tristan himself. I think you're after a female killer, someone highly motivated to get rid of the women connected to Tristan, as he's the object of their affection. They see these other women as the only obstacle to them being together. And if the same killer attacked Tristan's mother, you're looking for someone who was obsessed with him back then. Perhaps someone his mom would have disapproved of." *Like a woman he met at a strip club.*

"A woman. Right." Reid snorted.

Why would he disregard the notion outright? Just because he wanted to frame Tristan? To protect Christine, the woman he almost married? She knew from experience that "not quite married" didn't mean less love, even if it did sometimes make people drive off bridges.

Her nostrils flared, smoke burning her throat. "From what you've told me, the crimes don't require an excessive amount of upper body strength—the victims were drugged." And the dump site was the same as the kill site. "A woman would be able to lure female victims to the vicinity of the killing field, probably more easily and quietly than a man since women are more likely to trust female strangers." But a man could lure his girlfriend out to the dump site and blindside her. A detective just had to ask a woman to come along. No defensive wounds in any of those cases.

"There's a problem with that theory, though." Reid sniffed, coughed, and went on: "Your neighbors don't have doorbell cams, but I took the liberty of brushing your car for prints, specifically the engine in the back. Hot as hell when I arrived, but viable. Your car troubles were the result of tampering. Tristan's prints are on your engine block."

She narrowed her eyes at her house, then scanned the neighboring homes—evacuated now, the occupants surely pissed that her house-turned-bonfire had put their properties at risk. Finally, she drew her gaze back to the car, the paint darker than when she'd arrived. Prints on the engine block? It didn't make sense. What Reid had described was premeditated, not the work of a sleepwalker. It didn't fit Tristan's sleepwalking pattern anyway. And wide-awake Tristan had obsessive-compulsive tendencies—he was particular about getting dirty. He would have worn gloves. "No, they weren't."

His gaze clouded. "Are you calling me a liar, Doctor?"

"Yes."

Sammy turned to him. "I can get techs out here, too, Reid. Or at least ask what they found." He glanced at the car, but they didn't need a thermometer to know the vehicle was too hot to approach now.

Reid sniffed, then shrugged. "Fine. I can't prove it was him. I can prove it was foul play though—someone rendered that car useless. He was probably trying to keep you here so he could light you up. At the moment, he can't bury anyone in the places he'd like to. I've got patrols crawling by all the abandoned fields in the area. And we're systematically going through the most likely dumping grounds with dogs."

From abandoned fields to a very public spectacle of flame? "Detective, whoever tampered with my car, if it was tampered with... they'd know I wasn't driving it. They'd know I wasn't here. It only looks like I'm here." And even as she said it, another thought occurred to her: Had her malfunctioning car saved her life? But if someone had tampered with it to make it look like she was home, that person also knew she was a target... which meant they had to know the killer.

Fire roared in her ears. Crackling. Spitting. She was suddenly very, very tired, as if the fire had melted the energy from her marrow. *Done. I'm so done.* Maggie could no longer stomach being on the defensive, and she shouldn't have to be. She hadn't behaved perfectly through this, but everything she'd done, every visit she'd made, had been in the service of a greater good. If she had to answer for those choices, Reid should answer for his.

"Maybe you're just pissed at your brother, and getting him arrested is easier than competing with him." She glowered at Reid. "I heard you almost married his off-again-on-again girlfriend—that he took Christine from you."

"Ah, you talked to Eden, did you? That old woman's had it in for me since the day I..." He shook his head. "She hates me. Let's leave it at that."

"I imagine she does with the way you treat Tristan. She certainly seems to consider him family. And what about telling me I should get a gun? That's a fine way to get rid of a man, isn't it? Given what you know about my family's history, you might have assumed I had a bullet ready to go."

Sammy's eyebrows were at his hairline. "Reid... what the hell on *all* of that, but is she right? You're related to your suspect? If that's the case, you shouldn't be near this investigation at all. It's a conflict of interest."

Reid blinked. "We're not related."

"Come off it, you overconfident sack of pocket squares," Maggie snapped.

"Overconfident sack of...?" He sighed out the rest of the question, then went on: "Tristan's mother fucked my father and got pregnant; my mom found out about baby Tristan and took off. But I sure as hell don't consider that weirdo part of my family. Your patient is an absolute nutjob. Compulsive, hair-triggered, antisocial."

Well, that explained the grudge. Had Tristan's mother been killed for being a home-wrecker? "Trauma can make a person anxious—"

"So can guilt. And Tristan was obsessed with the details of his mother's death. He used to play with bugs incessantly, had hundreds of them tacked to a board in his room —started digging beetles out of the damn ground. That asshole relished what happened to his mom."

Maggie's chest tightened. Her throat hurt too, dry and scratchy with smoke despite their distance from the flames. "Even still, your anger about what his mother did to your family—"

"You can let that go right now." His words were forceful, but his gaze had softened. "His mother was good to me. After my mom moved out, she treated me like her own while Tristan was off with that stupid church. And I know for a fact that Tristan has a medallion that matches the one used to burn those symbols into the bodies. He's had it on his neck all these years, even though he knows that symbol was seared into his mother's dead flesh. He wants to relive it."

Tristan doesn't have the necklace. Her presence at Eden's

was no longer a secret, and Christine was not her patient —she didn't have to protect that woman's privacy. "Christine has that medallion. You should talk to the jeweler who made it. Christine has also been known to harass other women. And if Tristan's mother didn't want them to be together, Christine might have seen her as an obstacle."

Reid's eyes widened. Surprised at the notion, or just surprised that she knew? "Christine isn't a suspect. I looked through the phone records on our victims, and Christine never made a single call to any of Tristan's exes."

"She might have been smart enough to use a burner cell."

Reid ran a hand through his hair; it spiked up along the side. "The jealous lover angle didn't pan out. I investigated that initially, but Tristan hasn't had a relationship in years —just one-night stands, and all of those women are fine. A jealous lover would attack them too. And most of those women don't even remember his name, let alone care about him enough to hurt anyone. And they certainly didn't kill his mother."

"All the more reason for it to be Christine." Was Reid purposefully ignoring the medallion?

"It's not Christine," he insisted far too vehemently. It sounded like he was trying to protect the woman regardless of what the evidence suggested. Yeah, he definitely had a relationship with her—a current relationship. "Tristan is the one doing this," Reid said. "It has to be him."

"No, it doesn't, you just *want* it to be him."

The fire snapped, barking at them—cackling, laughing.

"Did you investigate this suspect for his mother's death?" Sammy asked finally. Sweat was running freely down the side of his face; his collar was damp. Maggie should be hot, too, sticky, but she felt nothing on her skin, only a blistering heat deep inside her chest.

Reid nodded. "I looked into his mother's homicide soon after I made detective. It had been years by then, so it wasn't a shock that I came up empty. But I watched Tristan like a hawk. When Tonya went missing three years ago, I interrogated him. And when someone dug Tonya's body up last week, I interrogated him again. It all fits." He turned back to Maggie. "I'm trying to find the truth, a goal we should share. So why are you protecting him?"

"I'm not protecting anyone." *Except Helena.* She drew her gaze to her house. Billowing smoke obscured the sky above the building like a dark cloud, brilliant ribbons of orange and white tightening their hold on the porch— strangling what was left of her home. Bile rose in her gullet, but she forced out: "I just don't believe your brother is guilty. And you've exhibited more than a few suspicious behaviors. But on the off chance that you're not the culprit, then Christine might have burned this place down because she didn't have a way to bury a new victim, as you said. Maybe you're right, maybe she is after me, and setting my house on fire was the easiest way to take me out. And Christine fits my profile. She makes more sense than—"

His nostrils flared, eyes shining, and she didn't think it was from the flames. "Christine's body was pulled from the blaze half an hour ago."

Maggie blinked at the fire. Christine was... dead?

That meant her house wasn't just some convenient disposal site. It was a warning.

If she wasn't careful, she'd be the next to go up in flames.

CHAPTER
THIRTY-TWO

MAGGIE'S FATHER still owned a house the next city over—the house where she'd sent Helena. No one was staying there now, but the thought of going there alone and being reminded of all the things she'd lost, being reminded that she was losing her father on top of everything else... it was too much.

She didn't know who she was anymore. Her skin was itchy with dried sweat and tight from the heat, her brain on fire. Her ribs had fused into a single shrunken panel of bone. Someone had tried to kill her. If the culprit wasn't Christine, who did that leave? Tristan, his brother the detective, or someone else entirely?

Reid was right about one thing: no matter who the perpetrator was, she was still in danger. Killing Christine in a house fire would not be satisfying for a suspect bent on a specific ritual. The killer would not have gotten to see the burn the medallion left on the flesh, would not have relished the moments spent scoring the bones beneath. Would not have gotten to wrap his victim in linen and bury her in the dirt.

How long did they have before the killer tried again? How long before this homicidal firebug killed someone else?

Owen's house was located in a quiet suburb thirty minutes from her house. Maggie had wanted to stay there in the street, to watch her home burn, mourning every ashy snowflake as it fell to the lawn, but she didn't have the heart to argue with Sammy. When he wrapped his arm around her shoulders and started walking toward his Jeep, she followed him without a word.

They'd only driven a few minutes before the shock started to wear off. "I think Reid's suspect is innocent," she said. Tristan could have been guilty and come to therapy to be absolved, but it rang false. Unless he had been hoping she'd stop him.

Which she hadn't. She'd seen the best-case scenario. She'd failed to recognize the other options, the additional complications. And now, another woman was dead.

"He might be innocent. It's hard to say right now." Sammy nodded and patted her leg, but not in a conde-scending way—pure support. When her brother vanished, Sammy had helped her put up flyers. And when she'd given up and stayed in bed, Alex had come over and tucked up under the covers with her while Sammy laid across their feet. Sammy had watched stupid television with her every day until his mother made him come home for dinner, and sometimes his mother brought dinner to them.

What had Tristan done after his mother died? He certainly hadn't had a brother to lean on, not a brother like Sammy—it sounded like Reid would have punched him before hugging him. Jeanna and Benedict Rose sounded like good supports, but Tristan wasn't a very forthcoming guy. Maybe instead of talking about his feelings, he sat in the dark and plotted revenge. Maybe his grief about his mother grew into fury while Maggie's loss had mellowed into heartache.

"Reid knows Christine," she said to the windshield. "The dead woman in my house. He was romantically involved with her."

Sammy glanced over. "How do you know that?"

Because I invaded a client's privacy and talked to his adopted family. "Just trust me, okay?"

He blinked, his brow furrowed, but he nodded. "I always do. But do me a favor and don't contact this patient —it'll only complicate things. You've told me all you know, right?"

She nodded. "All the relevant pieces." That wasn't entirely true, but if Tristan was being framed, she didn't want to give Reid more ammunition. And Sammy was right about not calling Tristan. The last time she'd talked to him, he'd threatened Helena. Contacting him now might irritate him, trigger him into doing something to Helena—or worse. At best, he'd just jerk her around some more. Anything else she wanted to know, she had to figure out for herself. Or, you know, let Sammy and the police handle it since she was currently homeless and car-less and... clothes-less.

Little-brotherless.

Kevin-less.

Nearly fatherless.

Sammy frowned and turned left onto Owen's road. The streetlights made the neighborhood glow in a ghostly way, as if the shimmering leaves above were watching them. The being-watched feeling wasn't fully inside her head. Sammy had made the detective call in for a protective detail, and when Sammy pulled up in front of Owen's house, the squad car was already sitting across the street with the lights off.

Sammy paused with his keys still in the ignition. "I trust you, Mags. And I need you to trust me too." He turned to her, his gaze earnest. "Reid Hanlon is a shark. He'll never stop if he thinks he's right—even when he should. Even if it breaks him. He's like your father in that way, but he's definitely jerkier."

Jerkiness didn't matter. "How often is he wrong?" she asked as they got out. Her limbs were so heavy she practically dropped to the driveway.

Sammy's face hardened. "I'll look into his relationship with the latest victim. But regardless of his track record, Reid should not be on this case with so many conflicts of interest."

Regardless of his track record... That meant he was rarely wrong or very good at making it look as if he were right. And this whole time, he'd been outright lying to her or withholding information—about being related to Tristan, about being involved with Christine, about the nonexistent prints on her car. Truth meant little to him. Lies were a means to an end. If he was framing Tristan, he'd do such a good job that no one else would be able to tell. Except maybe her. And Christine, of course, who was conveniently dead.

She pushed the thoughts aside as Sammy opened the front door. Owen and Alex were already there, sitting on the couch in Owen's traditionally furnished living room. Alex's earrings glittered as she stood, and Maggie tried not to think about how much they looked like Tonya's. Christine's. Five recent victims now—six including Tristan's mother. And who knows how many bodies they hadn't yet discovered?

Maggie kicked her shoes off; her feet were damp. *Gross.*

Imani was in the kitchen off to Maggie's right, the granite counter covered in platters of beans and meat, taco shells and salsa. Imani glanced over, saw Maggie enter, and kneed the oven door shut. Maggie was in her arms before she could nod despite the fact that she surely reeked of sweat and ash. Maybe freaky sex. She needed to shower. But what she wanted to wash off would not come clean anyway... and she'd need to ask one of them for clothes.

Maggie hugged Imani back, weakly but earnestly. The others followed suit, an assembly line of arms and support. She wanted it to be enough—and it almost was—but it felt as if her belly had been scooped out, her bones hollowed. She'd lost her home, her stuff. Yes, they were only things, but the ones that hurt the most were items she couldn't replace. Kevin's T-shirts, the ones she wore to bed, were all gone. Things that reminded her of her father, sentimental items... gone. Photos of her and Aiden, originals taken in the days before the cloud, so there were no digital copies that she could reprint—gone. There were a million other memories in that home that she'd never be able to re-create. And she could feel everyone's eyes on her, their gazes blistering like cinders. She could practically smell their sadness.

No, this would not do. She had to get out of her head.

She excused herself and spent a few quiet minutes in Owen's study, playing with his printer, blowing her nose to clear the smoke. It did not work. She wandered along the back hallway, then into the bathroom and splashed water on her face.

By the time she returned to the living room, Owen was shuffling cards in his wingback chair, tap-tap-tapping them against the coffee table, the hissing of the deck like

205

fluttering crows. Thank goodness. They'd clearly realized that she needed distraction more than pity.

She sat between Imani and Alex. Alex hugged her close, then released her. Imani had put together a plate for her, and it lay in the middle of the coffee table flanked by two wine glasses—Owen's and Sammy's—and the beers that Alex and Imani preferred. Sammy was gone. Probably washing his face as she had, trying to erase the ash that felt like it had been absorbed into her cells.

Maggie swallowed over the lump in her throat, resolutely keeping her eyes from the empty spot on the floor where Kevin usually sat—*used to sit*—and sucked a breath into her lungs. She could swear she smelled Kevin's cologne. Spicy. A little like cinnamon, a little like myrrh. A little like... him.

Tap-tap-tap, flutter-flutter-flutter.

She took a bite of the first taco. Perfectly seasoned, she was sure; Imani was a far better cook than any of them aside from Sammy. But it tasted like cardboard. She forced down the rest of the taco, the edges sharp like they wanted to cut her throat. The way the killer did.

"Holy shit!" Sammy yelled from somewhere down the back hallway. She jumped and dropped the second taco onto the plate. They all looked up as Sammy stalked into the living room holding up a printed photo of a clown, the colors vibrant, the teeth bloody. "Did you tape this to the back of the bathroom door?"

She smiled, and though she didn't feel the pleasure deep in her chest, it was better than focusing on things she'd rather not.

"Owen's going to kick your sneaky ass out," Sammy said, crumpling the picture in his fist. Owen blinked but said nothing. He did not like confrontation even if it was in jest.

"I'd like to see him try," she snapped back. "Doesn't he know I'm homeless?"

Sammy tossed the image into the trash can with a grimace. "Where the hell did you even get that?"

I printed it from Owen's office computer while you guys were busy feeling sorry for me. Get funny or get hurt... or get hurt and then get funny to forget about it.

Imani was still smiling. "The kids still talk about how you hired a clown for Sammy's birthday, but paid him extra to show up in the middle of the night. A week early."

"Hey, that clown brought over a super special gift card *and* the cast-iron pans Sammy had been lusting after."

Sammy pointed an accusatory finger at her. "This is why we can't have nice things." Alex and Imani looked at each other, then at Maggie, and collapsed into a fit of giggling at Sammy's horrified eyes. Maggie followed suit, but her chest... it felt like she was still inhaling smoke. Tight. Hot.

As if he'd heard the thought, Owen handed her the cards. "Deal. I'll get the snacks."

The game was Threes Wild—leave it to the middle school D&D crowd to create their own interactive tournament. Alex had taught them the base—Bridge—a card game Sammy claimed was the whitest of white people games, but this one had a twist. Every time you played a three, the other members got to throw cheese puffs at your head. If you caught at least one of them in your mouth, you won the hand no matter what the other players' cards were. If you played a four, you had to catch gummy bears. If you choked, you were disqualified.

Sammy was still shaking his head while she dealt the

hand. "I'm glad your house burned down," he muttered. "Now you'll be forced to buy better art."

"Or better yet, buy zero art," Alex quipped. "You know she'll just get scarier versions of everything."

And so it went. Soon the laughter drowned out the voices in her head—there was nothing but her friends, though the ache in her chest persisted.

But once the cards had been played, the wine drunk, and the cheese puffs eaten, the hollowness returned. When she finally dozed off, she slept in fitful bursts of nightmares. Her brother, screaming from inside the flames. Christine, blistered and burned, clawing her way from the ashes. And Tristan, grinning—predatory—as he stalked across the front lawn, his eyes dull and hostile in the way of stone-cold psychopaths, though the last thing she wanted to do was run. And near the morning hours, he came as he always did when she was under stress: the one who'd thrown her to the ground and taken a bite out of the back of her head. If Kevin hadn't come back when he had, if he hadn't helped her out of there...

I should have married him. I should have just said yes.

Her T-shirt—Owen's T-shirt—was soaked through when the sun came up.

She did yoga and meditated for half an hour, but her shoulders were so tight that even dressing was difficult. Owen had taken the liberty of washing yesterday's clothes for her—they smelled of lemons—but Alex had stopped by the department store on her way over last night and bought a week's worth of wardrobe while Maggie and Sam were dealing with the detective. She'd even picked things Maggie might have chosen herself—khaki slacks and a silky teal blouse for today. The outfit did not contain the charred scent from the night before, but the acridity stuck in her sinuses. She could taste smoke in her throat.

Owen was at the stove when she walked into the kitchen. Two plates sat on the table, and in the middle, platters of pancakes and honeydew without the snotty yogurt chaser.

"I'm heading to the office in a few," he said over his shoulder. "I'll reschedule your patients for you."

"I have the prison in an hour and a few patients this afternoon. But I'm not canceling."

The spatula stilled. He flicked the stove off and turned, his face drawn, his eyes sad and bloodshot—he looked as if he hadn't slept at all. *Way to go, Owen, make it all about you.* She didn't love the snarky thought, but she was too raw to feel bad.

"I know you want to keep your mind busy," he said, "but are you sure you don't want to take a day to regroup?"

"I'm sure." Her prison session was with a man who'd chewed his best friend's toes off while they were both high on some synthetic designer drug. What could be more distracting than being locked inside a room with that?

Besides, it was comforting to know where the danger was. And though she knew it was a passing notion, she was tired of feeling useless. She couldn't fix her house; she couldn't bring Kevin back; she couldn't cure her father. But she could help someone else, no matter how small the gesture. It was something.

Owen did not look convinced. "Why don't you let me come with you?" His voice was soft, like he was trying to persuade an obstinate toddler off a ledge. "I have to drop you at your rental anyway. I can drive you over to the prison and wait for you. After, we'll go pick up your car, and then we can get lunch."

"Absolutely not—you have your own work today. And someone from the police department is going to be following me, right?"

"I'm... not sure?" He dragged his eyes away, but not before she registered the pity in his gaze. "I think so, but—"

"That fire wasn't even as bad as the one at the circus," she muttered. "That one was in tents." *Intense. Get it?*

He raised an eyebrow, turned back to the stove, and finally left her alone. Her father was right—some people really did hate puns.

CHAPTER
THIRTY-THREE

THE POLICE WERE INDEED FOLLOWING her. The unmarked kept a respectful distance, or perhaps they thought they were full-incognito, but any halfway decent *Scooby-Doo* character would spot them in a minute. If they were better sneaks, they could use her as bait. The killer was clearly after her, and Reid seemed convinced that she was doing something "uncouth"—that she was protecting someone who didn't deserve it, and therefore would get what was coming to her. If he wasn't the killer, it seemed logical that he'd use her to lure the suspect out of hiding.

Maggie parked in the back of the prison lot and waved to the unit on the way inside. They looked at each other. Yeah, they'd thought they were hidden. *Losers.*

The prison sessions went by quickly and relatively calmly. Even the toe chewer seemed introspective, which lessened the burden on her heart, the pressure in her chest. But as soon as she left, that calm fizzled. Outside the prison walls, any of her patients could be lying to her—the detective might be lying too. She was driving straight back to the place where this had started, and she had no answers and little safety.

The Toyota's windows quaked like they were desperately trying not to burst outward with anxious energy. Even her bones were vibrating, a sickly hum that made her spine twitch, and they buzzed harder when she turned off the exit that led to the office. Either she'd made a mistake and left a killer free to murder again, or Tristan was innocent and she'd protected him, but had risked Helena in the process. At least if she could confirm where Tristan was going at night—if she could prove he'd been somewhere else when Christine had died—she could rule him out as a suspect. But she had no idea where he might be going at night, sleepwalking or not. A bench? A streetlight? Some dirt? What was she supposed to do with that?

And now someone was after her—had left a dead woman inside her home. Worst secret Santa gift *ever*.

Maggie gripped the wheel, resisting the urge to pound on it. *Dammit.* Owen was right: it would be a disservice to go to the office like this. Plus, if someone was watching her, she might be putting other patients in danger; she'd already risked Helena's life. How had she not considered that before? As a bonus, she'd avoid more pitying looks from Owen.

She sighed and snatched up her phone.

"Hey, Owen. You were right about needing a break. Can you cancel my patients?" Her voice sounded strained even to her. "No, no, I don't need company. I'm just going to visit my dad." *Let it go, Owen—let me go.* It would take him five minutes to clear her week, and by next week, she'd feel better and could give her patients the attention they deserved. By next week, hopefully the killer would be in custody.

For now, she'd go see someone who couldn't know how far she'd fallen. Who wouldn't know how desperate she was. Who would not mourn the loss of her brother's photos because he didn't remember the boy anyway.

———

"GET ME A SANDWICH, would you? The other girl said there's no cheese, but I could tell she was lying."

Maggie's father was allergic to dairy, had been for as long as she could remember.

She leaned back in the La-Z-Boy and pulled her cell from her pocket, trying to keep her attention on her dad and not the television. Their show was on, but at least he'd let her turn it down—her head had already been throbbing when she arrived. "I'll call down to the kitchen for some subs, how about that?"

"Sounds good, Mags. So what's new?"

I had a detective call me four times today. My house burned down. I'm cutting work and have the police following me. But —*Mags.* She jerked her head toward him. "Dad?"

His eyes shone, not with agitation about his sandwich, but with a deeper recognition. "Who were you expecting, the Easter Bunny?" He chuckled, then raised an eyebrow. "Before I forget... Did you bring flowers to your grandmother's grave? It was her birthday yesterday."

Her chest deflated. No, it wasn't anyone's birthday yesterday—no one that she knew. But hey, a little lucid was better than none. "I'll get some flowers today and run them by." She tried to keep her tone light, but her voice cracked. Her eyes were burning too. She always seemed to hold it together until Sammy or her father broke her down with a glance. Those punks.

"Mags, what is it?"

"It's been a... a hard week. My house burned down. I lost a lot of photos." Did he remember Aiden? Did he know that his son was gone—dead? That her significant other was dead? If so, she didn't want to remind him just so he could hurt for a few hours before he forgot again.

"Well, that's no good."

No good? That was like saying *A Song of Ice and Fire* was just okay, or that being locked in a barren bunker with a kickboxing cannibal was a *little bit* concerning. "That's quite the understatement."

"Eh. Most things are if you're in the right frame of mind."

"Your psychology nonsense won't work on me, Dad." It was a running joke between them, that they couldn't head-shrink the other. And it felt so damn good just to call him "Dad" and have him know what it meant.

But her father wasn't smiling; his gaze had gone somber—contemplative. Had she lost him again already? "If you have photos that you really miss... just go back your-self. Find a forensic sketch artist, show him the shots you do have for reference, and describe in painstaking detail the bits that are missing. Pay the artist as much as it takes to get exactly what you need. What else are you going to buy, some fancy VCR?"

Her heart lightened, just a little—was that hope niggling in her chest? That was... a great idea. She reached across the expanse between their seats and squeezed his arm. "Thanks, Dad. That's perfect."

"And for god's sake, get a digital copy this time. You never know when you might leave the stove on again."

The stove... Oh. She was a terrible cook, had nearly burned his house down at age fifteen making mac and cheese. Of course he'd assume it was her fault, especially since she hadn't told him that someone tried to kill her. Heck, maybe he thought she was still fifteen—locked perpetually in her teenage years. Yikes. She'd rather take a job testing rectal lightbulbs.

"Nothing you can't fix if you use your head." He tapped his temple with one skinny finger, then turned his gaze back to the television. "Can you turn this up? And can you find me a sandwich? The other girl said there's no cheese, but I could tell she was lying."

She blinked. He wasn't looking at her anymore, but she could tell even in profile that the light had gone out of his eyes. So fast—it always happened so fast. *Bye, Daddy. See you later.*

But she'd accomplished what she came here for. For twenty minutes, she'd been herself again. "I'll make a call about the cheese, okay? And I'll be sure to stop by your mom's." Whether he believed she was going to the woman's house or her grave, the statement was safe enough.

He nodded. "It's her birthday. She loves daisies, so be sure to—"

"I will." All these years later, and he could remember in painstaking detail the way his mother had smelled. The flowers she liked. The rest of them had to pick allergenic weeds by the roadside and sit on empty graves just to feel closer to their loved ones, while her father got to believe they were still there, ready to accept a bouquet of...

She blinked. Daisies. *Flowers.*

The television noise faded in her ears. After the sleep-walking episode, Tristan said he'd had flower petals on his hands. It was one thing to dream, but quite another to have proof that you were playing in a garden.

215

It wasn't a garden. It probably wasn't a park either—the detective had been trolling those all week.

But a *cemetery* would have all the elements Tristan had described to her: the benches, the lights, the flowers. Not a lot of security, so it might be easier to avoid detection. And even if this notion had occurred to Reid, a cadaver dog would be of no use when there were legally planted bodies every ten feet.

If Reid was even a little bit right about Tristan being obsessed with his mother's death... perhaps it made sense for him to visit her gravesite.

But there was more, she realized, perhaps the very thing that had been keeping her brain tense and her chest constricted. With Christine dead, Tristan's companion for a decade, it felt as though they were drawing nearer to some endgame. Whether Tristan was the culprit or not, perhaps someone would involve his mother—the catalyst for all of this. Full circle.

Either she'd find a less-murdery explanation for her patient's nighttime activities, or she'd find another body.

Maybe more than one.

CHAPTER
THIRTY-FOUR

THE POLICE UNIT was parked outside the retirement home when she emerged from the hallway into the lobby. She could see the officers from her spot inside the building, the car facing the road as if that made them any less conspicuous. Maggie found a seat in the back of the lobby behind a half wall topped with ferns and pulled out her cell.

It only took a few minutes on the obit archives to find what she was looking for: a copy of the obituary announcement for Tristan's mother published in the local paper, very old-school. It listed the name of the church in bold near the bottom.

The church itself was surely the one that Benedict Rose and Tristan's mother attended, maybe Tristan himself if he was as religious as Reid seemed to think. And Maggie was lucky; the cemetery attached to it was huge. She tapped the button to look at a close-up of the grounds. Flowers, check. Streetlights, check. And... benches.

How did you miss this, Maggie? He told you he started sleepwalking after his mother's death, and you figured he was meandering around a park? You're as dumb as a damn cabbage.

She hit a few more buttons in service to her newly formed escape plan, then repocketed her cell. Maggie squinted through the ferns at the parking lot. The dark shadows of the officers' heads were barely visible, but they were there in the car. Too far away to make her out tucked behind the plants, but they'd see her if she walked out the front door.

If she inadvertently led the officers to Tristan, he'd end up with a bullet in his head just like her father's patient because of Reid's carefully orchestrated campaign against him. She'd never know for certain if he had been guilty, or if he was framed by a killer on the force. And Maggie did believe that Tristan was sleepwalking. She believed he was digging. What she didn't know was whether he was hurting anyone.

Perhaps today, she'd figure that out.

She took the long way around the back of the lobby, her head held low. The officers were still in the same place when she slipped out the back door.

Maggie walked.

The air on her neck raised the fine hairs along her spine, but for once, she did not feel watched. The sun beat down, hot against her flaming hair, warming the flesh on the backs of her exposed hands. The storefronts on either side promised ice cream and novelties and shoes; the people wandering about the road promised complication.

She went on, putting distance between herself and the retirement village—the officers. *Am I doing the right thing?* That might be the wrong question. Perhaps *will this lead to the outcome I want?* was better suited. Right and wrong had become merged into a sickly shade of gray days ago.

She glanced at her cell, then up at the road as an unfamiliar blue sedan pulled to a stop at the curb. Her breath caught, but then she noted the Hytch sticker. Her shoulders relaxed.

The driver asked no questions outside of where to go, which was good. "I didn't want the police to follow me" would not have helped him to feel confident about taking the fare. The drive to the cemetery was laced with heady silence but no pitying gazes, no pressure outside of what existed in her own head. This wasn't by the book, wasn't even fully by her guts, but she knew what her father would have chosen, and he was the one who managed to sleep at night even before the stroke erased his mistakes from memory. She knew what her mother would have done, too, though Mom might have passed around a bucket of Glocks.

Some family traditions they had.

The ride took twenty-seven minutes, and by the time the driver slowed to a stop in the church parking lot, her spine was tingling with nervous energy. Rolling hills stretched beyond the tall iron gates, the cemetery bordered on three sides by walls of lumbering pines. The wind against her face felt stale, steeped in misery and death.

There were no locks on the gates. No guard to stop her as she made her way over the grass, then onto the gravel walkway. Not even a lawn care person in the vicinity, though the cemetery appeared well-maintained. Not a single weed crept about the gravestones.

So where? Where to look for Tristan's mother? Should she seek out dead flowers, like the ones he'd been rolling in? What color had he said?

But a second voice, this one more fervent, whispered back: *You'll know it when you see it.*

She glanced behind her. The iron gates loomed in the distance, and she was breathing hard—had she been running? She slowed her pace as she went on, but the wind was practically howling at her to retreat. The erratic thumping of her heart sounded like footsteps.

A bench, Maggie. Look for the bench.

There was only one that she could see on the far side of the cemetery, standing vigil beside the gravel path. She hustled that way. The hairs on her neck prickled, threat this time—the sensation of prying eyes. Maggie whipped around, but saw no sign of another person. Only leaves scampered behind her, propelled into skittering tornados by the blustery wind.

Gravel crunched beneath her shoes like the raspy snarl of breath from an emphysemic lung, punctuated by a final grinding hiss as she stopped beside the wrought iron bench. The thing had seen better days, the seat beaten and faded by the elements. Around it, row upon row of tombstones loomed, a veritable human garden. A few of the headstones were marked by planted flowers, but most of the graves were covered in grass, the fresher ones topped with browning sod trying desperately to root before frost rendered the blades as dead as the corpse beneath. But halfway up the fourth row, a single grave contained neither sod nor grass. She started that way, her heart in her throat.

The patchy greenery here wasn't from ill-rooted sod, nor was it from someone taking a shovel to the earth to plant a row of mums. No flowers at all around the dirty headstone, but that didn't mean they hadn't existed in the past. And the earth itself...

Heat lanced her lungs with fingers of bright current. Her heart battered itself against her ribs. The ground was zombiefied, the dirt torn apart as if someone had been trying to claw their way out. Perhaps they had. Was she looking at a crime scene the police hadn't yet discovered?

She dropped to her knees, scooping handfuls of dirt

aside, expecting with every scratch that she might see the gray, worm-infested fingers of a cadaver. Should she feel guilty about the lightning in her veins, the electricity snapping through her brain?

Maggie went at the ground harder, panting, staining her khaki pants, maybe the teal blouse, too, but stopped short when she scraped a slab of compacted soil hard enough to abrade her fingertips. Rough here, the dirt pounded solid by time and passing feet. Maggie yanked her hands from the earth and squinted at her index finger; the nail had been torn. She was bleeding. And in her mind's eye, she saw Tristan's fingers. His injured hands.

If a body had been hidden here recently, the dirt should be loose—Tristan hadn't buried someone in this spot. Though there might be another grave with an extra body inside it.

Maggie drew her eyes to the headstone.

IN GOD'S CARE was carved inside a cross on the top of the stone, and in smaller letters beneath, as if her name was an afterthought: ABIGAIL SIMMS. The front of the headstone was filthy. But from this angle, she could see a pattern in the grime, the streaks of brown and black, thicker at the top, degrading to fine lines that vanished near the base of the stone. Bloody claw marks.

The gray sky glowered down at her. The world smelled of soil—of grubs and impending thunder. Maggie sat back on her heels. She suddenly felt the agony of what had happened here in her bones, the desperation as palpable as the breeze on her face. This damage to the stone, to his fingers, was not that of a killer trying to create a place for a new victim. It was frantic, borne of terror. Of loss.

Perhaps that made sense. Tristan's mother died, the episodes started, then settled. Tonya vanished, which triggered a brief resurgence. The detective showed up to interrogate him, it triggered another bout of sleepwalking, and since then, Reid had been dredging up those memories over and over and over. Tristan hadn't come here to bury a person. Maybe his subconscious had been trying to save one without recognizing that he was already too late.

Maybe she'd have done the same.

But the question remained: how was this related to the missing women? There was certainly a connection. Was Tristan just losing it? Clawing at his dead mother's grave by night while he slept, kidnapping women and murdering them while he was awake? Did he come here after he buried the bodies elsewhere? Was someone messing with his head? The jealous stalker angle had made so much sense, but her best suspect was a charbroiled corpse. That left Reid himself, but why would he be killing these women? Were they substitutes for Christine? Was he jealous of his brother?

A sound came suddenly from behind her, the vivid snapping of a twig. She whirled around, leaping to her feet so fast she almost toppled over. And she was soon extra glad that she'd managed to stay upright.

Tristan Simms stood near the base of his mother's grave, his hands clenched at his sides, his eyes dark with fury.

CHAPTER
THIRTY-FIVE

I IMMEDIATELY REGRET THIS DECISION.

But it was too late to back out now. And a moment's hesitation could get one killed... or kill someone else.

So though she tasted the fear like iron on her tongue, though her heart was thundering in her temples, she remained still, her shoes sinking in the soft earth. He'd caught her at his mother's ruined grave—her hands were dirty too. Did he remember that he'd done this? He couldn't possibly think that she had decimated his mother's plot for fun. But his eyes... he was upset, and it certainly looked like he was mad at her.

"Helena's safe," he said.

She blinked. Well, that was certainly good news, but it did not ease the tension in her spine. "For how long?"

"Forever. I just needed... help."

Her mouth was so dry it was hard to speak, but she managed: "I met your stalker detective—Reid Hanlon. Why do you call him Rich?"

"It's short for Richard. Because he's always been a dick."

Ah... that was actually pretty funny and very "brother."

MEGHAN O'FLYNN

But she couldn't laugh—she could barely breathe, though his gaze was on the ground at her feet. "Is this where you come at night, Tristan?"

He shook his head. "I haven't been here in years. Or... I don't think I've..." He sighed at the ground. "I *was* here." But the inflection felt off. Was he really only now realizing this?

"If you didn't know you'd been coming here, then why are you here now?"

"I traced your cell," he said, as if spying on your psychologist was the most natural thing in the world. She drew her eyes to the surrounding landscape—the trees, the endless rows of headstones, the far-off iron gates. Not another living creature roamed the vicinity. There was no one here to help her if he attacked.

But did she think he would? The rage in his green eyes had dulled, if it had ever been anger at all—she could no longer tell for certain. His muscles were not taut as if ready to pounce. His voice was soft, and too even to be fighting a bout of frenzied wrath. If he was a psychopath, she might be more worried—they had a remarkable ability to appear calm before an attack. But Tristan Simms was no psychopath. She was willing to stake her reputation on it... and apparently, her life.

It always happened so damn fast.

She swallowed hard. "Knowing that I'm being followed doesn't make me feel particularly safe."

"I wanted to make sure you were okay. That no one... hurt you."

"Why would anyone want to hurt me?" It was a dumb question—she could think of five reasons to kill her off the top of her head, her stupid puns being a strong number six —but open-ended questions left lots of room for answers.

"Why did someone hurt Tonya?"

Ah, he'd answered a question with a question. Great, he knew all the shrink tricks. The breeze blew, brushing Tristan before it hit her nose—musky. And the energy matched, a heavy vibration like what you'd feel at a young child's funeral: sorrow edged with a gut-twisting fear that your kid was next.

"I need you to drop the act, Tristan. Women are being murdered. Someone tried to kill me last night. So if you want my help, you need to tell me everything. Right now."

"That's fair." He hung his head. "I didn't know Tonya was dead for sure until the detective showed up to interrogate me last week."

"And Lillian?"

He raised his face. "I didn't even know she was missing until she came up dead. I thought she ghosted me."

Huh. Was that true? He had said that his girlfriends often left him, sometimes suddenly. He wasn't on social media at all. Was it actually possible that he didn't realize they were missing? Sammy had said they were only now connecting the cases, so if Lillian's disappearance hadn't been linked to the other crimes until her body was found, Reid wouldn't have known she existed until the other day. A single picture at a beach might not have made Tristan a suspect with whatever cop had snagged her missing persons file.

"How'd you end up at the crime scene?"

"I was walking around, trying to figure out where I was going at night. I got an alert about the body." He shrugged one shoulder. "And before you ask, I'm sorry I lied about my mother... and my father. Richie's father. I spit it out without thinking."

She wasn't concerned with that, not now. That'd be like worrying about the terrible lemonade served onboard a sinking ship. "Let's deal with one issue at a time, from most pressing to least. And we'll assume that you had nothing to do with your mother's death."

"My... mother?" His gaze flicked to the grave and back to her, his shoulders tightening, eyes bright with understanding. "I didn't, of course I—"

"The detective thinks you did. He thinks that you killed them all, that you screwed with my car, that you—"

"He's right."

Ruh-roh. "Excuse me?"

"About the car. Rich can trace the GPS you installed when you refurbished the interior—he can get into that much more easily than tracking your cell."

You didn't have any trouble tracking my cell. Her back was slick with sweat. "You were trying to protect me? That's a weird way to go about it." But she'd considered the same, that someone had sabotaged her car to trick the killer into thinking she was home.

"I didn't want Rich following you, getting to you. He's dangerous. My mother..." His eyes tightened, a glint of anger brightening like the flash of sunlight on a murky pond. *There's the fury.* "He killed her; I'm sure of it. I can't prove it, the guy is sneaky as hell, but he hated me after he found out that my mom and his dad hooked up—"

"But he didn't hate *her*." She didn't realize she'd been thinking it until the words were out of her mouth, but... it was true. Reid Hanlon was a good actor, but not that good. "Reid cared about your mother. She slept with his father, but he seemed genuinely sad about her death. The way he's behaving toward you is more indicative of a justice-driven detective than a serial killer trying to cover his tracks. And why would he set you up? Of all the people he could have picked, you're the last one to go down without a fight. You have considerable resources to protect yourself, and the brass could have pulled him off the case at any moment just for being related to you."

"Maybe Rich killed my mother and not the other women, but figures he can pin her death on me too."

"You think... there are two killers out there? Rich and—"

He shrugged. "My mother wasn't killed the same way as the others, so it's possible. And I might still... be responsible for the more recent victims. Not on purpose," he amended when she raised an eyebrow. "I'm safe while I'm awake. But when I'm asleep... I just don't know." His voice trembled. "But I *did not* kill my mother. I didn't have a single episode before she died."

Maggie frowned. What he was saying didn't make sense. "Your mother and these other women... they *were* killed the same way, Tristan. Reid told me." She might have imagined that he'd made that part up, but Reid had said it in front of her best friend the prosecutor. Sammy would have known if Reid was lying.

Tristan was already shaking his head. "She was buried, but it was different—there were bugs. And my girlfriends didn't start vanishing until Tonya. That means the killer hurt my mother then waited seven years before they killed anyone else."

"Maybe there were other bodies in the meantime that you don't know about. How good are you at keeping track of your exes?" Clearly terrible since he didn't even know Lillian was missing. And Tristan'd had more than his share of one-night stands.

His brow furrowed. "I guess that's possible, but it seems way more likely that this is someone else copying her death. Maybe even... me." He dropped his gaze to the soil once more—the grave. He shuddered.

He really had no idea—he really thought he might be guilty. But she no longer believed that. She took a step forward. "Tristan, you're wrong. The killer is using the same medallion as a burning implement, the same bone-scoring techniques, something that the police did not release to the public. This killer has to be someone who has intimate knowledge of your mother's—"

"Wait... a medallion?" He raised his head. "Rich never said anything about a medallion."

"I thought it was your job to know things." But he wouldn't know things that the detective hadn't committed to an online record. And Reid was nearly as protective of his evidence as she was of her patients' privacy... but not quite. "It was about this big." She showed him with her thumb and forefinger. "I was told that Christine had it."

"She has mine, but..." His face changed so suddenly it was like he'd become a completely different person. Slack and pale, his eyes wide. Haunted. A ghost of himself.

"Tristan?"

He swallowed hard. "My medallion... it wasn't the only necklace." He raised his fingertips and pressed them to a spot in the middle of his chest, perhaps where the medallion would have sat... where his mother was burned? But that wasn't what stopped her heart. He was touching his chest in exactly the same place Benedict had when he'd mentioned Tristan's mother.

"Benedict made them for all of us; Mom had one too. It was the only piece he ever duplicated. Protection or something, to keep us connected to each other and to God."

Benedict had made the medallions for everyone—for Tristan, his mother, himself. And... *If I had to guess, I'd say it's religious, but that's just a gut feeling.* She imagined the giant

THE DEAD DON'T DREAM

glittering cross on the wall, sparkling with jewels, then the earrings—Tonya's earrings.

The world around her went black and then pulsed back in vibrant pre-storm colors, the green so verdant it hurt her eyes. Her lungs were suddenly open wide, revelations swirling through her head and locking into place faster than the leaves flying past on the rushing wind. Tristan clutched at his chest, his shirt knotted in his fist.

That explained how the killer knew about the women who ended up dead, why Tristan's one-night stands were spared. Benedict only knew who he was creating custom jewelry for; he'd have asked for their information. Maybe some of those women had gotten a phone call from Christine and decided to leave Tristan alone—once they'd stopped corrupting Benedict's surrogate son, they hadn't needed to die. But the ones who stuck, all the girls Benedict blamed for ruining Tristan... they were buried out there. Somewhere.

Her guts twisted, a nest of rodents scurrying amidst flaming thorns. That was why Christine had died. She was useful for a time—perhaps the jeweler believed she was helping to protect Tristan with her threatening phone calls. And Christine throwing a fit at Eden had made it appear that Tristan wasn't into her. She wasn't a threat. But Maggie herself had alerted Benedict to the fact that the woman was still sniffing around Tristan. He'd seen Christine as an accomplice in his task until Maggie had outed her.

Her ribs ached; her heart spasmed. Her jaw was clenched so hard that her whole face throbbed. She understood what it was to be shocked at your parent's actions, the surprise you felt when you found yourself at your own mother's sentencing hearing, but to realize your foster father was a murderer? That he killed your mom and the women you loved? Tristan was like Mannie's children, registering the crimes of their father with horrified disbelief —*X marks the spot*. But Tristan's mother had been innocent.

And that wasn't the most significant issue tugging at her brain, stabbing like shards of glass into her gray matter. They'd only recently begun finding the bodies. But Benedict was an old man; it was highly unlikely that he'd only now begun killing. What had his motives been before Tristan had given him a place to focus his predilections? How many more dead women were there that hadn't yet been discovered? How many before Tristan's mother?

Tristan was staring at the headstone, his face waxy with shock.

She tried to keep her voice steady as she asked: "How much jewelry did you have made, Tristan?"

He took a shuddering breath. "More than a dozen pieces." When he met her eyes, they were glazed—numb. Devastated. Green around the gills, too, like he might puke. She could guess what he was going to say before he opened his mouth.

"I think we need to call Rich."

CHAPTER
THIRTY-SIX

MAGGIE STARED through the two-way mirror into the interrogation room, astonished that she was even here. Tristan had taken her to get her car, and the detective met them at the station where Reid listened carefully to Maggie's assessment of Tristan's mental health, and then to their story—their theory about Benedict Rose. And though he'd referred to Tristan as Maggie's "best friend" twice, Reid actually seemed to believe them.

Now, she was watching the interrogation for inconsistencies in Benedict's demeanor, standing at the window like a Peeping Tom. There was not so much as a chair in this glorified closet, just a small table topped with a television currently playing the scene inside the interrogation room in real time.

Reid eased himself into the seat across the table from the bearded jeweler. "Did you kill Christine Archer, Mr. Rose?"

Just ripping the bandage right off, eh?

Benedict's eyes widened. She leaned nearer to the double-sided mirror, looking for the micro-expressions that were common of those who were lying... or who were panicking. She couldn't see his mouth well, but the muscles around his eyes twitched with irritation—less common in those who were purposefully being deceitful. "I thought you wanted to talk about Tristan."

That's what Reid had told him when he'd asked him to come in. She supposed it wasn't entirely a lie, just mostly, though Reid's gaze had remained carefully, if not fictitiously, genuine. He was a pretty good liar, that Reid. She didn't appreciate all the fibbing when it was directed her way, but she could see the benefit now.

"That's not an answer."

Benedict crossed his arms—defensive. "Of course I didn't hurt that girl. Harlot though she was, that's between her and God."

Well, that certainly didn't feel like a no. Even if he was denying it, he was also hinting that he wouldn't blame a deity for smiting her. If he saw himself as the curator of said deity's judgment, would he blame himself or God?

"Maybe you were worried about your daughter, Benedict." Reid shrugged and glanced at the mirror, as if to ensure that she was paying attention. "Jeanna and Tristan have a special relationship, right? They're thick as thieves. And Tristan's always buying things for her little girl."

"My daughter is none of your business. And neither is my granddaughter."

"Is Robin Tristan's child?"

Maggie balked. *What?* That hadn't even occurred to her. Hadn't Tristan said Jeanna was his sister? And if she remembered right, Jeanna was raped. That was one of the things Tonya had loved about Tristan, his sympathy and care for his sister in the aftermath of that attack.

Benedict's eyes sharpened. "Tristan sure does give her

money like that child belongs to him. But they would never tell me even if it was true. I didn't raise them to... do that."

"Whether it was intended or not, maybe you think he should marry her if you believe he's that baby's father. But to do that, he'd need to be on a righteous path. Getting rid of bad influences would certainly help. Maybe he'd even come back to the church in despair if all his women keep dying, right?" The stream of accusations was so thick, Maggie felt like she was wading in it. *Tristan should be here to see this too.* But he had no professional reason to be, and every reason to distance himself.

Benedict's nostrils flared. "Tristan's on a bad path, that's for sure. Takes after his mother—her sins caught up with her. But I can't save anyone, Richie. Only God can do that."

Reid laced his fingers on the tabletop. "You're the one who always told him that his mother's death was his fault."

Ouch. That was rough, but Maggie believed it. Even Reid, a man who had spent the last several years investigating his brother, didn't seem to think Benedict had done right by Tristan. It made her soften toward him... just a little.

"Abigail's death was *her own* fault—that's what I've always said. But he didn't help, playing with fire like he does. Poor Abby never found her way, and his antics just drove her deeper into the arms of those fornicators."

"Like my father?" He smiled—nice teeth. "But surely, a quick round with a priest could fix what my father did. Penance and all. I grew up Catholic, Benedict; confession is like a magic eraser. You didn't need to kill anyone."

"Confession isn't perfect, Richie, not for true believers. Even our Pope now... he's not a man of God." He practically spit out the words. Man, if the Pope wasn't a good enough

Catholic, anyone else might as well give up and wait for a lightning bolt to strike them in the ass.

Reid was practically rolling his eyes—deep brown, steeped in intelligence. Kinda handsome now that he was on her side. "Yeah, that Pope, all about peace. Wrath and hellfire's better, right? Blood on the doorframes? Locusts?"

"Fire is what's *real*—like hot metal from the smelter."

The smelter... Ah, the bone scoring tools. *How did I miss this?* She hadn't been at the shop looking for a killer, but this was blatant—overt. And though she'd seen people go from Dr. Jekyll to Mr. Hyde more than once, his mannerisms in that shop just didn't fit. Even now, watching him spout off about the very things that should indict him, Benedict as a killer felt... *off.*

"I've got evidence, Benedict. Compelling evidence. DNA —your DNA."

"Whatever you think you have, you're wrong." But his eyes dulled—uncertain.

"What I think I have is a case. I can link you to Lillian Russell's crime scene. I found out an hour ago that they discovered two gray hairs with her body, and I'm quite certain that they'll match your beard."

Well, that had happened fast. While she and Tristan were solving this case in the cemetery, Reid had been figuring it out here. No wonder he had been so willing to accept their statement as fact. That was, if Reid was telling the truth. There was no law against lying to suspects during an interrogation.

Benedict didn't seem to realize the latter. His jaw dropped, beard parting to reveal the cave of his mouth.

"I can prove you were at that crime scene," Reid repeated. "That you had a motive to kill Tristan's mother and to kill the women who might have been leading your son astray. And I have that." He pointed at the man's chest, just below his wild beard. The chain was barely visible around the hump of fat at the back of his neck, but in the bright lights of the interrogation room, she could see the outline of a circular object beneath his shirt. The medallion. She could almost smell the burning flesh, though that might have been the room... or her nose. Ash liked to stick in the sinuses.

Benedict frowned. "This?" He reached for the necklace and drew it from beneath his button-down—shiny, metal, and the right size to have made the marks on those women. She squinted, trying to see the details, but could only make out the oblong shape engraved in the center, the bands of dead space on either side. "It's Saint Benedict—my name-sake. For protection. I made one for all of us." He stopped speaking suddenly, his eyes narrowed as if to say *but I didn't make one for you, Richie, because you're* not *a part of this family*.

"Protection, huh?" Reid leaned nearer to the jeweler, over his hands, shoulders rippling like he was trying not to lunge across the steel. "Can you think of anything those dead women might have needed protection from?"

Benedict's brow furrowed, but the small muscles around his eyes remained still this time, a strong indicator of untruth. He slipped the medallion back beneath his shirt and crossed his arms once more, but it felt more like deflection, a pause to consider what to say. The hairs on the back of her neck rose, prickling beneath that old, healed scar.

No, this was all wrong... the evasion was out of character. Benedict was a righteous man—a zealot. Men like that bled for their beliefs, they died for their beliefs. They killed for them. And they were the first to scream it from the rooftops, especially if they knew they'd been caught.

Fire is what's real. That might as well have been a confession. So why had Benedict suddenly become mute on the matter of his convictions?

"It's not an uncommon symbol," Benedict said. His forehead was damp, glistening with sweat.

"But the piece itself *is* uncommon. Because you only do custom work." Reid mirrored Benedict's movements, crossing his wide forearms across his chest. "If you have an alibi for last night, I suggest you cough it up now."

"I was at home."

"Anyone who can verify that?"

His eyes blazed, but it felt more like fear than defensiveness. "No, I was alone. Since my wife died, I don't spend much time outside the house."

"How did your wife die, again?"

Maggie stared. Reid already knew how this man's wife had died—he had to know.

"She just didn't wake up one day. God had a reason."

"Were you getting along at the time?"

Benedict paused, nostrils twitching. *That's a no.* "How dare you, boy. You're just like your father. Dirty, trying to drag good people down to meet the devil with you."

"What were you at odds about, Benedict? Did she want to go back to work once Jeanna was grown, use that pharmacy degree she'd spent years earning? Did she want basic human rights despite being a woman?"

The jab hit home—Benedict's eyes brightened with fury. "The stress... that's what killed her. My wife was the one who pushed Jeanna to go off to college—pushed her away from God. And just look what happened."

"Robin, you mean?"

He sniffed. "I love that child. But thank goodness my wife died before she had to see what her choices had done. Before our girl showed up pregnant with no father in sight and no ring on her finger." *Damn*. "And before you accuse me of something downright awful, no good Christian would end a life before God believes it's time." Benedict's jaw was hard as stone. "Get me my lawyer, Richie."

Reid smiled. "As you wish, *Benny*." He shoved himself to standing hard enough to make the chair teeter on two legs before pattering back down, then stalked from the interrogation room. Maggie could not take her eyes from Benedict's stooped form. Less like defeat and more like... devastation.

She frowned. Was Benedict Rose a religious zealot? Sure. Was there circumstantial evidence linked to him, his hair at the crime scene? Maybe. But she would have bet her most gruesome clown painting that he'd see murder as a "smite him to hell" kind of sin. He valued the afterlife far more than this one; he had seemed appalled at the notion that someone might have killed his wife. And his granddaughter had no fear of him—he'd shown her genuine affection despite the way she'd come into the world. He bent the rules for those he loved.

She turned as Reid opened the door to her Peeping Tom closet.

"What do you think?" he said as he closed the door behind him, so close she could smell his sweat. No cinnamon gum, just the musk of a long day.

"He's clearly devout." And he *was* lying—he was definitely lying. Yet something wasn't clicking right in her head. Maybe her mojo was off since she'd just lost her entire house to a serial killer who'd tried to murder her. *Duh.* "I know you have evidence against him," she said slowly. "But he doesn't *feel* right to me."

Reid raised an eyebrow. "Because he's a kindly grandfather?"

"No because..." *He's not jealous. He's not the stalker type.* "He doesn't fit the profile." A psychological profile could change, of course, but not this much. Unless she had been *that* wrong to begin with.

"Sometimes, the worst criminals look the most normal. Unless you changed your mind and think your best friend Tristan seems more like a serial killer. I'd put him away just for that nickname he gave me." His eyes glittered—was that a joke?

"He's not my best friend. He's not my anything."

The glimmer faded. Reid sniffed. "We've got a team on it. We'll trace Benedict's steps for every one of those killings, but between his car's GPS and that gray hair, we've got him at three of the scenes already. A confession would have been nice, but..." He shrugged.

Tristan was right—they *were* fast at tracking car GPS. She stared through the mirror. Benedict was rubbing the spot on his chest again, his face drawn. "He changed his tune so quickly, Reid. Went from righteous fire and brimstone to asking for his lawyer."

"He realized he was caught."

"I don't think so. I think if he'd done it... he'd be proud." Benedict raised a finger and swiped at his eye—crying. Not an ounce of pride in him, not anymore.

"He's protecting someone," she practically whispered. Someone who had hurt the women Tristan cared about. And with Benedict in custody, the real killer would have to act quickly if they had something special in mind for Tristan himself... or plans for some other unlucky woman.

"We should have DNA confirmation on those crime scenes tomorrow—if he has an accomplice, we'll know. But even if he does have a partner, it's highly unlikely that they'll do anything tonight with Benedict in custody. Why prove our main suspect innocent if it means we'll arrest them instead?" Reid glanced at the mirror, then turned her way once more. "I hope you'll be able to rest easier now that this is over." His eyes blazed with what appeared to be genuine remorse.

"You're done interrogating me, huh?"

"I'm finished being mean to you," he said. "But that doesn't mean you and I are done talking. We work well together."

Weird that it sounded like an invitation.

Weird how she still felt very much unsettled.

CHAPTER
THIRTY-SEVEN

TRISTAN

Tristan blinked his eyes, but it didn't edge the blur from the corners. The room came to him in hazy pieces. Where was he?

His home. He recognized the floor-to-ceiling windows, the black couches, the gas fireplace—currently blazing. The glass wall in front of him led to the pool. He wasn't sure how he'd gotten here, but at least he knew he wasn't a killer. That softened the tightness in his chest though it did little to help him figure out what had happened.

He'd left the precinct. He'd driven home. He'd made himself a drink like he did after a long day—and they were all long days. And then... blackness.

Tristan tugged one wrist toward the ceiling, then the other, but his brain wasn't working; his arms refused to listen. Wait... no. It wasn't his brain or his arms—a rope. A chair.

He shook his head, trying to clear it. A dream? Surely a dream. He'd been reliving his mother's death with his sleepwalking, trying to intervene—that's what Maggie had said. Was this... some version of that?

Tristan wriggled, his brain focusing. The restraints were not in his head or the remnants of some nightmare —definitely bound, though not with rope. The dining chair he was secured to sat in the middle of his living room, the duct tape around his wrists so tight that it was cutting off his circulation. His fingers from middle to pinky were numb, and the others pricked with pins and needles.

Tristan's heart throbbed in his temples, which only intensified the wooziness in his brain. Even if he was free, he felt too dizzy to stand. *Shit*. What the hell was going on? The killer had been captured—Benedict was with Richie. Had he gotten out after questioning, come here to finish the job? Was that even possibl—

Creeeee...

The noise from the hallway made him turn, but his head was heavy too, his eyes still blurry as if he were trying to see through dirty water. A hazy outline like a half-formed apparition came into view, the thunks of footsteps echoing in his ears. Her hair... long and dark and shiny. And there she was, an angel glimmering in the firelight.

Goosebumps bristled on his arms, but it was a muted feeling, blunt against his flesh. He wasn't sure why Jeanna had decided to come by, but he'd never been more happy to see her. "Jeanna, thank goodness. Help me. Super quick, I don't know where he is."

Jeanna smiled, her dark hair shimmering like night waves. He scanned the room feverishly, but there was very little here that would help if Benedict returned. Would he hurt Jeanna? Tristan didn't think so, but Benedict had hurt Tristan's mother, had killed so many others... Why not Jeanna too? Maybe the vodka cup on the coffee table would make a good weapon. No, the shards would be too small to do major damage. The fire poker—could he get to the fire poker?

Jeanna was still standing near the hallway like a statue, surely as stunned as he was to find himself in this position. "Seriously, Jeanna, I'll explain after, please—"

"We've waited long enough, Tristan," she said as if she hadn't heard him. She approached, her movements jerky in the firelight, too fast for his bleary eyes to follow.

What was she talking about? He shook his head again, once more trying to clear it, trying to understand, but he failed.

She climbed into his lap, one leg on either side of his thighs, her breath hot against his throat. His belly heaved—acidic. No, this was all wrong. She was his *sister*. The closest they'd ever been physically was a supportive hug, a high five on his way out the door.

"Jeanna, stop, what are you—"

"Don't let the devil put ideas in your head. The devil puts ideas in my head, too, but I don't listen. Not anymore." She lowered her mouth to his, the pressure intense, his lips smashed between their teeth.

He clenched his teeth together, blocking her tongue, trying to pull away with his sluggish muscles, every movement a slow-motion reminder that he was useless—helpless. "Stop," he said, but it came out muffled. He shook his head free, and she finally pulled her face back to look at him. Her eyes glittered the same way they did when she spoke of Robin—pure joy. As if every piece of her life had finally fallen into place.

She's crazy. Not a normal person in an abnormal situation—literally insane.

"Jeanna, why are you here? I'm tired; my brain isn't working right. Tell me what's happening. Tell me like I'm five years old." Stalling—he was stalling. *Please let whatever she drugged me with wear off soon.*

"Christine's gone now. They're all gone. You, me, and Robin... we can be a family."

They were already a family. She was his *sister*. "I don't want kids, Jeanna."

"You wanted Robin."

"I helped you because *you're* family, not because I wanted a daughter."

"Want one or not, you have one."

No, he absolutely did not. He didn't know who Robin's father was, but it certainly wasn't him. "Jeanna, I'll always be here to help you. I love you like a sister."

"I know you love me; Nana and Dad, they know too. That's why this is so perfect."

"Did your dad put you up to this? Did he say we should... be together?" Jeanna would have believed him. She believed anything the old man said. Robin was only here because Benedict had told Jeanna that she needed to have the baby—that if she had an abortion, she had no father. All Jeanna's dreams, gone in a single violent thrust. No wonder she lost her mind.

"I don't need him to tell me that we should be together. Everything I've ever done has been for you. The phone calls, telling those women they couldn't possibly have a chance—"

The threats? "That was you?"

"I think we should make it official. Get married. Stop living in sin."

"Untie me, Jeanna. We can talk about all this."

She smiled and fingered the pendant at her clavicle—Saint Benedict. Her gaze darkened. "I know about all the things you used to do with Christine. The games you liked to play."

Uh-oh.

Jeanna's fingernails tightened against his shoulders—sharp, painful. "This is what you like, right?"

"You were watching me?" he croaked. She was crushing his rib cage with her bony hips. Or maybe he was just imagining Christine, Lillian, Tonya, all of them gasping for breath. Jeanna had killed every woman he'd ever cared about because... she thought they'd be together, raise Robin together? *That's why she started killing my lovers three years ago—that's when she needed a father for her baby.*

He turned his head, one way then the other as if he might shake her claws from his body.

"I don't have to watch you. I know what you like. And I'm better for you than Christine."

"Of course you're better. You're family."

Jeanna stiffened. The words had not come from his sister, nor was the tone his. But he did recognize the voice.

Maggie. The doctor was halfway into the room from the back deck, her hands out at her sides, her silhouette surrounded by muted orange haze. Dirt marred the knees of her khaki pants. Was she really there, or was it just his fuzzy brain? The world was more solid at the edges, he realized, though it was still hard to focus his eyes.

"It's okay, Jeanna," Maggie said. "I know you don't want to hurt Tristan. You love him more than anyone else ever could."

Jeanna's fingers softened against his shoulders. She pushed herself to standing, and the moment the pressure on his thighs eased, his calves lit up with a stabbing, needling pain. His hands were numb. Even if he escaped the restraints, he wouldn't be able to take Jeanna down before she hurt Maggie. He was useless.

But Jeanna hadn't drugged Maggie the way she had him. Jeanna would be at a distinct disadvantage against the doctor.

Jeanna seemed to realize this at the same time. She lunged backward, toward the fireplace—damn, she'd remembered the poker.

Maggie advanced, undaunted by the weapon. "I know I don't mean anything to you. But I'm the only one who knows that he feels the same way." Maggie edged closer, but stayed to the left side of the room. It was as if she were purposefully avoiding the chair—avoiding coming nearer to him, like a burglar avoiding laser beams that would set off an alarm.

Jeanna raised the weapon higher, wielding it like a baseball bat. "You don't know anything."

"I know enough. I know that what your dad did to you wasn't right. Making you feel like you couldn't go to school. Making you feel like—"

"He didn't do anything to me!"

"Good families don't control each other, Jeanna. Your mom supported you, maybe even got your father on board with college until someone attacked you. I don't know how she died—I don't know if your father killed her. I don't know exactly how you feel. But I do know what it's like to want to control *something* when the rest of the world feels unstable." The pain in Maggie's voice was palpable—speaking from experience, not from a psychology manual. "But you can't control Tristan," she finished.

"We belong together," Jeanna said, but her words were a thin whine. Maggie was getting to her, the same way she'd gotten to him in their first session.

Maggie lowered her hands to rest on the thighs of her khaki pants. "If you love him, you need to let him choose. The way your father should have done for you."

"Dad let me go to school, and my mother *died*."

"Your mother wasn't your fault."

"Of *course* she was."

Tristan felt the words in his guts as if each had ripped open a different wound. Tears glittered in Jeanna's eyes. But she couldn't really believe that, could she? He had never heard Benedict blame Jeanna for her mother's death, but... he might have. He'd certainly blamed Tristan for his own mother's death, albeit subtly.

"Sometimes things just happen." Maggie took a single step closer... no, to the side. Tristan had to crane his neck to see her. Was she backing toward the archway to the foyer? "Jeanna, let him go. If you don't, Robin won't have any parents." Maggie glanced his way, her eyes boring into his. He understood.

"I'll take care of her," Tristan said, though speaking to Jeanna made his belly sour and his heart beat triple-time. Jeanna turned to him, her mouth set in a small, shocked *o*. "I'll make sure that Robin has everything she needs. I'll make sure she goes to college." And he would. He didn't want Jeanna, hadn't wanted a child, but Robin deserved a better hand than she'd been dealt.

"We'll both make sure Robin has what she needs," Jeanna said to him, her voice low and dangerous. Her gaze darkened as if she'd made some pivotal decision, and oh god, whatever it was would mean bad things for the doctor. Because there was only one way Jeanna was getting out of this room to care for Robin herself: she had to destroy the witness.

Jeanna turned away from him, her arms coiling into

ropy bundles of tendon and muscle as she tightened her grip on the weapon. She lunged.

There was no time to cry out. Jeanna flew toward Maggie like a feral animal, the sharp end of the poker glinting with firelight. He had never felt more helpless, tied up with his tongue a lump in the bottom of his mouth. Maggie was going to die. Like his mother. Like Tonya. Like all the others.

Maggie jumped to the right, beyond his line of sight—

A blurred form leaped from the darkness at her back. Before Tristan had time to register what he was seeing, Jeanna was on the floor, screeching, the arm with the poker pinned behind her.

"Knock it off, you're going to stab yourself a new asshole," the man on top of her said. *Richie?*

Maggie skirted the scuffling on the floor—his deranged sister, his half brother who hated his guts—and knelt beside the chair. "Got yourself in a bind, eh?"

He was too stunned to reply, and she didn't seem to expect him to. Maggie tugged at the tape around his right hand. Pins and needles exploded through his forearm, his nerves screaming. She released his other hand, then bent lower to work on his ankles.

"You're my hero," Tristan said.

Maggie snorted, but Richie replied, "Why thank you." Rich glanced Maggie's way. "I told you to go home, Doctor Connolly."

"Hey, I helped. And we work well together, you said so yourself."

Tristan squinted at Maggie, then at Rich, who was still smiling as he secured the cuffs around Jeanna's wrists. Tristan's chest tightened, and it had nothing to do with Jeanna. He rotated his ankles, trying to force blood into his toes.

Richie yanked Jeanna to her feet, spittle glittering on her lips, tears on her cheeks. She whimpered. "Tris, help me. Tell them it's all a misunderstanding. Tell them!"

He met her eyes. "She's crazy," he said, and watched her face fall. But Tristan did not feel sorry for her.

Not one bit.

CHAPTER
THIRTY-EIGHT

MAGGIE CRACKED the Toyota's window and let the chill breeze dry the sweat from her hairline.

She'd left Tristan's home soon after the detective led Jeanna away in cuffs. Reid had called an ambulance, too, but Tristan had seemed more intent on talking to Maggie than getting treatment for his minor injuries.

Owen was probably waiting for her at his house with a pot of chicken soup or chamomile tea, whatever home remedy he figured might help with the loss of all her possessions. He was only trying to be kind, yet she couldn't bring herself to make the turn when the exit came up.

Her other friends seemed worried too. Alex and Imani had both texted to ask if she wanted to go out for pizza or Thai, respectively. But she didn't want to explain the dirt on her new clothes, how she'd snuck away from her police escort, how she'd ended up at the precinct watching Reid interrogate the wrong man. Or how she'd ultimately ended up confronting a killer in the dark living room of her patient who, *oh yeah*, she'd had naughty dreams about. She was tired of explaining and even more tired of thinking.

Her office was deserted, as she'd hoped, not a single light on inside the building, just the steady glow from the downstairs lobby and the parking lot floods that made the asphalt glitter. The silence inside the building was absolute, eerily quiet after the excitement at Tristan's home. A heavy, depressive feeling weighted her chest as she climbed the stairs, the let-down of adrenaline—her body trying to find homeostasis. But though she knew this logically, she did not like the way the silence seemed to exacerbate her unease. Her nerves were bristling with agitation. Her head throbbed.

She made her way to the third floor. The pressure in her chest persisted. She'd push through that and check her email, maybe catch up on her paperwork. Try to redeem herself since she'd completely missed Jeanna's murderous intentions. She felt like a hack. But at least she could use that sinking feeling as motivation to solve someone else's problems. Guilt without purpose would eat you alive.

Maggie's chair was where she'd left it, her water bottle still sitting on the corner of her desk, the painting exactly where it should be. The gouges on the drawers glared at her, but she'd get metal filing cabinets this week. She'd make sure this didn't happen again, not that she expected it might—the culprits for the robbery and the homicides had both been caught.

So why didn't it feel like this was over?

Maggie slid into her seat and hit a button on her keyboard, waking up the monitor, then sipped from her water bottle while she scanned her email list. Her throat was still dry, irritated from yesterday's smoke. Sammy had sent her a message about a new client; he was convinced this one was innocent. Could she do an evaluation ASAP?

She smiled. Sammy always knew exactly what she

needed. She should buy him some more cast iron. Maybe she'd even forgo the delivery clown this time... *nah*.

Maggie took another swig from her water bottle, pulled the keyboard closer, and typed the appointment into her planner. But every time she blinked, she saw Tristan's "sister" Jeanna behind her eyelids.

Jeanna loved Tristan, but enough to kill? Had Jeanna tracked her father's gray hair into the crime scenes accidentally? That was possible—they did live together. And Tristan's mother... she wouldn't have approved of him marrying his sister, but would Jeanna have risked killing her? The second Tristan found out, he'd have left her murderous ass.

She sighed. In a household like that, where normal human urges got bastardized as "unclean" or "sinful," unhealthy cognitive defenses were necessary just to feel sane. But Jeanna had taken things too far. She'd been delusional, imagining that she and Tristan had a life together, a future, a child, perhaps even denying that her rape had taken place.

And Maggie had missed all of it. Then again, she hadn't asked Jeanna anything personal. She'd brought up Christine's earrings and showed her a... a photo of... of Rich...

Her hands dropped to the desktop. Her fingers were suddenly heavy—the keyboard wasn't working. The room spun. And the hairs on her neck were prickling violently, the voice in her head whispering in staccato bursts: *Threat. Being watched. Not alone.*

Maggie leaned back in the chair and drew her eyes to the door—someone was there. Who was that? Not Jeanna, for sure not Jeanna; she was locked up. Jeanna's father was still at the station, too, and the figure was small. Too small to be a man... right?

She blinked, but her eyes refused to focus. She put her palms flat on the desk and rose, the edge of her pinky cold against the paperweight—the snake. Bile rose in her gorge. She felt like she might vomit.

"Hello, child." The words came at a distance.

I should have seen this one coming. Of course it was the domineering matriarch who had overruled Jeanna with her own daughter, whose name was on the jewelry store—the one pulling every string. She'd probably told Jeanna to make those phone calls to Tristan's exes, told Jeanna to go see Tristan tonight. Convinced Jeanna that Tristan was hers. And she'd done everything she could to make it so.

Maggie closed her fingers around the glass; the heavy, slippery glass. Those gray hairs at the crime scenes had never been Benedict's. And Reid wouldn't know until the DNA came back... tomorrow.

"Hey, Eden." The words were mushy in her mouth. "You come to... see a guy about... a snake?"

One chance, Maggie. You have one chance. Focus. Pretend you're trying to hit a target through the trees.

Eden stepped into the room; her figure wavered. Maggie inhaled deeply, called on every last reserve of strength she possessed, and slung her arm toward the figure.

I should have gone back to Owen's.

That was the last thought she had before the blackness took her.

CHAPTER
THIRTY-NINE
TRISTAN

Tristan eased his foot off the gas. Though he felt okay now, it was probably best to be careful after whatever drugs Jeanna had given him. But he had something he needed to do tonight, and he did not feel that it could wait.

Bringing the doctor Chinese takeout shouldn't seem so vital, he knew that logically. He also knew that it was the least he could do since she'd saved his life. And Maggie shouldn't be alone, not until he figured out what this nagging pressure in his chest was, even if she would be mad at him for tracking her phone. Again.

Jeanna—he couldn't believe it was Jeanna. She'd always seemed like such a... well, a priss. She wouldn't even stand up to her dad. The thought of her luring his girlfriends into the tall grass and murdering them...

You never really knew all the dark things that lurked within a person, but that was crazy. Seriously crazy. Full-on bat-shit crazy. How had he missed that level of derangement?

Maggie's rental car was parked in the front of the lot. Her office light was on.

He took the elevator to the third floor, the Styrofoam containers perfuming the air with salt and MSG. Did she like Chinese food? He thought so—who didn't, right? All the information he'd gotten on her, and he hadn't researched her favorite meals.

That was the main reason he was here: to promise not to pry into her life, or the lives of her patients—to tell her that Helena was safe and always would be. He'd been desperate, trying to ensure that she didn't call the cops and alert Rich about... well, anything. But it seemed his brother was not the culprit in his mother's death. He'd been wrong. All these years, he'd been wrong.

That was bothering him, too: his mother. It might not have been Richie who killed her, but it wasn't Jeanna either. He could understand her killing his girlfriends—in a whacked-out crazy way—but that one he could not accept. Had his mother's death merely created the blueprint for Jeanna's crimes? Then who had killed his mom? It had to be someone close to Jeanna if she had inside information on the killer's ritualized pattern. Perhaps it was her father after all. Hopefully Richie would sort that out soon. He'd gone long enough without answers.

The elevator slowed, then stopped.

Maggie's outer office door was closed, which he expected. He raised his hand to knock, then tried the knob. It turned.

The waiting room was empty. "Doctor Connolly?"

No response. He traversed the waiting area, then stepped into the back hallway. Maggie's stained-glass lamp painted the carpet outside her half-open door in rainbow colors. "Doctor?"

Nothing. His heart ratcheted into overdrive. The hairs on his arms stood. And as he approached the door, he smelled something tangy beyond the strong scent of Chinese food. Though he could not identify what it was, he knew that it wasn't right—that it was dangerous.

He pushed into the office, the door swinging wide. Silence invaded his eardrums. Tristan dropped the bag to the floor.

The room came to him in pieces, a single blink loaded with a million snippets of information. A body lay before him, curled around her midsection. Her hair was stained a sickly ruby—a lake of blood bloomed beneath her head. A section of skull above her ear was caved in like someone had taken a hammer to a watermelon. But the lake had stopped widening. The body was not moving. The doctor? No. Softer, wider through the midsection. Gray hair around the wound.

"Maggie?"

He stepped carefully over the body, squinting down at her, looking for signs of life, but saw only the claret that marred the floor, an amoeba of shining crimson. So much blood. And now he could see her face. Eden—it was Eden. She didn't appear to be breathing.

Where was Maggie? Was she okay? Had she left to get help? No, she'd have called the police from here.

He dragged his gaze from Eden's ruined skull. Two chairs sat undisturbed in the middle of the room. The sofa table with a baseball glove remained untouched beneath the window. The desk...

Behind the desk.

Feet.

Oh no.

He vaulted to the desk, his heart in his throat, and stumbled around the corner, praying that she was warm— that she was alive. Was Maggie on the floor here, prone and cold, as bloody as the body near the doorway? For a moment he believed she was dead, her eyelids closed, her face aimed at the ceiling, but no, that wasn't blood—just her hair, fanned around her head.

He hit his knees. "Maggie! Wake up, honey! Wake up!"

Honey—had he just called her honey? But she wasn't awake or she'd have yelled at him for that, and what was he even saying? He didn't call anyone honey. Not ever.

He touched her face; her skin was clammy. Tristan didn't see any injuries on her, which was of some relief, though his knee was wet. Was she bleeding after all? He looked down. Shards of glass glittered on the carpet. Her water bottle had shattered.

The drugs. That bitch had poisoned her.

"Maggie! Wake up!"

She moaned, a tiny, thin noise, but it was there. His heart soared.

"I'm here." He pulled out his phone and tugged her against his chest. Her breath on his neck was soft but present.

"I've got you, honey," he said, the word so sweet on his tongue. He wasn't entirely sure what that meant, but he was certain that his world would be far darker without Doctor Maggie Connolly in it.

CHAPTER
FORTY
EPILOGUE

HE DREW his fingers over her rib cage, his tongue lashing wildly at the tender spot between her legs. Maggie closed her eyes and moaned. It was the sweetest sound he'd ever heard.

Oh, she'd been through a lot these past few weeks—a brief hospital stay, a fight with a murderer. Losing her home.

But he was going to make her forget.

He let his fingers dance on her nipples. She widened her legs for him. *Oh yes, Maggie. Yes.*

Look at me. But he couldn't ask her. She was in charge—that was how she liked it.

Then she looked at him all the same. She couldn't see his face, of course, not beneath the thick fabric of his mask. The only part she could see was his lips, the pink of his tongue. And his eyes. He could not see her face either, but he knew what she looked like—knew all too well.

Beyond the closed door, the club moved, a living, breathing entity, but they'd taken a spot in one of the private rooms tonight. And though she was the one leading, always the one leading, he never felt more powerful than when she spread herself on the bed for him.

She shuddered and arched her back, and he pulled his face from her. When she bucked against him, he drew his fingers down to stroke the soft folds between her legs.

She propped herself onto her elbows. How beautiful she was, just leaning there against the bed, looking at him. If he had his way, he'd never leave this room.

And then she moved. Maggie pushed herself up, quietly, slowly rising until she stood naked before him—toe to toe. She grabbed his face, and for one terrible moment, he believed she might remove his mask, but instead, she tugged his chin down toward her lips. She tasted like sex— salt and spice and musk.

And then her lips were gone; his mouth was cold. Her hand on his neck made him tremble.

She pointed to the bed. To the leather straps so carefully positioned along the headboard. The restraints that were there just for him.

He did exactly as she asked—he always did. And as she climbed on the bed and eased herself down onto him inch by painstakingly wet inch, he lost himself in her rhythm, slow at first, then harder, faster. She threw her head back. She scratched at his chest.

And then Maggie was screaming. Oh, what he'd give to hear her scream his name.

But she wouldn't. She didn't know who he was even though he loved her.

And he wouldn't tell her.

He wasn't about to ruin a good thing.

———

Did you like *The Dead Don't Dream*? Maggie's story is just getting started. Continue the Mind Games series with *The Dead Don't Mind*. Grab it now on meghanoflynn.com, then read on for a sneak peek!

———

"*THE DEAD DON'T MIND* IS A SHARP, FAST-PACED PSYCHOLOGICAL THRILLER THAT KEPT ME GUESSING UNTIL THE FINAL PAGE. O'FLYNN HAS CREATED A SERIES SO ENTHRALLING, AND A CHARACTER SO CLEVER, I NEVER WANT THE BOOKS TO END. AN ABSOLUTELY BRILLIANT AND TWISTED STORY."
~*BESTSELLING AUTHOR EMERALD O'BRIEN*

THE DEAD DON'T MIND
MIND GAMES #2

A mute child holds the key in this addictive serial killer thriller for fans of *Bones* and *The Blacklist*.

THE DEAD DON'T MIND
CHAPTER 1
REID

DETECTIVE REID HANLON had never been one for flamboyance, though he did have a penchant for the dramatic. Not in word or deed, but in the little pops of color he immersed himself in, the flair that made up a daily existence. His home was decorated in soft mossy grays, but his art was an eclectic mix of vibrant yellows and milky whites and deepest cerulean. His suit today was tailored, gray—not bad-looking at thirty-nine, if he did say so himself—accented by a brilliant purple tie. Bright, almost theatrical.

But the room in which he stood... the florid vividness here was too much. The scene cut deeply, cruelly, despite his twenty years on the force. If he ever found himself numb to the horrors of the job, that was a sign that he should quit. So when Reid's jaw clenched, he welcomed it as a manifestation of his still-kicking humanity and leaned into the revulsion. Breathed in the copper. Let the distress seep into his bones.

It wasn't that the house itself was odd. It was hard to make a cookie-cutter middle-class abode strange without triggering a citation from the HOA. Average-sized rooms, coffee tables hewn in richly stained mahogany. The walls were builder's grade beige, plenty of opportunity to spice things up with a painting or three, the canvases changeable with mood or season. There were no paintings here now, but the plaster did not lack color. Blood splashed the walls like exuberant child's art, patterns and swirls that would make perfect sense to the forensic analysts who would soon arrive to dissect the angles of penetration and the resulting spray pattern.

It was often small things that made the difference for the analysts—a tiny dot on a far wall or the level of shine on a congealing puddle. The freshness of the scene should help. Lucky, that. He might not be here at all had it not been for the tiny smudge of claret on the inside of the window glass.

"I was on my bike when I saw the... the... the blood," the child had said. Ten years old, swimming in an oversized sweatshirt that matched his giant blue eyes, his freckled cheeks damp with tears.

"You have good instincts, Mr. Kole Bishop," Reid had said. "Sharp like a hawk." They liked phrases like that here in Fernborn, Indiana—it softened the blow, made one imagine the flight of the hawk instead of the wriggling death clutched in its talons. The child had blinked and offered a trembling smile, but the glassy terror that had shone in little Kole's gaze had made Reid's heart hurt.

Reid dragged his attention from the window. So many angles to analyze. So many penetrations.

So much blood.

Reid knelt beside the man of the house. Ted Darren lay prone with the back of his head angled against the couch leg, his neck twisted oddly. Not obviously broken, but snapping the man's neck would have been overkill. The couch was soaked in crimson, pools of it glittering and wet in the light from the floor-to-ceiling windows. Deep wounds bisected his abdomen and chest. Blood pooled beneath his legs; the killer had hacked at the tendons behind his knees and ankles, presumably to ensure that he couldn't run. More lacerations gouged chunks of muscle from his forearms, exposing the bones. Defensive wounds. Darren had seen the weapon coming. Perhaps an ax from the way the tissue folded inward below his jaw—a fatal blow to the jugular.

Who was he kidding? He *knew* it was an ax. He just didn't want it to be an ax, because that meant it had happened again, just like it had happened two districts over. The fact that he even knew about that case was a fluke; Detective Tengreddy in Point Harris had called him just last week for insights. What were the odds? Did the killer know Reid had been contacted? Perhaps striking here wasn't a coincidence after all—

"Detective Hanlon? Forensics is here."

Reid squinted at the body. "Not yet," he said to the dead man. "Not yet." He didn't need to look at the flatfoot in the doorway, probably still pale the way he'd been when Reid arrived, his watery brown eyes darting everywhere except the corpse.

"But—" Officer Marshall began.

"Please," Reid said, pushing himself to his feet. "I'll let them in as soon as I'm done walking through." He needed to see the house as it had been before. He wanted to see it as the killer would have, surrounded by silence as acute as flensing wounds. Surrounded only by the victims.

Marshall stared at him for an extra heartbeat, his eyes beseeching, or maybe just anxious, then backed out. Reid waited until the door clicked shut, then turned for the stairway, the railing honed in a dark wood that matched the coffee tables. Teddy Darren, or perhaps his wife, had a fine eye for detail. He kept his hands in his pockets as he made his way to the second floor, elbows tucked in so as not to brush the walls or the rail. Blood on the stairs—strange for this perp. But he could already hear the rushing water, part of the killer's trademark.

The water was louder at the top of the stairs and louder still as he approached the rooms. Reid edged through the already open master bedroom door.

Diane Darren—quite the unfortunate bit of alliteration she'd married into—was still tucked under the covers in the master bedroom, but he could see her... or parts of her. Her cloudy eyes were wide to the ceiling, mouth gaping as if shocked, sandy curls cascading limply over the pillow. She'd died quickly from the yawning chasm beneath her jawline, dissected muscle and severed windpipe. Nearly instant death, which was a minor consolation prize, like coming in first in a shit-eating contest.

He stepped nearer, squinting—his mouth tasted like pennies. No severe injuries to the backs of the arms; no time for defensive wounds. But the killer had hacked at her anyway, slicing through the sheets and the fascia that covered her abdomen. The intruder had started his reign of terror up here—no way Diane had slept through the brawl in the living room. The commotion upstairs had probably woken Ted, who'd fallen asleep on the couch. Did the killer know he was walking into a divided sleeping situation? The killer had not left blood on the stairs at any of his past crimes. The deviation screamed "unplanned."

Reid could see the case notes from the last murder in his head: *Injuries made in a downward trajectory, multiple slashing wounds with a low force profile.* From the angle here, the killer had almost certainly been crouched beside the bed or kneeling as if in prayer—that was consistent with his past crimes, as was his efficiency. He was always fast, dispatching each victim and moving on before the other occupants had time to react.

But though Diane had died quickly, Ted had not. Downstairs, the killer had made shallower cuts, not using his full strength. Yet Reid was quite sure he hadn't lost his nerve. He had incapacitated the man first, only later made sure that Ted was dead. Unlike his other crimes, he hadn't wanted that killing to be quick. He had *hated* that it was quick.

What was different about Teddy?

Reid was still considering this as he made his way into the hallway. The rushing water was louder here, yelling for his attention, trying to drag him into the bathroom on his right. But the bathroom was always the killer's last stop.

He took a breath and imagined the upper floor was silent—the water would not have been running when the killer first strode down this hallway. Perhaps he'd have heard the whimper of a wakening child. Perhaps the creaks and groans of his own footsteps. From the fine dots along the baseboard, the ticking drip of Diane's blood off his blade.

The imagined *drip, drip, drip* from the ax grew louder; the water faded in his ears. The room to his left—the boy's —was empty, as he'd been told it would be. Reid paused just outside the door of the last room on the right, steeled himself, and stepped over the threshold.

The bubble-gum pink walls were studded with posters of horses and colored-pencil drawings of the same. The child lay on the bed beneath an oversized photograph of her on a white steed. If the girl had been a brunette, he could almost have imagined that she was asleep, but as it was, her white-blonde hair was bathed in the dramatics of extinction, dark with blood—one hard blow to the back of her neck. But, like her mother, she didn't suffer. Her left arm was still wrapped around a stuffed unicorn, the horn specked with congealing crimson.

His stomach clenched. That unicorn. Her little fingers wrapped so carefully around the horn. It made Lily Darren look alive, and she *felt* alive to him, as if her essence were still here. Downstairs, he had felt only the energy of life passed, the muted, heady silence that came with dead things. But here in this room, he almost believed the child might suddenly sit up and look at him. Maybe beg him to save her.

The hairs on the back of his neck prickled, an uncomfortable but insistent tingle that spiked into needles of panic with a sudden flash of movement in his peripheral. *I'm not alone.*

Reid whirled, hand on the butt of his gun. And straightened. His own face stared back at him from the full-length mirror that hung on the half-open bathroom door, a second entrance to the killer's final destination. Waxy and pale— he did not look well.

His shoulders relaxed. A trick of the mind; because he

wanted the child to be alive, perhaps. Or maybe it was because the incessant whoosh of rushing water almost sounded like breath. It was also possible that Marshall had allowed the forensics team to enter, and he'd missed it because of the running water and his focus on blotting out the noises in the home. But he did not hear the chatter of instruments or voices, just the pressured hiss of the bathtub. Although...

He frowned. The floor was dry; the hallway had been as well. By the time police had arrived at the last crime scene, a waterfall had been cascading down the stairs. The scene before that had featured soggy carpet. Had the killer forgotten to plug the tub?

Unplanned. Definitely unplanned. What was he missing?

Reid stepped nearer to the bathroom, his shoulders squared—

Clink!

He froze. Reid might have imagined that this, too, was a trick of the mind, but then the sound came again. *Clink-clink!* Bright and fast and decidedly real.

He drew his weapon. "Police!"

The clinking stopped. He stilled, listening, weapon aimed at the half-open door. There shouldn't be anyone else here. The youngest boy was at camp, according to the neighbors, and everyone else was accounted for—dead, but present.

"Come out with your hands up!" He didn't believe he was talking to the killer. Probably an animal. Did the children have a cat? But he was not going to risk an ax to the head just because he believed it unlikely. Better cops than him had died for less egregious errors.

He watched the bathroom door. No footsteps

THE DEAD DON'T DREAM

approached the other side; he saw no shadow beneath. He edged to the side of the jamb and toed the door the rest of the way open.

Reid's heart shuddered to a stop. He lowered his weapon.

The bathroom was simple enough, more beige walls and white furnishings, more mahogany cabinetry. The bathtub faucet was running, the drain open—the tub was empty and clean. But that was where the normalcy ended.

A blond-haired boy sat on the closed toilet lid, toes curled underneath him, arms wrapped around his knees. His fingers and pants were bathed in ruby, nails coated in thick, curdled-looking red. A tiny toy car sat in a smeared puddle near the base of the toilet. He held an ax clutched in his fists near his knees, the sharp edge still dripping, the handle dark with blood.

GET *THE DEAD DON'T MIND* ON MEGHANOFLYNN.COM!

"*THE DEAD DON'T MIND* IS A SHARP, FAST-PACED PSYCHOLOGICAL THRILLER THAT KEPT ME GUESSING UNTIL THE FINAL PAGE. O'FLYNN HAS CREATED A SERIES SO ENTHRALLING, AND A CHARACTER SO CLEVER, I NEVER WANT THE BOOKS TO END. AN ABSOLUTELY BRILLIANT AND TWISTED STORY."
~*BESTSELLING AUTHOR EMERALD O'BRIEN*

WICKED SHARP

A BORN BAD NOVEL

A mountain hike with your serial killer father. Good Samaritans who aren't as innocent as they appear. What could go wrong?

CHAPTER 1

I HAVE a drawing that I keep tucked inside an old doll house —well, a house for fairies. My father always insisted upon the whimsical, albeit in small amounts. It's little quirks like that which make you real to people. Which make you safe. Everyone has some weird thing they cling to in times of stress, whether it's listening to a favorite song or snuggling up in a comfortable blanket or talking to the sky as if it might respond. I had the fairies.

And that little fairy house, now blackened by soot and flame, is as good a place as any to keep the things that should be gone. I haven't looked at the drawing since the day I brought it home, can't even remember stealing it, but I can describe every jagged line by heart.

The crude slashes of black that make up the stick figure's arms, the page torn where the scribbled lines meet —shredded by the pressure of the crayon's point. The sadness of the smallest figure. The horrific, monstrous smile on the father, dead center in the middle of the page.

Looking back, it should have been a warning—I should have known, I should have run. The child who drew it was no longer there to tell me what happened by the time I stumbled into that house. The boy knew too much, that was obvious from the picture.

Children have a way of knowing things that adults don't—a heightened sense of self-preservation that we slowly lose over time as we convince ourselves that the prickling along the backs of our necks is nothing to worry about. Children are too vulnerable not to be ruled by emotion—they're hardwired to identify threats with razor's-edge precision. Unfortunately, they have a limited capacity to describe the perils they uncover. They can't explain why their teacher is scary or what makes them duck into the house if they see the neighbor peeking at them from behind the blinds. They cry. They wet their pants.

They draw pictures of monsters under the bed to process what they can't articulate.

Luckily, most children never find out that the monsters under their bed are real.

I never had that luxury. But even as a child, I was comforted that my father was a bigger, stronger monster than anything outside could ever be. He would protect me. I knew that to be a fact the way other people know the sky is blue or that their racist Uncle Earl is going to fuck up Thanksgiving. Monster or not, he was my world. And I adored him in the way only a daughter can.

I know that's strange to say—to love a man even if you see what terrors lurk beneath. My therapist says it's normal, but she's prone to sugarcoating. Or maybe she's so good at positive thinking that she's grown blind to real evil.

I'm not sure what she'd say about the drawing in the fairy house. I'm not sure what she'd think about me if I told her that I understood why my father did what he did, not because I thought it was justified, but because I understood him. I'm an expert when it comes to the motivation of the creatures underneath the bed.

And I guess that's why I live where I do, hidden in the New Hampshire wilderness as if I can keep every piece of the past beyond the border of the property—as if a fence might keep the lurking dark from creeping in through the cracks. And there are always cracks, no matter how hard you try to plug them. Humanity is a perilous condition rife with self-inflicted torment and psychological vulnerabilities, the what-ifs and maybes contained only by paper-thin flesh, any inch of which is soft enough to puncture if your blade is sharp.

I knew that before I found the picture, of course, but something in those jagged lines of crayon drove it home, or dug it in a little deeper. Something changed that week in the mountains. Something foundational, perhaps the first glimmer of certainty that I'd one day need an escape plan. But though I like to think I was trying to save myself from day one, it's hard to tell through the haze of memory. There are always holes. Cracks.

I don't spend a lot of time reminiscing; I'm not especially nostalgic. I think I lost that little piece of myself first.

But I'll never forget the way the sky roiled with electricity, the greenish tinge that threaded through the clouds and seemed to slide down my throat and into my lungs. I can feel the vibration in the air from the birds rising on frantically beating wings. The smell of damp earth and rotting pine will never leave me.

Yes, it was the storm that kept it memorable; it was the mountains.

It was the woman.

It was the blood.

GET *WICKED SHARP* ON MEGHANOFLYNN.COM

"FULL OF COMPLEX, ENGAGING CHARACTERS AND EVOCATIVE DETAIL, *WICKED SHARP* IS A WHITE-KNUCKLE THRILL RIDE. O'FLYNN IS A MASTER STORYTELLER."

~PAUL AUSTIN ARDOIN, *USA TODAY* BESTSELLING AUTHOR

FAMISHED

AN ASH PARK NOVEL

SUNDAY, DECEMBER 6TH

Focus, or she's dead.

Petrosky ground his teeth together, but it didn't stop the panic from swelling hot and frantic within him. After the arrest last week, this crime should have been fucking impossible.

He wished it were a copycat. He knew it wasn't.

Anger knotted his chest as he examined the corpse that lay in the middle of the cavernous living room. Dominic Harwick's intestines spilled onto the white marble floor as though someone had tried to run off with them. His eyes were wide, milky at the edges already, so it had been awhile since someone gutted his sorry ass and turned him into a rag doll in a three-thousand-dollar suit.

That rich prick should have been able to protect her.

Petrosky looked at the couch: luxurious, empty, cold. Last

week Hannah had sat on that couch, staring at him with wide green eyes that made her seem older than her twenty-three years. She had been happy, like Julie had been before she was stolen from him. He pictured Hannah as she might have been at eight years old, skirt twirling, dark hair flying, face flushed with sun, like one of the photos of Julie he kept tucked in his wallet.

They all started so innocent, so pure, so...*vulnerable*.

The idea that Hannah was the catalyst in the deaths of eight others, the cornerstone of some serial killer's plan, had not occurred to him when they first met. But it had later. It did now.

Petrosky resisted the urge to kick the body and refocused on the couch. Crimson congealed along the white leather as if marking Hannah's departure.

He wondered if the blood was hers.

The click of a doorknob caught Petrosky's attention. He turned to see Bryant Graves, the lead FBI agent, entering the room from the garage door, followed by four other agents. Petrosky tried not to think about what might be in the garage. Instead, he watched the four men survey the living room from different angles, their movements practically choreographed.

"Damn, does everyone that girl knows get whacked?" one of the agents asked.

"Pretty much," said another.

A plain-clothed agent stooped to inspect a chunk of scalp on the floor. Whitish-blond hair waved, tentacle-like, from the dead skin, beckoning Petrosky to touch it.

"You know this guy?" one of Graves's cronies asked from the doorway.

"Dominic Harwick." Petrosky nearly spat out the bastard's name.

"No signs of forced entry, so one of them knew the killer," Graves said.

"*She* knew the killer," Petrosky said. "Obsession builds over time. This level of obsession indicates it was probably someone she knew well."

But who?

Petrosky turned back to the floor in front of him, where words scrawled in blood had dried sickly brown in the morning light.

> Ever drifting down the stream—
> Lingering in the golden gleam—
> Life, what is it but a dream?

Petrosky's gut clenched. He forced himself to look at Graves. "And, Han—" *Hannah*. Her name caught in his throat, sharp like a razor blade. "The girl?"

"There are bloody drag marks heading out to the back shower and a pile of bloody clothes," Graves said. "He must have cleaned her up before taking her. We've got the techs on it now, but they're working the perimeter first." Graves bent and used a pencil to lift the edge of the scalp, but it was suctioned to the floor with dried blood.

"Hair? That's new," said another voice. Petrosky didn't bother to find out who had spoken. He stared at the coppery stains on the floor, his muscles twitching with anticipation. Someone could be tearing her apart as the agents roped off the room. How long did she have? He wanted to run, to find her, but he had no idea where to look.

"Bag it," Graves said to the agent examining the scalp, then turned to Petrosky. "It's all been connected from the beginning. Either Hannah Montgomery was his target all along or she's just another random victim. I think the fact that she isn't filleted on the floor like the others points to her being the goal, not an extra."

"He's got something special planned for her," Petrosky whispered. He hung his head, hoping it wasn't already too late.

If it was, it was all his fault.

GET *FAMISHED* AT MEGHANOFLYNN.COM.

"FEARLESS, SMART WRITING, AND A PLOT
THAT WILL STICK WITH YOU."
~*AWARD-WINNING AUTHOR BETH TELIHO*

SHADOW'S KEEP

CHAPTER 1

FOR WILLIAM SHANNAHAN, six-thirty on Tuesday, the third of August, was "the moment." Life was full of those moments, his mother had always told him, experiences that prevented you from going back to who you were before, tiny decisions that changed you forever.

And that morning, the moment came and went, though he didn't recognize it, nor would he ever have wished to recall that morning again for as long as he lived. But he would never, from that day on, be able to forget it.

He left his Mississippi farmhouse a little after six, dressed in running shorts and an old T-shirt that still had sunny yellow paint dashed across the front from decorating the child's room. *The child.* William had named him Brett, but he'd never told anyone that. To everyone else, the baby was just that-thing-you-could-never-mention, particularly since William had also lost his wife at Bartlett General.

His green Nikes beat against the gravel, a blunt metronome as he left the porch and started along the road parallel to the Oval, what the townsfolk called the near hundred square miles of woods that had turned marshy wasteland when freeway construction had dammed the creeks downstream. Before William was born, those fifty or so unlucky folks who owned property inside the Oval had gotten some settlement from the developers when their houses flooded and were deemed uninhabitable. Now those homes were part of a ghost town, tucked well beyond the reach of prying eyes.

William's mother had called it a disgrace. William thought it might be the price of progress, though he'd never dared to tell her that. He'd also never told her that his fondest memory of the Oval was when his best friend Mike had beat the crap out of Kevin Pultzer for punching William in the eye. That was before Mike was the sheriff, back when they were all just "us" or "them" and William had always been a them, except when Mike was around. He might fit in somewhere else, some other place where the rest of the dorky goofballs lived, but here in Graybel he was just a little...odd. Oh well. People in this town gossiped far too much to trust them as friends anyway.

William sniffed at the marshy air, the closely-shorn grass sucking at his sneakers as he increased his pace. Somewhere near him a bird shrieked, sharp and high. He startled as it took flight above him with another aggravated scream.

Straight ahead, the car road leading into town was bathed in filtered dawn, the first rays of sun painting the gravel gold, though the road was slippery with moss and morning damp. To his right, deep shadows pulled at him from the trees; the tall pines crouched close together as if hiding a secret bundle in their underbrush. Dark but calm, quiet—comforting. Legs pumping, William headed off the road toward the pines.

A snap like that of a muted gunshot echoed through the morning air, somewhere deep inside the wooded stillness, and though it was surely just a fox, or maybe a raccoon, he paused, running in place, disquiet spreading through him like the worms of fog that were only now rolling out from under the trees to be burned off as the sun made its debut. Cops never got a moment off, although in this sleepy town the worst he'd see today would be an argument over cattle. He glanced up the road. Squinted. Should he continue up the brighter main street or escape into the shadows beneath the trees?

That was his moment.

William ran toward the woods.

As soon as he set foot inside the tree line, the dark descended on him like a blanket, the cool air brushing his face as another hawk shrieked overhead. William nodded to it, as if the animal had sought his approval, then swiped his arm over his forehead and dodged a limb, pick-jogging his way down the path. A branch caught his ear. He winced. Six foot three was great for some things, but not for running in the woods. Either that or God was pissed at him, which wouldn't be surprising, though he wasn't clear on what he had done wrong. Probably for smirking at his memories of Kevin Pultzer with a torn T-shirt and a bloodied nose.

He smiled again, just a little one this time.

When the path opened up, he raised his gaze above the canopy. He had an hour before he needed to be at the precinct, but the pewter sky beckoned him to run quicker before the heat crept up. It was a good day to turn forty-two, he decided. He might not be the best-looking guy around, but he had his health. And there was a woman whom he adored, even if she wasn't sure about him yet.

William didn't blame her. He probably didn't deserve her, but he'd surely try to convince her that he did, like he had with Marianna...though he didn't think weird card tricks would help this time. But weird was what he had. Without it, he was just background noise, part of the wallpaper of this small town, and at forty-one—*no, forty-two, now*—he was running out of time to start over.

He was pondering this when he rounded the bend and saw the feet. Pale soles barely bigger than his hand, poking from behind a rust-colored boulder that sat a few feet from the edge of the trail. He stopped, his heart throbbing an erratic rhythm in his ears.

Please let it be a doll. But he saw the flies buzzing around the top of the boulder. Buzzing. Buzzing.

William crept forward along the path, reaching for his hip where his gun usually sat, but he touched only cloth. The dried yellow paint scratched his thumb. He thrust his hand into his pocket for his lucky coin. No quarter. Only his phone.

William approached the rock, the edges of his vision dark and unfocused as if he were looking through a telescope, but in the dirt around the stone he could make out deep paw prints. Probably from a dog or a coyote, though these were *enormous*—nearly the size of a salad plate, too big for anything he'd expect to find in these woods. He frantically scanned the underbrush, trying to locate the animal, but saw only a cardinal appraising him from a nearby branch.

Someone's back there, someone needs my help.

He stepped closer to the boulder. *Please don't let it be what I think it is.* Two more steps and he'd be able to see beyond the rock, but he could not drag his gaze from the trees where he was certain canine eyes were watching. Still nothing there save the shaded bark of the surrounding woods. He took another step—cold oozed from the muddy earth into his shoe and around his left ankle, like a hand from the grave. William stumbled, pulling his gaze from the trees just in time to see the boulder rushing at his head and then he was on his side in the slimy filth to the right of the boulder, next to...

Oh god, oh god, oh god.

William had seen death in his twenty years as a deputy, but usually it was the result of a drunken accident, a car wreck, an old man found dead on his couch.

This was not that. The boy was no more than six, probably less. He lay on a carpet of rotting leaves, one arm draped over his chest, legs splayed haphazardly as if he, too, had tripped in the muck. But this wasn't an accident; the boy's throat was torn, jagged ribbons of flesh peeled back, drooping on either side of the muscle meat, the unwanted skin on a Thanksgiving turkey. Deep gouges permeated his chest and abdomen, black slashes against mottled green flesh, the wounds obscured behind his shredded clothing and bits of twigs and leaves.

William scrambled backward, clawing at the ground, his muddy shoe kicking the child's ruined calf, where the boy's shy white bones peeked from under congealing blackish tissue. The legs looked...*chewed on.*

His hand slipped in the muck. The child's face was turned to his, mouth open, black tongue lolling as if he were about to plead for help. *Not good, oh shit, not good.*

William finally clambered to standing, yanked his cell from his pocket, and tapped a button, barely registering his friend's answering bark. A fly lit on the boy's eyebrow above a single white mushroom that crept upward over the landscape of his cheek, rooted in the empty socket that had once contained an eye.

"Mike, it's William. I need a...tell Dr. Klinger to bring the wagon."

He stepped backward, toward the path, shoe sinking again, the mud trying to root him there, and he yanked his foot free with a squelching sound. Another step backward and he was on the path, and another step off the path again, and another, another, feet moving until his back slammed against a gnarled oak on the opposite side of the trail. He jerked his head up, squinting through the leafy awning, half convinced the boy's assailant would be perched there, ready to leap from the trees and lurch him into oblivion on flensing jaws. But there was no wretched animal. Blue leaked through the filtered haze of dawn.

William lowered his gaze, Mike's voice a distant crackle irritating the edges of his brain but not breaking through— he could not understand what his friend was saying. He stopped trying to decipher it and said, "I'm on the trails behind my house, found a body. Tell them to come in through the path on the Winchester side." He tried to listen to the receiver, but heard only the buzzing of flies across the trail—had they been so loud a moment ago? Their noise grew, amplified to unnatural volumes, filling his head until every other sound fell away—was Mike still talking? He pushed *End,* pocketed the phone, and then leaned back and slid down the tree trunk.

And William Shannahan, not recognizing the event the rest of his life would hinge upon, sat at the base of a gnarled oak tree on Tuesday, the third of August, put his head into his hands, and wept.

GET *SHADOW'S KEEP* ON MEGHANOFLYNN.COM.

"MASTERFUL, STAGGERING, TWISTED... AND COMPLETELY UNPREDICTABLE."
~*BESTSELLING AUTHOR WENDY HEARD*

"Intense and suspenseful...captured me from the first chapter and held me enthralled until the final page."
~*Susan Sewell, Reader's Favorite*

"Cunning, delightfully disturbing, and addictive, the Ash Park series is an expertly written labyrinth of twisted, unpredictable awesomeness!"
~*Award-winning Author Beth Teliho*

"Dark, gritty, and raw, O'Flynn's work will take your mind prisoner and keep you awake far into the morning hours."
~*Bestselling Author Kristen Mae*

"From the feverishly surreal to the downright demented, O'Flynn takes you on a twisted journey through the deepest and darkest corners of the human mind."
~*Bestselling Author Mary Widdicks*

"With unbearable tension and gripping, thought-provoking storytelling, O'Flynn explores fear in all the

best—and creepiest—ways. Masterful psychological thrillers replete with staggering, unpredictable twists."
~*Bestselling Author Wendy Heard*

LEARN MORE AT MEGHANOFLYNN.COM

WANT MORE FROM MEGHAN?

There are many more books to choose from!

Learn more about Meghan's novels on

https://meghanoflynn.com

ABOUT THE AUTHOR

With books deemed "visceral, haunting, and fully immersive" (*New York Times Bestseller Andra Watkins*), Meghan O'Flynn has made her mark on the thriller genre. Meghan is a clinical therapist who draws her character inspiration from her knowledge of the human psyche. She is the bestselling author of gritty crime novels and serial killer thrillers, all of which take readers on the dark, gripping, and unputdownable journey for which Meghan is notorious. Learn more at https://meghanoflynn.com! While you're there, join Meghan's reader group, and get exclusive bonuses just for signing up.

Want to connect with Meghan?
https://meghanoflynn.com

Made in the USA
Coppell, TX
17 October 2023